P9-DIW-542

EIGHT IN THE BOX

EIGHT IN THE BOX

A NOVEL OF SUSPENSE

. . . .

RAFFI YESSAYAN

BALLANTINE BOOKS | NEW YORK

Published in the United States by Ballantine Books, an imprint of The Random House Publishing Group, a division of Random House, Inc., New York.

BALLANTINE and colophon are registered trademarks of Random House, Inc.

LIBRARY OF CONGRESS CATALOG-IN-PUBLICATION DATA
Yessayan, Raffi.
Eight in the box : a novel of suspense / Raffi Yessayan.
p. cm.
ISBN 978-0-345-50261-2
1. Serial murderers—Fiction.   2. Boston (Mass.)—Fiction.   I. Title.
PS3625.E87E38 2008
813′.6—dc22   2008005055

Printed in the United States of America on acid-free paper

www.ballantinebooks.com

2 4 6 8 9 7 5 3 1

FIRST EDITION

Book design by Barbara M. Bachman

For my wife, Candice

PART ONE

. . . .

The people have always some champion whom they set over them and nurse into greatness. . . . This and no other is the root from which a tyrant springs; when he first appears above ground he is a protector.

—PLATO, *The Republic*

CHAPTER 1

Richter slipped his arm down the cool shaft of the dryer vent, feeling the dampness of the metal through the latex glove. He slid the bolt lock, gave the door a shove and was inside. Locking the door behind him, he reattached the dryer hose to the vent cover. Let the police work a little to find out how he'd gotten in.

It took a moment for his eyes to adjust to the darkness. Richter breathed in the basement smells of detergent and mold and was overpowered by the pungent odor from a cat litter box. A scant amount of light from the casement window outlined the stairs leading up to the first floor. The door at the top of the staircase had been left open for the cat.

Perfect.

How nicely the City of Boston's streetlights lit up the first floor. A narrow hallway led to the living room with its French doors. Richter entered the room, careful not to bump into anything.

The walls were pale, although he couldn't make out the color. Artwork by a child with some talent hung, carefully framed and matted, on each wall. A vase on the coffee table held dried roses and Queen Anne's lace—a nice touch, the sort of thing Grandmother would have enjoyed. It was a comfortable room. He could see himself relaxing on the couch, watching one of his old movies.

He moved out of the light and stepped into the dining room, stopping to look at the family pictures on the mantel. The built-in hutch, with its leaded-glass doors, was filled with old-fashioned teacups and saucers. The dining room led into the kitchen and back around to the front hall where he had entered. He'd completed his private tour of the lovely old Victorian.

Now he had more important things to attend to.

Richter made his way up the stairs. The moonlight shining through the stained-glass window on the landing created a kaleidoscope of muted color on the pine floors. The stairs creaked, but at midnight Susan McCarthy would be in a deep sleep. Her bedroom light had gone out two hours earlier.

Richter walked down the carpeted hall. He turned the cold glass doorknob, and the door to Susan McCarthy's bedroom yawned open.

CHAPTER 2

Assistant District Attorney Connie Darget sped through another red light before turning onto Prospect Hill Road in Roslindale, one of the old neighborhoods of Boston now being taken over by trust-fund babies. This was one of the few perks of his job. The pay was terrible, but who else besides a cop could fly around the city in the middle of the night with total disregard for traffic laws? He had activated his emergency lights, the wigwags, the strobes, the flashbacks. Driving to a murder scene made Connie feel alive, like a kid sledding down the Blue Hills, not knowing if he'd be able to stop before shooting out onto the highway below.

He stopped in the middle of the street, a few houses down from number twelve. That was as close as he could get. He left the flashbacks on so the cops wouldn't tow the Crown Vic.

Two ambulances were situated in front of the house, with a half dozen police cruisers blocking incoming traffic. It was warm for February, close to fifty degrees at two o'clock in the morning. A suit jacket was all he needed over his shirt and tie. Most of the residents of the quiet, middle-class neighborhood were outside, but the extensive yellow tape kept them a good distance away.

Connie overheard the grumblings of the crowd as he made his way toward the scene. He played up to his audience, brushing past them with a practiced expression of intense focus.

"Why won't they tell us anything?" a woman asked.

"I don't know, but it's a bad sign when the paramedics are still waiting on the sidelines," said a man in pajama bottoms and a sweatshirt.

"They're probably all dead!" the woman said, her voice rising. "I've
seen this kind of thing on TV. If the victims are dead, then their bodies
get treated like a crime scene."

TV can teach you something after all, Connie thought.

The media had taken over the parts of the street that were not taped
off. Television reporters were interviewing neighbors, fishing for sound
bites for the morning news. Connie flashed his credentials to a uniformed cop and moved toward the crime scene.

As one of the young prosecutors handpicked by the district attorney
to represent the office at all murder scenes, Connie had access to a world
most civilians never imagined. Members of the Homicide Response
Team were supposed to oversee the integrity of each investigation. In
reality, they stayed out of the way and let the homicide detectives from
the BPD run the show. Connie flipped the smooth, black leather bill-
fold with its gold badge back into his jacket pocket.

After his first few homicides, he noticed that the police gave him
more access to crime scenes, maybe because he looked the part of a sea-
soned detective. With his cleanly shaven head and BPD notepad, he
blended right in. And he was a city kid, like most of the cops, not some
rich carpetbagger from the suburbs who'd been afraid to come into the
city until his politically connected parents got him a job in the DA's office.

Connie skirted the taped perimeter. He never walked through a
crime scene unless he checked in with the detectives first. He saw a cop
he recognized and walked over to get an update.

After a quick handshake, the officer leaned in close. "Connie, one
vic, a female, Ocean Frank before we got here. That's all I know. They
haven't told us shit, other than to keep the crowd back."

"How'd she die?" Connie asked.

"No idea."

"Who's here from Homicide?"

"Mooney and Alves. They're inside."

"I should've known," Connie said. "Only Sergeant Mooney would close off this much of a street as a crime scene. He's got half of Rozzie taped off."

"That's why he's the best." The cop pointed toward the side porch. "That looks like Alves now."

Connie had met Detective Angel Alves on his first day as a virgin prosecutor in the South Bay District Court. Not even four months ago Alves had been promoted to Homicide, but the two of them had stayed in touch. Connie watched as Alves directed two patrolmen to the back of the house before turning toward the street. Connie raised a hand to catch Alves's attention. Even at a murder scene at two in the morning the detective looked sharp in his tailored suit. They made eye contact and Alves waved him over.

"Good morning, Conrad," Alves said, extending his hand.

"Please don't call me that," Connie said, shaking his hand. "You sound like my mother."

"Okay, *Connie,* nice of you to show up." Alves looked pointedly at his watch. "We've been here an hour. The reporters made better time than you." Alves tilted his head toward the cameras that were focused on them.

"I only got paged twenty minutes ago." Connie shook his head. "Those guys in Operations are useless. Once they called so late I showed up after the scene had been cleared. Then I got chewed out by the DA. I don't like to rat people out, but I'm calling their captain about this."

"Do what you have to. Nobody's going to think you're a rat. We've got another ugly scene here."

"Another?"

"Remember Michelle Hayes, just before Christmas? She disappears and all we find is a bathtub full of her blood."

"I thought we had her as a domestic."

"We did, originally. She'd been through a nasty divorce. But the guy had an airtight alibi. Out of town on a corporate team-building junket, where the whole office goes into the New Mexico wilderness for the weekend to play Boy Scouts. Probably spent most of their time shopping in Santa Fe. No other suspects, so the case goes cold. Until tonight."

"Who's our victim?"

"Susan McCarthy. Also recently divorced, but still friendly with the ex. She got the house and kid in the settlement. According to her parents, the ex took the daughter to Disney World for February school vacation. We're assuming it's Susan's blood in the tub, but we won't know till the DNA comes back. The crime lab is looking for known samples to compare."

"Any motive?"

"Nothing. Tonight's the first sign that the Hayes murder wasn't isolated. We've got a sick bastard on our hands, Connie. Whoever did this has the same MO."

"Copycat?"

Alves shook his head. "We never released the details. The media never picked up on the story. We're not as lucky tonight." Alves motioned again toward the reporters circling them. "I heard a few of the uniforms calling him the Blood Bath Killer. Wait till the *Herald* gets ahold of that."

"What do we have so far?"

"Not much." Alves took out his notepad. "We've got the district detectives canvassing the neighborhood for witnesses and the crime lab processing the house. Sarge is upstairs with a few of the civilians from the crime lab. Last time, the guy left us nothing to work with. He may have made a mistake this time."

"What's that?"

"We found a sneaker print in the dirt by the cellar door. No signs of a forced entry, so it may not mean anything. We're taking a plaster mold, just in case. If he didn't come in through the basement, then we're thinking McCarthy may have let him in. Maybe they had a date and then he decided to kill her."

"Who found the scene?"

"Nine-one-one call. Never says a word, leaves the phone off the hook. Just like the Hayes case. Dispatcher figures someone accidentally hit the preprogrammed emergency button. Kids do it all the time. We have to send a cruiser out anyway. Uniforms get here in less than five minutes. Side door's wide open. Kitchen phone's still off the hook. Then they find the bathtub and the blood. Looks like our boy wants to personally call us out to see his work."

"Where's the bathroom?"

"Upstairs. You're not going to throw up on me, are you?"

"I'll never live that one down, will I? That woman's body was rotting for days before the neighbors smelled the stench. And you clowns didn't warn me to put VapoRub under my nose."

"Just busting your chops." Alves smiled. He turned and led Connie into the kitchen. The kitchen looked perfectly ordinary, nothing out of place except for the telephone receiver dangling from its cord.

"The guys that answered the call knew what they were doing. They didn't touch anything. We're going to take the phone off the wall and fume it for prints. And we'll need elimination prints from all family members."

Much of what Connie knew about police work he'd learned from Angel Alves, especially during ride-alongs when he could watch Alves in action. Walking through this normal house, knowing that a person had been killed upstairs, Connie remembered one of the first lessons Alves taught him, about the importance of watching a person's hands. As Alves put it, "No one is ever going to shoot or stab you with their eyes or their feet. If someone's going to kill you, it'll be with his hands."

As they made their way to the second floor, Connie thought about the terror Susan McCarthy must have felt as she took her final breath. He paused at the top of the stairs and looked down the hall where a woman had lost her life. How true Alves's words were.

CHAPTER 3

Swiping his key card through the scanner, Connie entered the South Bay District courthouse. He started toward the stairs leading to the district attorney's satellite office. Shit. He was covering arraignments this morning, a bad way to start the week. Another swipe of his card and he wove his way through a maze of desks to the front counter of the clerk's office. There he picked up the stack of police reports from the weekend arrests. Busy weekend. Hopping over the counter into the front lobby, he jogged up the main staircase to the third floor.

Through the glass doors of the DA's office, he saw the secretaries answering phones and checking in witnesses who had been subpoenaed to court. At least ten people were crammed into a waiting area designed to hold five. It was like standing room only at Fenway for a Sox–Yankees game, except no one was happy to be here. They were either victims or witnesses to crimes. The last thing they wanted to do was come to court and testify.

"Good morning, ladies," Connie said as he hurried past the secretaries, careful not to make eye contact with any of the witnesses. He hated treating them like homeless people asking for change, but he had work to do and no time to answer the questions they were sure to ask.

The long corridor ahead of him was on the north side of the building, a wall of windows broken up by the assistant district attorneys' work cubicles. Except for Liz Moore, the supervising ADA, none of the lawyers had their own offices. Their cubicles faced out onto Roxbury's

Dudley Square and toward the distant, mirrored glass of the John Hancock building.

As he came around the corner, Connie almost ran into Nick Costa, who was leaning back in his swivel chair. Nick looked sharp in one of his trademark tailored suits and Italian ties, his expensive wardrobe complementing his Mediterranean looks. And he didn't have to live beyond his means to look good. He was well taken care of by his parents: Greek immigrants who had achieved the American dream by founding a floral shop that had grown into the largest chain in the Boston area. Connie stuck with the two charcoal gray suits his father had bought for him when he was sworn in to the bar. "You're tardy," Nick said. "It's almost nine."

Connie pointed to his pager. "Homicide Response. I was supposed to pass it off on Friday, but one of the Gang Unit ADA's had a wedding. It sucks having two sleepless weekends in a row. Wearing this pager is like hazing for DAs. Every time you start to doze off, the damn thing beeps. The hardest part is being out at a crime scene all night and then handing the case off to the Homicide DAs."

"I thought I saw you on the news. The 'suspicious death' in Rozzie."

"How'd I look?"

"Like Mr. Clean with that shaved dome of yours," Nick said, running his fingers through his hair.

Mitchum Beaulieu hung up his phone and stood up from the neighboring partition, a red thermos cup of home-brewed tea by his lips. He tapped Nick on the shoulder. "Let the man tell his story." Mitch Beaulieu stood over six feet tall with the muscular, lanky build of a swimmer. He had light brown skin, scattered freckles and neatly trimmed reddish-brown hair. People told him that he looked like Malcolm X, and he milked the resemblance for all it was worth, going so far as to wear the same style of eyeglasses.

"Hey, Red," said Connie. "Didn't see you hiding there."

"What time did you get called out?" Nick asked.

"Two. Hardly got any sleep."

"Why are they saying it's suspicious?" Mitch asked.

Connie put the police reports down on his desk, crouched in a baseball catcher's stance and leaned in, lowering his voice. "Suspicious death is the understatement of the year. I get the page for a possible homicide. I throw on a suit and tie, fire up the Crown Vic and head to this old Victorian on Prospect Hill."

"Lights and siren?" Mitch asked.

"Lights, no siren," Connie said. "Victim's already dead. Didn't want to look like a jackass in front of the cops, pulling onto the scene with the sirens blasting."

"Did you see the body?" Nick asked.

"There *was* no body. All they found was a bathtub full of blood, like that murder back in December. They never had a suspect or a solid lead on the first case. They didn't even find the woman's body. Now it looks like they have a serial killer on their hands."

"What did it look like?" Mitch asked.

"What did what look like?" Connie said.

"The tub full of blood."

For an instant Connie was back in the narrow hallway of the Victorian, the metallic smell of blood in the air, Mooney barking orders. "To be honest? Kind of surreal—seeing all that blood, knowing that someone's body was drained." Connie straightened up and stretched his legs. "Got to get ready for arraignments. And I still have discovery I need to turn over in the Jesse Wilcox case. It's coming up for motions soon. I ain't letting that bastard walk again."

"Christ, Connie, who cares about a drug case?" Nick said. "You can't start telling us about a murder and then shut us off."

"I've already told you more than I should have. If Alves finds out, next time I'll be outside the yellow tape, doing the Dunkin' Donuts run."

Nick waved him off. "You don't want to tell me, fine. But don't treat me like some asshole on the street."

Connie took a breath. "Sorry, okay? I'm just wiped out. I was at the scene for six hours."

"Who found the blood?" Mitch asked, taking another sip of tea.

"Two patrolmen responding to the call. And the killer may have made the call himself. Seriously, that's it."

"The killer called the police himself?" Nick repeated. "I definitely want to hear more about this later."

Connie picked up his police reports. "Where's the rest of the crew?"

"I think they're in court," Mitch said.

"Is Andi in yet?" Connie asked. "I'm going to grab her and see if she can help me out in arraignments."

"Don't go grabbing her in the courtroom," Nick joked. "I don't care what you guys do on your own time, but that's not appropriate behavior for a courthouse."

"Wow, that's funny," Connie said. "I keep forgetting how funny you are."

Nick shrugged. "If you're going to date an intern, you need to have a sense of humor about it."

"Hey, boys, let's get going," Liz Moore called out to the three of them. "It's almost nine. I don't want to hear the judges complaining about you being late again."

Liz Moore was a no-nonsense woman, raised in the rarefied air of power, prestige and acute social awareness. Her father, Arthur Moore, was a lawyer active in the civil rights movement. Ever the politician, he claimed allegiances with both the militant Malcolm X and the pacifist Dr. Martin Luther King, Jr. Not only was he a leader in Boston's black community, but he was also one of the most successful lawyers in the state.

Now his daughter was admired for her fairness and openness, and respected for her ability in the courtroom. And, Connie thought, it didn't hurt that she was gorgeous.

"How much longer do we have to work like this?" Mitch said. "We've been down two ADAs for months."

"Stop whining," Liz said.

"I'm serious," Mitch said. "Didn't the DA promise us more bodies? We've been shorthanded for too long. One of us is going to drop the ball on a serious case."

"Mitch," Liz said, "the gods of justice have heard your prayers. We're getting a new lawyer tomorrow."

"Does he have any experience?" Mitch asked.

"No, *she* doesn't," Liz said. "I'm expecting you guys to help her out so she'll actually be of some use to us. But for now why don't you help me by getting your asses down to court?"

Liz Moore promoted a team atmosphere among the lawyers at South Bay. Connie appreciated the way she had made it a requirement that they look out for one another. As a black woman who had accomplished so much in a profession dominated by white men, Liz made it clear she didn't want the competitive atmosphere of big law firms to tarnish what was clearly her courthouse.

"All arraignments to the first session," the courthouse PA system boomed. "All pretrial hearings to the second session, all motions to the third session, and all trial matters to the fourth session."

"Let's go put some bad guys away," Nick said.

CHAPTER 4

Detective Angel Alves entered the BPD's crime laboratory and moved around the reception desk toward the examination room. He was aware of every step, fueled with the energy from his first major case since being promoted to Homicide in the fall. Two murders in two months linked to the same killer. He tapped on the glass window, and Eunice Curran waved him in. A blast of cool antiseptic air hit him as he opened the examination room door.

As director of the crime lab, Eunice Curran was considered by most cops to be the best forensic examiner. Single and in her mid-forties, she had devoted the last ten years to making hers one of the most professional, accredited forensic crime labs in the country. The cops appreciated how she and the criminalists who worked for her used solid scientific methods in collecting evidence so their testimony held up in court.

"Hey, Angel," she said. "Coffee?"

"No thanks. Already had two."

"Then you must need something. You never stop in just to say hello." She winked at him.

"I can't stop in every day. My knees get weak when I see you. Then I spend the rest of my day thinking about your beautiful eyes. If Marcy found out, she'd kill me."

"I keep forgetting about that wife of yours." Eunice smiled. A nice smile. Perfect white teeth. "You ever get tired of her, you know where to find me." Eunice was kind of a plain Jane, but she took good care of herself and she was fun to talk to.

More than anything else, Alves liked her for her brains. Intelligent women had always attracted him. That was why he was still so much in love with Marcy, a part-time English professor at UMass Boston in Dorchester. But even though he played their banter off, he found it exciting when Eunice Curran, in her white lab coat, explained science that he didn't fully understand. The lyrics from an old Robert Palmer song popped into his head: *A horn section you resemble, and your figure makes me tremble, and I sure would like to handle what's between your ears.*

"Let me guess why you're here today," said Eunice. "The Blood Bath Killer."

"Don't let Mooney hear you say that. He doesn't want to give this guy a nickname and a cult following."

"I'll be careful around the Sarge," she assured him.

"We just got back from the crime scene. Same as the last case, we need to know if the amount of blood we have here is consistent with a death."

"Hard to tell. Like I told you last time, the *average* human being"—and all traces of the flirty Eunice Curran vanished, he could see—"has about four and a half to five liters of blood in their system. This will vary with the size and weight of an individual."

"I have a couple of pictures of Susan McCarthy. She was about five seven, medium build," he said, showing her the photos. "She weighed about a buck-twenty, buck-thirty."

Eunice gave a nod.

"How much blood was in that bathtub?"

"I'm not sure. It was like the Hayes crime scene; the blood mixed with water. Judging from the temperature of the water, Ms. McCarthy had probably been set down in a warm bath, just like Hayes. Based on the deep red color and the thickness of the liquid that we found in both bathtubs, I'd say they were consistent with suicides. But then we would ordinarily find a *body* in the bathtub along with the bloody water."

"She was alive when she was put in the bath?"

"I think so. There are other ways to drain a person of her blood, but the easiest way is to have the heart do the pumping for you."

"So he puts his victims in the bathtub and slits their wrists. Are they incapacitated in any way? Unconscious, maybe?"

"No trace of drugs in the blood."

"So, maybe he hits them over the head and knocks them out. Who knows? But whoever lost that blood is definitely dead, right?"

"Angel, I can't say so with any scientific certainty, and this isn't my specialty, but if that was Susan McCarthy's blood in the tub, my guess is she's dead. There's no way of determining the ratio of blood to water, but it certainly seemed like there were at least three or four liters of blood in the tub. She wouldn't have lost all her blood, but that's all she would need to lose before her heart would stop beating. The blood matched Susan McCarthy's type. You'll have the DNA results as soon as I get them."

"Anything else in the tub besides blood and water?" he asked.

"Some hair, but that was it."

"What about everything else your guys collected from the scene?"

"I've got them going over the bed linens. We inspected each room with visible ambient light. Then we used an alternate light source for fibers and biological stains that fluoresce. Nothing. So we went to the trace evidence vacuum. It doesn't look promising. McCarthy kept a pretty clean house and our killer is very careful."

"What about the footprint?" Alves asked.

"We got an excellent cast," she said as she walked over to the evidence table and picked up the plaster imprint. "The sole of the sneaker is made from a mold with the New Balance name on it. That was helpful. Otherwise I'd have had to send it to the FBI. Size ten and a half. Right foot. I don't know the model, but New Balance should be able to help you with that."

"You mean you can't tell me the height and weight of the guy who wore the shoe?" This time Alves winked at her.

"Welcome to CSI Boston," she said, lowering her voice and raising her eyebrow. "Not only can I tell you the guy's height and weight, I can tell you his race, his mother's maiden name; and if it's a clear enough mold, I might be able to give you the name of his firstborn child."

"That's pretty good," Alves said. "But I wouldn't quit my day job if I were you. Anything else you can tell me about the shoe?"

She nodded, back to business once more. "It has pretty distinctive characteristics in the tread pattern. There seems to be an imperfection from the manufacturing process." She showed him the cast. "The C in Balance looks like an O. A flaw like that would have made it an 'irregular.' "

"The kind of shoe they sell in outlet stores at a discount."

She nodded. "And the shoe has some distinctive random wear characteristics," she said. "Right here you can see that it's worn out more on the right, especially toward the heel. Everyone has his own walk, so shoes wear differently. I also found some nicks and gouges left by sharp stones or broken glass."

"Can you make a match?"

"You bring me the shoe that left this print and I can make a positive ID."

"I'll have the guys from ID come up and take a picture of the mold."

"Good idea."

"Thanks, Eunice. I'll give Sarge the update."

"Anytime, Angel Eyes. And if you want to continue this discussion later, I'm free for dinner."

CHAPTER 5

Alone in the conference room, Andi Norton heard the commotion as the guys moved down the hall toward her. They looked like a group of cute young boys on their way to face a playground challenge.

She had her red hair pulled back and draped over her shoulder. That morning it had looked like a deep red silk scarf in contrast to her sharp navy blue suit, the skirt of which she'd had tailored to show off her slender legs. "Well, if it isn't the three musketeers," she said.

"That's right," Nick said, flashing a smile. "We're on a mission to clean up the streets of the city."

"Andi, I need your help in arraignments," Connie said. His hands, by his side, were flexing, like he was anxious to get started.

"I'm all yours," she said.

"We know that," Nick said. "But he needs your help in arraignments."

Connie punched Nick in the arm.

"That hurt."

"I know," Connie said.

Andi followed him as they walked ahead of the others down the stairs to the second floor.

Connie was taking two stairs at a time and Andi was having trouble keeping up. "Slow down," she said. "I'm going to break my ankle with these heels."

"We're late. We need to get squared away before the judge takes the bench. You do the arraignments. I'll start the paperwork and step in if you need help."

"Great," Andi said, "I can use the ice time." Every day she spent in court, Andi felt more like a real lawyer. After interning in the office for almost nine months, she felt she had developed a solid understanding of the law. "Connie, do you think I'll be ready for a jury soon?"

"I think you're ready now. I've got one set for tomorrow that I was going to give you. A simple drug case, hand-to-hand to an undercover."

"Are you serious?" Her entire body pulsed with adrenaline. This was more than she'd been hoping for.

"I've got to start working on the Jesse Wilcox case. If I lose the motion and the drugs get suppressed, then I've blown another shot at taking him off the street."

"Is he the one that—"

"Beat a drug case last year. It was the last trial I lost. Then Alves pinched him on this new case a few weeks before getting bumped up to Homicide."

"When's the motion?"

"Not for a couple of weeks, but I want to finish looking over the file tonight and make sure discovery's complete. I'll get together with Alves later this week if he frees up some time. Everything's riding on this motion."

"So, is tomorrow's trial definitely mine?"

"I'll check with Liz to make sure it's okay. You've been doing a great job. I don't think she'll have a problem with it, especially if I second-seat you. And hey, you are one lucky gal. It took me a year before I had my first jury trial. It would be a neat trick if we can get you one while you're still a student."

Andi studied the tall, serious man in front of her. Unlike guys she had dated in the past, Connie hadn't been frightened away by her young daughter. He had understood that she had to put Rachel and her career ahead of everything else. She fixed her eyes on his. "Connie, thanks for everything. You've taught me so much that I feel like I'm better than most of the lawyers I go up against. If Liz lets me try the case, I'll do a good job. I won't make you look bad."

He nodded. "I know you won't. Because you're going to spend tonight prepping. And you'd better have your opening ready to run by me first thing in the morning."

With that, Connie opened the door to the first session for her. The noise of the courtroom hit her like that of the annual wedding gown sale at Filene's Basement. Thank God she had chosen South Bay for her internship. So many of her classmates were stuck in suburban courthouses with garden-variety drunk-driving cases and barroom fights, day after day. Instead, she had drug distributions, gun cases, even serious assaults.

And she got to meet Conrad Darget. There was no pretense with Connie. The combination of his clean-shaven look and his muscular body was a nice bonus. And there was that excitement, that helplessness she felt when he hugged her, like there was no escape.

His eyes were the most unusual she'd ever seen: two different colors, one hazel, one blue. The two together were beautiful—mesmerizing, she liked to think, like each held a separate part of his personality. The logical prosecutor. The thoughtful man.

To the other ADAs, Connie may have been Mr. Clean. But for Andi Norton he was starting to look more like Mr. Right.

CHAPTER 6

The corridor on the second floor of police headquarters at One Schroeder Plaza seemed especially long this morning. Angel Alves opened the glass door that led into the Homicide Unit and walked into Sergeant Wayne Mooney's office. Mooney had his back to the door and Alves knew he must be lost in thought. "Sarge, I just spoke with Eunice. She confirmed that McCarthy's probably dead."

Mooney swiveled around to face him. The sergeant nodded and drew his hand over the crime scene photos spread out on his desk. "We're not waiting around for DNA results. You and I both know that she *is* dead. Now let's see what we can do to catch this bastard."

"I thought we should at least check with the crime lab. She also said that both vics were probably alive when they were put in the tubs. What I can't figure out is why he would go through all that trouble to make them look like suicides and then take the bodies."

"He's not trying to make them look like suicides. I think he's performing some kind of sick ritual. I just don't know what it is yet."

That quickly, Mooney became engrossed in the photos. In the bright morning light Alves could see a thicket of gray hairs rapidly conquering the brown on Mooney's head. Not bad, considering most guys on the job for more than twenty years had gone completely silver or had no hair at all.

"What else did you get from Eunice?" said Mooney. "They find anything useful in the house?"

"No."

Mooney was chewing on his pen, studying the Hayes crime scene photos. "What about the shoe print?"

"They got a decent mold. It's a New Balance. Eunice thinks it's an irregular. Says she can make a match if we find the shoe."

"Pull up a chair. When we catch this sick fuck, that mold will be great corroboration at trial."

Alves watched as Mooney sorted through the stack of reports on his desk from the Hayes murder, pulled one out and seemed to cross-reference it with one of the photos.

"We need to find a common thread between the two vics. Why were they killed? Why the hell is he draining off their blood?" Mooney asked. "What's he doing with their bodies? They've got to have something in common that brought this guy into their lives."

"They were both divorced, successful businesswomen," Alves said.

"Lucky in their careers, unlucky at love. We know that Hayes wasn't dating anyone. Was McCarthy? We canvassed the neighborhood last night. No one saw her getting dropped off by anyone. If she was seeing someone, last night would have been the perfect time to have him over, with the kid and the ex both out of town."

"She wasn't dating," Alves said. "Her parents said she didn't want a parade of guys coming in and out of her daughter's life. She thought it would hurt the kid. It sounds like she had no intention of dating until her little girl graduated college." If he were ever out of the picture, he knew Marcy would put the twins before her own needs.

"What else?" Mooney asked.

"Both of their exes were out of town at the time of their murders," Alves said. "Each has an alibi. But we can keep digging."

"I talked to Walter McCarthy a few hours ago. The man's destroyed. I'll get a better read when I see him in person, but I don't think he had anything to do with this. You're right. The killer must have known that they'd be alone. Did he know their exes would be out of town too? How would he know that?"

"Maybe our guy's a travel agent or works for an airline," Alves said. "I'll check to see if there were any similarities in their travel arrangements. I've got a decent contact with the feds."

"When you finish, I want you to run over to Fidelity to see if any of McCarthy's friends knew she'd be alone this weekend. Maybe she was seeing someone she was hiding from her family. Or maybe there was someone she wasn't interested in who couldn't take no for an answer. I'm going to shoot over to Roslindale to see McCarthy. He and the kid are due in at Logan at ten. I'm having them picked up."

"What do you think you'll get out of him, Sarge?"

"I'm wondering if they used any of the same contractors that Hayes used on her house." Mooney pulled a report off the stack on his desk and handed it to Alves. He said, "Successful, single mothers always use housecleaners, landscapers, plumbers, handymen. There might be a link there."

Mooney stood up and hitched his pants, putting his gun and holster back onto his belt. He took a fresh battery out of the charger and clipped it onto his police radio and slid it into his back pocket. "There's another way our guy could've known they were alone. He could've been watching them. The house next to McCarthy's didn't look lived in. Everything was overgrown. Someone could have watched her from that yard. I want to see if there was a similar vantage point near the Hayes house. Then I'm going to start canvassing both neighborhoods. I don't like to rely on what people tell the uniforms. I'd rather ask them face-to-face."

Alves skimmed the names of the contractors on the report Mooney had given him. "Sarge, remember this guy that Hayes hired to fix her ceilings? He was her next-door neighbor, a plasterer right off the boat from Ireland. He seemed a little cagey. I'd like to take another run at him."

"The plasterer didn't kill anyone," Mooney said. "He was terrified that we were going to get him deported. Call me when you finish up at Fidelity."

Alves knew he was getting the bum's rush. Mooney was anxious to get going.

CHAPTER 7

Alves watched the sun as it began its descent over the Mission Hill housing development, his old neighborhood. The ugly three-story brick deathtraps that he grew up in had been razed and replaced by charming town houses, the city trying to give people a sense of home. Alves was standing on the second-floor catwalk that ran between the north and south wings of One Schroeder Plaza. The plaza had been named for two heroic police officer brothers, one gunned down by bank-robber radicals in 1970, the other shot during a pawnshop heist in 1973. It had been a busy day but there were no new leads and he was tired.

"How'd it go?" Mooney asked. Alves hadn't heard his sergeant behind him.

"Not so good, Sarge. Sorry I never called."

"Don't sweat it," Mooney said. "Anything new?"

"McCarthy worked with so many people they took up my whole day, but no one gave me anything we didn't know. Most people knew she was divorced and that she and her ex were still friendly. She had custody of the kid, but she let the ex take her whenever he wanted. Since the split, she'd devoted herself to her daughter and her job. There was no man in her life. She'd never have gone out on a blind date or looked through the personal ads."

"What about your friend with the airline info?" Mooney asked.

"He had nothing for me," Alves said. "The two exes booked their airfare online with different airlines."

"I came up empty too," Mooney said. "McCarthy wasn't aware of any contractors working on the house. Susan had custody of the house, but he took care of all the upkeep, including the yard work. He still had a forty percent interest in the house, if and when they ever sold it. I think he was trying to get back with her. Being her maintenance man was a perfect way to keep himself in the picture."

"How's he holding up?" Alves asked.

"He's a mess."

"You see the kid?"

"No," Mooney said. "They'd dropped her off at her grandparents' on the way over. All the shit we see, nothing bothers me more than seeing the kids when something like this happens. The only thing worse is when a kid dies." Mooney was staring toward the fading sun. He looked angry, like he was mad at himself for having allowed Susan McCarthy to be murdered. Mooney didn't have any kids of his own, and Alves wondered how this tender streak had developed in his otherwise tough sergeant.

"You find anything else in the house?" Alves asked.

Mooney closed his eyes and turned away from the sun. He took something out of his jacket pocket. "We looked through her Black-Berry," he said, handing the device to Alves. "Everyone listed was a relative or a business contact. Get a subpoena from the DA's office so we can check out her call history."

"Did the neighbors see anything?" Alves asked.

"Most of them weren't home. Maybe we'll go back later."

"Sure," Alves said. "But, Sarge, can we get a little sleep tonight? Marcy and the kids haven't seen me since yesterday morning and I'm running on fumes."

Mooney watched the last sliver of the orange sun duck behind the skyline. "You know what's bothering me more than anything? I still can't figure out how the bastard got in the house if she didn't let him in. And I don't think she let him in. Look at the struggle that took place in the bedroom. I'd have to say she didn't see him till he was in her room."

Mooney looked down at his watch like he was surprised to find it there on his wrist. "Oh shit, we gotta go."

"Where?" Alves asked.

"The media room. Press conference with the commissioner and the DA. They're hoping to go live on the five o'clock news."

"Do we have to say anything?"

"No. Just stand behind the brass and look good," Mooney said. They started walking toward the bank of elevators. "When we're done, we'll go talk with the rest of the neighbors. Then you can go home to your family and get some sleep."

"Thank God."

"Thank me, not God," Mooney said. "Make sure you get a good rest. In the morning we're going to start looking into every corner of McCarthy's life. I want to know where she did her grocery shopping, where she bought her clothes, where she took her dry cleaning, where she got her keys made, what movie theaters she went to, her favorite restaurants, everything. We'll cross-check it with everything we know about Hayes. These two women came in contact with this sick fuck someplace and we need to find that place."

CHAPTER 8

Andi Norton fished the car keys out of her bag before starting down the stairwell of the courthouse. A habit she'd learned in a self-defense course in college. The parking lot was poorly lit—a couple of the streetlights had been out for months—but the courthouse was close to the police station. Pick up Rachel at Mom's, toss something in the microwave for a quick dinner, read Rachel a story and send her off to bed, then get to work on the trial. As Connie had suggested, she was going to spend her night writing out her direct exam questions for her witnesses and practicing her opening. Connie had done a nice job keeping her nerves under control earlier, but the truth was that this "simple" trial was getting her stressed out.

She'd parked her silver Camry, a hand-me-down from her parents, in the far corner of the lot. Instinctively, she scanned the area for anyone suspicious before closing the courthouse door behind her. From halfway across the lot she could see the car's dull finish, dirty with street salt. She had some of her mom's leftover lasagna in the fridge. That wouldn't take long to heat up. Rachel could have her bath before dinner to save time.

Footsteps behind her, soft at first, then ringing as they drew closer. Someone else was in the lot. Maybe one of the cops heading out on a detail or one of the ADAs working late. She turned, ready to smile, but saw a dark figure in a hooded sweatshirt. She tried to pick up her pace, but the footsteps quickened. Why hadn't she changed into her sneakers? The high heels were useless. Looking over her right shoulder she saw the man in the gray hood closing the gap between them.

Panic rose in her chest and she tried to run. Why hadn't she parked the car closer to the stairs? She clenched the key chain in her right hand, all her keys sticking out between her knuckles like spikes. They weren't brass knuckles, but they would have to do.

She was no more than ten feet from her car but the man's heavy breathing was loud. The battery on her automatic door lock and panic button was dead. She would have to use her key to unlock the door, the same key that was her only weapon. She felt a hand on her left shoulder, and then a tug on the bag in her right hand. A muffled voice said, "Run your shit!"

She was being robbed.

Maybe worse.

Give him the bag, she thought. Isn't that what they taught her in that self-defense class? Give up your wallet, your purse, your keys, your car. Give him whatever it is he wants so he doesn't hurt you. But what if he wasn't going to rob her? What if he was going to throw her in the car and kidnap her? What if he planned on killing her? What if he was the man who'd killed those women? What else did they teach her in that class? Fight! Fight like hell. And make lots of noise.

Andi spun around to her left, leading with her elbow, catching him squarely in the jaw. She let her momentum carry her as she followed with an immediate right cross to the side of his head, the whole time screaming as loud as she could. She didn't get his face with the keys like she'd wanted to, the hood of his sweatshirt protected him. Before he could react, she swung her right foot up and kicked him in the groin. Her pointy shoes came in handy, maybe the best weapon she had. He was hunched over, clutching himself, gasping for air, and she was getting ready to give him another boot when she heard more footsteps running toward them.

Even in the poor light she recognized Connie's familiar frame running toward them. She stepped back as Connie hit the mugger with his shoulder, knocking him down hard onto the asphalt. Connie stayed with him, putting his knee in the man's back to hold him down before jerking off his hood.

With a jolt, Andi Norton recognized Nick Costa, who lay moaning, trying to breathe, blood running from his split lip.

Connie hopped up. "What the hell are you doing?" he asked.

Nick spit blood. "Trying to have some fun with Andi. Figured I could scare her." He was fighting to catch his breath.

"You idiot!" she yelled. "You *did* scare me. What's your problem?" She swung her bag at Nick, hitting him, and he yelped.

"I guess you figured wrong," Connie said. "Are you all right?"

Nick nodded his head, unconvincingly.

Connie helped him to his feet. "You just got your ass kicked."

"Yeah, and I'll be sure to tell everyone about that in the morning," Andi said. "As if I don't have enough stress getting ready for my first trial, you have to pull this crap."

"I'm sorry, Andi," Nick said, getting some wind back. "I understand your being angry and all, but I think you and your goon here"—he nodded toward Connie—"have punished me enough." He wiped the blood from his lip and stared at it for a moment before licking it off his fingers. "You're one tough chick."

She shook her head, stunned that he would pull such a dumb stunt. "I did give you a pretty good beating, didn't I?" she said, trying to play it off.

"I learned my lesson," Nick said. "I won't be harassing any more pretty redheads in deserted parking lots."

"You're lucky she's wearing a skirt or she really would have tuned you up." Connie laughed.

"Ain't that the truth." Nick coughed.

A wave of accomplishment swept over her. She'd handled a dangerous situation. She'd impressed Connie. She smiled to herself, turned back to her car, started it up and backed out of her spot. It felt good to see them both jump out of the way. She leaned out of her window, blew a kiss at Connie and said, "I'll talk to you later. And you, Nick, need to come up with a creative story to explain what happened to your face." She accelerated, leaving the two of them looking after her.

CHAPTER 9

Standing in his garage, Connie unlocked the dead bolt on the heavy wooden door and bumped it open with his hip. He'd bought the 1960s ranch with the attached two-car garage a couple of years earlier as a fixer-upper. Thanks to the summers he'd spent working for contractors during college, he was a pretty decent carpenter, plasterer and painter. He'd recently finished fixing up the basement so he could actually enjoy having his own place. The white house with green trim had been painted pink when Connie first saw it. That was probably why he'd gotten it so cheap.

Walking into the kitchen, he threw his keys on the counter and headed down to the basement. He flopped onto the couch and turned on the television. He could finally relax, knowing that the pager wasn't going to disturb him. He still had some work to do, but at least he didn't have to think about the drug case he'd given to Andi. She'd do a great job with it. He didn't have any worries about that. And he'd seen a new side of her tonight. It had been fun watching her kick Nick's ass in the parking lot. He'd never dated anyone who handled herself like that.

It was almost seven o'clock. He had TiVo'd the broadcasts from Boston's major news stations and now he could watch them at his leisure. Once he got it started, he sat engrossed in the coverage of Susan McCarthy's disappearance.

Sgt. Mooney and Angel Alves stood behind the district attorney and the police commissioner at a press conference. The logo of the BPD, a gray badge with its prominent 1854 on a background of deep blue, was fixed above their heads. Face time for the DA and the commissioner. Neither of them said anything significant beyond the fact that McCarthy was missing. They'd done a good job of giving vanilla answers.

Connie recognized one of the reporters with a reputation for sensational reporting. The man was positioned so his viewers could see his squared jaw and perfectly coiffed white hair as well as his station's logo on his microphone. "Isn't it true that Susan McCarthy is dead? That the physical evidence you have is a bathtub full of her blood?" His intense gaze swiveled smoothly from the podium back toward his cameraperson. Before either man could answer, the reporter continued his cross-examination. "Isn't it also true that there was a similar murder a couple of months ago? And isn't it true that the police are referring to the assailant as the Blood Bath Killer?"

The other reporters now began shouting questions. The DA responded to the barrage by saying that both matters were under investigation. His answer seemed like a resounding "yes" to everything. And that quick, the world knew there was a deranged killer prowling the neighborhoods of Boston.

Channel 7 followed the press conference with file footage of the Boston Strangler murders that had rocked the city between 1962 and 1964. Albert DeSalvo, the Strangler himself, was the city's most infamous serial killer, so what better time to revisit those crimes? The Strangler preyed on women alone in their homes, getting in by posing as a maintenance or delivery man. He then sexually assaulted his victims, strangled them with their own stockings or bathrobe ties and left them in obscene sexual poses.

The report segued to coverage of Susan McCarthy's daughter and distraught ex-husband getting off a plane and being hurried into an unmarked police car. Walter McCarthy's hair was disheveled; his clothes were wrinkled and the circles under his eyes made him look as though he hadn't slept in days. The girl looked confused and frightened by the reporters and cameras. She was maybe seven or eight years old and her long blond hair looked like maybe her father had tried to fix it for her.

She probably didn't really understand what had happened to her mother. Maybe she'd been told that her mother was dead, but she was too young to understand what that meant. Her father might have told her something that was easier for a child to comprehend, like that her mother was now an angel in heaven with some previously deceased relative, maybe a grandparent, and that since Mommy was now an angel she would always be with her and watch out for her.

Connie thought about how this little girl's world had been instantly altered. This one incident would affect her for the rest of her life, as it would every member of Susan McCarthy's family.

Connie was hungry. How many hours ago had he eaten his boiled eggs and tuna? The flickering images faded to coverage of the grieving family and friends, who talked about what a good, caring person Susan was.

What were people supposed to say about Susan? Should a jealous sister say that she hated Susan because Susan was always their mother's favorite? Should a co-worker competing for a promotion say that Susan was a backstabbing brownnoser? No one was going to say anything bad about Susan McCarthy now that she was dead.

Connie's grandmother had often used the expression "Never speak ill of the dead," but he'd always thought it ridiculous. Did it mean you shouldn't speak ill of Hitler? Mussolini? Stalin? What about mass murderers? Nobody could speak ill of Ted Bundy, who killed college students at the University of Florida and women throughout the Pacific Northwest? Or Richard Speck, who killed an apartment full of nursing students during one bloody night of self-gratification? Or Jeffrey Dahmer, who raped, sodomized, murdered and ate people in his apartment in Milwaukee?

Nobody was going to "speak ill" of Susan McCarthy, just like they never said anything bad even when a drug-dealing gangbanger was killed on the city's streets. Connie was sure that the day Jesse Wilcox turned up dead from lead poisoning on some street corner, his mother would be on the television saying he was a good churchgoing boy. Every one of these gangbangers was a *good kid who'd just turned his life around when this tragedy struck him down.* Alves liked to joke about how there must be a serial killer who specialized in knocking off drug-dealing gang members who'd just turned their lives around.

When he looked back at the screen, the voice-over was talking about where Susan McCarthy had gone to school, where she worked, where she volunteered her time: Rosie's Place, a women's shelter for survivors of domestic violence. An elderly neighbor talked of how "Suzie" bought her groceries every Saturday and shoveled her walk in the winter. A blank-faced newspaper boy said "Mrs. McCarthy" would leave him a bag of homemade cookies with his tip every week. It was amazing how many people had been affected by her death.

Connie felt as though he really knew her. He wasn't getting a complete picture of who Susan McCarthy truly was, but she was certainly the type of person he'd have liked to have had as a friend when she was alive.

The segment ended with a Boston Police hotline number anyone could call with information on Susan's disappearance. Authorities were still calling it a disappearance, and she was officially considered a missing person. But Connie had been in that bathroom. Susan McCarthy was dead. No phone calls to a hotline were going to change that fact.

It was getting late. He had to fix some dinner and get to work. He turned off the television and closed his eyes. He truly believed that she was in a better place.

CHAPTER 10

Richter lifted Susan McCarthy out of the refrigerator. He didn't like leaving her in there all day, but it took time for the rigor mortis to dissipate. Now, twenty hours after, her limbs were moving smoothly. He could have worked out the rigor with a little massage and slow movement of the joints, but waiting was easier. He wasn't in any hurry.

He placed her on the large, white enamel table he had once used to fold his laundry. At first glance it looked like a vintage laundry table from the 1920s, but it was actually an antique embalmer's table he'd purchased at a bankruptcy auction at an old, family-owned funeral home.

Susan McCarthy's skin was cold but still soft. All those years of moisturizers had paid off. The peaceful look on her face told Richter she was enjoying Wagner's *The Flying Dutchman,* music he'd selected especially for her.

With the first few notes, he thought of the scene in *Apocalypse Now* when Robert Duvall's Lieutenant Colonel Kilgore explains how they're going to attack a Viet Cong village as helicopters fly in low out of the rising sun with massive speakers blasting *The Ride of the Valkyries.* Over the years Richter had collected all of Wagner's work.

Richter studied Susan's face. The minute lines under her eyes showed her age, but he appreciated her maturity. The bloodshot eyes were always a problem, though. Ocular petechia. It happened every time, an inescapable result of oxygen deprivation. Fortunately, you can pretty much find anything you need on the Internet, even dealers in old medical supplies.

He was pleased to see that the music had relaxed her, and the cold table didn't seem to bother her much. He anticipated spending some good time with Susan after her transformation, but he didn't want her to be uncomfortable in the meantime. The news reports told about how generous and loving a person she was, how she was admired as much for her character as for her mind. He'd made an excellent decision in selecting her.

Her face looked angelic in repose, her naked body somehow innocent. Richter began gently washing her skin with antiseptic soap. Now it was time for the real work. With great care he made an incision in her neck exposing her carotid artery. Raising the artery with an aneurism hook, he made another small incision and placed a tube inside the artery, securing it with string. He followed the same procedure with the other carotid artery as well as both femoral and axillary arteries.

The tubes were connected to a gravity tank suspended four feet above Susan's head. The ten-gallon tank was filled with straight thirty-index arterial fluid, the strongest solution on the market. He had "acquired" the embalming materials from the same funeral home where he had bought the table. They had a full stock of fluids and powders, although they weren't for sale legally. A late-night visit with bolt cutters and the discipline to take only what he needed before he replaced the padlock with his own assured him that the theft would never be detected.

Before removing the clamps on the tubes, allowing the arterial fluid to flow through her arteries and return the color to her skin, Richter inserted drainage tubes in the corresponding veins that allowed the remaining blood to flow out of her body.

But first he had the messy job of removing her organs and filling her abdominal and thoracic cavities with embalming powder and cotton.

Unfortunately, there was no real way to preserve the organs and prevent decomposition. So this was a necessary step.

Tomorrow, once her body had absorbed all of the fluid it could take and he had stitched her up again, he'd dress her in the blue suit he had taken from her closet. Then she could join the others in the next room. He had a feeling Susan McCarthy was going to fit in just fine.

CHAPTER 11

Wayne Mooney parked his car at the bottom of Prospect Hill. He knew from experience that the best time to go through a neighborhood undetected was between two and four in the morning. Breaking-and-entering artists did their best work during those hours.

Mooney was wearing dark sweats. It would be easier to cut through the yards without a suit. He walked up the driveway of the nearest house, into the shadows of the backyard, away from the glow of the streetlights. He stood at the base of the hill looking at the rear of the houses on Prospect Hill Road.

Mooney didn't walk up the hill. He cut across the yards at the foot of the hill until he got closer to the McCarthy house. Then he made his way through a half dozen yards and over a couple of chain-link fences before the house came into view.

Navigating his way through a minefield of toys scattered in one yard, he found himself behind the house adjacent to McCarthy's. Looking up toward the house, he had a perfect vantage point from which to watch Susan McCarthy's bedroom. The view would be even better when he got closer. He hopped the fence. Two decades after making it through the Boston Police Academy, he knew he could still beat most of the younger guys in the obstacle course.

He moved through the neighboring backyard, which was overgrown with shrubs and briars. According to neighbors they'd interviewed last night, the old house hadn't been lived in for some time, not since the elderly woman who owned it retired to her summer house down the Cape. Inside, the house was fully furnished as if she just got up one day and left without packing. The exterior of the house showed signs of deterioration, some of the shingles curling up and others rotted off.

Mooney stood on the side of the house where he had an unobstructed view of Susan McCarthy's bedroom. It was the perfect place to sit and watch her, completely hidden by the neglected boxwood hedges. From his post, he also had a clear view of the basement door where the criminalists had recovered the shoe print. He focused on the door for a moment, scanning the surrounding area. He knew what he needed to do. Get into the McCarthy house. And he was going in through the basement door.

Mooney took a step toward the house and someone knocked his legs out from under him, locked both his arms and took him to the ground. A jolt of pain shot through his chest, his face mashed into the moist dirt. He struggled to free one of his arms and managed to land a few elbows. There was the familiar racking of a semiautomatic, and he saw the shadow of a gun aimed at his head.

"Boston Police. Don't move!" the man with the gun shouted.

The first man regained his hold, Mooney's arms and legs immobilized. He knew enough not to struggle and get himself killed by a couple of overanxious uniforms. And he knew they were uniforms, even though they wore civilian clothing. The one with the gun was wearing black jeans and an oversized black Chicago White Sox baseball jersey. Gang Unit, or maybe the Anti-Crime car from District 5.

"Morning, guys," Mooney said, struggling to turn his head toward the barrel of the gun. "Sergeant Mooney. Homicide. Check my pocket."

Mooney saw the look on the young cop's face change. Mooney had never seen the kid before, but the kid now recognized Mooney. Maybe he had seen Mooney at the scene last night.

"Oh shit, Sarge, we're sorry," he said, putting his gun back in its holster. "Jackie, let go of him," he said to his partner. "It's Sergeant Mooney."

"How do you know? Check his credentials."

"Trust me, I know. Just let him up."

The big guy let go of him. Mooney stood up, brushed the dirt off and tried to get the circulation flowing in his arms and legs. Maybe he couldn't compete with these younger guys after all. "I didn't even know you were behind me. You guys Anti-Crime?"

"Yeah, we're in the K-Car on last halves. I'm Mark Greene," he said, extending his hand to Mooney. "My partner's Jack Ahearn. Sorry if he roughed you up."

"Roughed me up? I didn't even know what hit me. You guys do a good job. What are you, some kind of judo guy?"

"Wrestler, sir," Ahearn said.

"High school? College?"

"Both."

"You're pretty good."

"I know, sir."

"What are you doing out here, Sarge?" Greene asked.

"Since this is my murder investigation, why don't you tell me what you guys are doing here?"

"We just figure sometimes these killers return to the scenes of their crimes. We've been sitting on the house since midnight. Came here straight from roll call."

"Good thinking," Mooney said. "Unfortunately, if he was coming back, I'm sure we just scared him off."

"Do you need us to help you with anything, Sarge?" Greene asked.

"I'm trying to figure out how this guy operates. I think I know how he got here undetected and where he hid while he cased the place. Now I just need to get into the house the way he did. I'm pretty sure I've solved that mystery. But before I go breaking into the house, why don't you guys call for a marked car so everyone knows we're the good guys?"

CHAPTER 12

Fumbling through the junk piled on his nightstand, Alves found his cell phone and answered it on the fourth ring. "Yeah."

"He slid his arm in through the dryer vent."

What time was it? Four fifty-six, according to the bedroom clock's digital readout. Was that Wayne Mooney's excited voice booming in his ear?

"The exhaust vent for the clothes dryer is so close to the basement door, you can reach right in, knock off the hose and unlock the door. I just did it myself."

Sergeant Mooney was at the McCarthy house at five in the morning?

"That's how he got into the house without waking Susan McCarthy. That's why the only struggle was in her bedroom, when he startled her awake. She didn't let him in. She was being watched, probably from overgrown shrubs at the house next door. The killer knew she was alone and he knew how to get in the house because the dryer vent was right in front of him." Mooney finally took a breath.

Silence.

Alves glanced at Marisela. Such a beautiful name, but she liked to be called Marcy. She seemed to be breathing regularly. Good. The phone hadn't woken her up. Maybe she was finally getting used to the calls at all hours. He watched her closely in the dim bedroom light. Maybe her breathing was just a little too regular. She hadn't stirred since he'd picked up the phone, hadn't shifted to accommodate his body's movement. She was pretending to be asleep. "Sarge, do you know what time it is?" Alves tried to keep his voice down. "What are you doing out there?"

"Woke up at two and couldn't get back to sleep, so I figured what better time to come out here than the middle of the night, just like the bad guy."

"The neighbors are going to think the killer's back."

"I have a marked unit with me. This is our first break, Angel. Now we know the footprint by the cellar door is probably his. And the dryer vent has rough metal edges, so there's a possibility he left some hair or fiber evidence when he reached in to open the door. The crime lab's coming to check it out. What size was the footprint?"

"Ten and a half, New Balance."

"I'm going to the New Balance Factory Store in Brighton as soon as they open. I know they sell irregulars. Back in the day, I used to buy my running shoes there. Nice discount for anyone in the BPD Runners Club. They should have no trouble figuring out the sneaker model. Maybe they can tell us where and how many might have been sold locally in the last couple of months."

"Should I meet you there?"

"No. I want you to keep working on how these two women crossed paths with the killer. Have you run it through ViCAP yet? There have to be some other missing-persons cases where foul play is suspected."

"Nothing there. I even spoke with an FBI agent in Quantico to make sure I hadn't missed anything."

"Then go back and look at our unsolved homicides and missing-persons reports from the past year. Look for successful, divorced women who lived alone or were home alone the last time they were seen alive. This isn't the first time our guy has killed. He's killed before and he's decided to start taking the bodies and leaving the blood behind for us."

"Sarge, I don't think serial killers change their MO."

"I don't think he has *changed* his MO, he's still *developing* it. He's performing some sort of ritual that he's perfecting. There are some sick thoughts going through this guy's head, and I'd say he's getting more daring with every kill. The first time he probably left the body right where it was and took off in a panic. Or maybe he dumped the body. I'm sure he didn't start by killing Michelle Hayes, draining her blood and taking her body."

"I'll give it a shot and let you know if I come up with anything."

He brushed the long brown hair off Marcy's cheek. He felt her stiffen. In that moment he hated Mooney for calling so early. Two more hours and he'd be having coffee with the guy anyhow. He couldn't have waited to fill him in?

Mooney read the silence. "Angel"—his voice was tight and tinged with anger—"in a homicide investigation, you have to follow every lead. You take what you've got and investigate the hell out of it so that you can catch this guy before he kills again. And he will kill again. If you don't think Homicide's for you—"

"Sarge," Alves began, "I didn't mean to—"

"I need you to chase down the evidence so we can figure out how these women came across this guy and ended up dead. That'll be the most important piece of this puzzle. Once we know how *he* found *them, we'll* find *him.* I'll be at New Balance. You go through those missing-persons reports. I'll see you at headquarters in a couple of hours."

Alves flipped his phone closed and sat up in bed trying to focus his eyes with the light from the clock. He looked at Marcy. He never wanted to let the job come before his family, but Mooney was right. This was Homicide.

He leaned over and kissed Marcy on the cheek. "Happy Birthday," he whispered.

"Are you leaving?" she asked, without moving, her eyes shut tight.

"I have to. Sarge has already been up for three hours."

"So we can't have a life because your boss is an obsessive maniac?"

"He's doing his job. How can I complain? He's not asking me to do anything he wouldn't do."

She lay there quietly, facing away from him. He heard her short, quick breaths. He was screwed.

"Marcy, we both knew this was going to happen. But we decided that this was the best thing for us right now. Homicide is going to look great on my résumé. And we need the money if we're ever going to get out of this tiny house and send the twins to private school. You were more than happy with the thirty hours of guaranteed overtime every week. Well, this is why it's guaranteed."

He was making sense, but he knew she was not in the mood to hear it. She'd been comfortable with their old life, when he had a regular shift and they could sit and have a cup of coffee together in the morning. Still, she had to understand that he was doing this for her and the kids. He gave her another kiss on the cheek. This time he whispered, "I love you." He stood up, and with the help of the kids' night-light in the hall, walked toward the bathroom.

CHAPTER 13

Nick Costa stepped out of the clerk's office with the police reports for the day's arraignments. Behind him he heard knocking on the glass entrance. A pretty blonde was trying to get his attention. Just his luck that a good-looking juror would show up on a day when he didn't have a trial scheduled.

Nick checked his watch: It was only seven thirty. He opened the door a crack. "I'm sorry, Miss, but jurors aren't allowed in until the courthouse opens. You're about an hour early."

"I'm not here for jury duty," she said. "I'm with the DA's office."

Nick stammered for a moment, then caught himself. "I didn't mean to offend you," he said, extending his hand. "My name's Nick Costa."

"Monica Hughes," she said. She had a firm handshake, almost too firm, and she made some serious eye contact. Someone, probably her father, had told her the importance of a good handshake and eye contact. It didn't come naturally for her. She gripped his hand as if she were trying to crush it, jerking his arm up and down.

On the other hand, thought Nick, she had a great body, tall and athletic. Not an ounce of fat on her, and blue eyes to go with her short blond hair.

"I'm with the DA's office too," Nick said. "I think you're going to be tagging along with me today in arraignments."

"I didn't mean to snap," she said, taking a moment to grab a breath.

"It bothers me when people assume I'm a juror or a victim because I'm a woman."

Nick nodded. "Sorry for making that assumption," he said. "Listen, let me show you around. The clerk's office and probation department are at those counters," he said, pointing straight ahead past the metal detectors and the security checkpoint. "The courtrooms are this way." He gestured toward the stairs.

She walked two steps ahead of him as they made their way up the stairs. A swimmer, he figured, or a runner. Hell, she could probably finish the Boston Marathon without breaking a sweat.

"You ever been in a courtroom or argue in front of a judge?" Nick asked as they reached the second floor.

"No."

"Not even an internship?"

"Nothing."

"So you really are new at this? Get ready, because you're about to take a crash course in the criminal justice system." It was clear he was going to have to teach her everything. Not a bad assignment at all.

"I've seen courtrooms on TV. I'm not worried."

He laughed out loud. He knew she wouldn't appreciate it, but he couldn't help it. "You better be worried. It's a lot different in a real courtroom, when you're the one standing up there arguing in front of the judge. Let's see if the first session is open," he said, pointing down the hall. "I'd rather show you around before the courtroom is crowded."

Nick directed her down the corridor. On second thought, maybe she was too good-looking. How was he supposed to concentrate on his work?

The door to the courtroom was locked, but he jiggled the handle and it popped open. One of the advantages to working in the same courthouse every day was that he got to know all of the little idiosyncrasies of the building. He held the door for her. They entered the courtroom with its white walls and pale woodwork, and he saw the look of surprise on her face.

"This isn't at all what I pictured," she said.

"I told you. Get that TV crap out of your head."

"I was expecting dark wood-paneled walls and ceilings with antique chandeliers. This place looks so modern and bright. It's so . . . *plain.*" She pointed toward the front of the courtroom and the two tables separated by a podium in front of the bench. "Which table is ours?" she asked.

"The one on the right," he said. "We are the prosecutors, you know."

"Right," she said with a smile. "Thanks. You know? I like this place. I think I'll be just fine."

"Don't get too cocky. You're still in an empty courtroom. This place will be a circus by ten o'clock. We arraigned more than eight thousand new cases in this courtroom last year. That's almost seven hundred a month."

"Do you guys get a lot of jury trials?"

Wow, she *was* ambitious. Her first day on the job, she hadn't even done an arraignment and she was trying to figure out how many jury trials she was going to have. "If we're lucky we average about two a month."

"That's all?"

"If you were at a firm you'd be lucky to get one a year."

"Yeah, but I'm not at a firm. I'm in a courthouse that had eight thousand arraignments last year, remember?"

"What a wiseass." He laughed. "Very few cases go to trial," he explained. "Most of them plead out or get dismissed. There are times when you think a case is definitely going but something goes wrong at the last minute. Your witnesses don't show up, the defendant defaults, the Creole interpreter doesn't show up or you don't have enough people to sit a full jury."

"You actually have days when you can't get twelve people to show up for jury duty?"

"*Eight,*" he said. "District courts use six-person juries with two alternates." He gestured toward the jury box with its eight empty seats. "You could go to trial with six jurors, but if you lost one for any reason—

illness or family emergency—you'd have a mistrial and have to start all over."

She walked toward the front of the room and stood at the podium. She looked back over at the empty courtroom and jury box, and then turned toward the judge's bench. "How long have you been with the office?" she asked, her head tilted up at the seal of Massachusetts high on the wall behind the bench. It wasn't an innocent question. She wanted to know how experienced he was, if she should take his advice.

"A year," he said. "I've been at South Bay the whole time. There's so much turnaround, I'm already one of the more experienced prosecutors here. Liz has been around for three years. Most people leave the office if they don't get promoted to superior court within three years. Some with political aspirations put a year or two in as a prosecutor so they can say they're 'tough on crime.' But most of us are here to get trial experience that you can't get anywhere else. That's how we justify making less money than the secretaries at most big law firms."

"How many trials have you had?" she asked, still facing the judge's bench. She didn't seem overly impressed by his long-winded explanation.

"Ten, over the past six months," he said. "Most of them were dogs, but the defendants wouldn't plead guilty, so I took them to trial. They weren't the sexiest cases, but in the end I'd done ten openings, ten closings and a bunch of directs and crosses."

She turned toward him, looking at him directly. "What's your record of wins and losses?"

The one question he had hoped she wouldn't ask. He didn't want her to know he had lost every one of his trials. "No one around here cares about wins and losses as long as you try the case."

"Still, you must keep track of your record."

"Really, I don't. If I start counting wins and losses I might get gun-shy about trying a case. The way I see it, if a defendant refuses to change his plea to guilty—no matter how weak or strong my case is—then bring in the jurors, give me eight in the box, and let's start the trial."

Nick could see that Monica wasn't impressed with his explanation, and he was starting to lecture her. Here was this gorgeous woman, his captive audience for the day, and he was boring her before their first cup of coffee. He needed to change the subject or he was going to blow this perfect opportunity.

"Shit," Nick said, looking up at the clock and heading back toward the door. "It's eight o'clock. We'd better get upstairs and start prepping these files."

CHAPTER 14

Connie sat at the far end of the conference room watching Andi Norton as she practiced her opening statement. She faltered a few times, and whenever she paused she mumbled a deadening "um..." Still, he had to test her ability to concentrate under stressful conditions. Better for her to panic now than in front of the jury. Connie looked around the room—the bored juror routine. Andi stopped mid-sentence. From the corner of his eye he saw her scrambling to collect her thoughts, finally shaking her head in frustration. "What's wrong?" he asked innocently.

"You know what's wrong," she hissed at him. "Why did you do that to me?"

"You need to focus on your case and nothing else. You can't worry about what the jurors or the judge are doing. If someone comes into the courtroom during the trial, you don't turn to see who it is, even if it's the DA himself."

"Connie, give me a break," she said. "I'm not even a goddamn lawyer and I'm about to start a trial." Her face flushed with intensity.

"I love the emotion you show, but you need to tone it down a bit or you're going to turn the jurors off. This is a drug case, not a murder."

"I'm so scared my hands are shaking." She held her hands out for him. "Can you see that?"

He took her hands and gave them a gentle squeeze. "I can't see it. And if I can't see it standing this close to you, no one else can see it.

How about some pointers to help calm you down? First, let's talk about your case. This is a marijuana distribution case, right? The defendant sold a dime bag to an undercover cop, a misdemeanor. That's not the crime of the century, is it?"

"No."

"The defendant has no record, so even if you convict him, he'll probably get probation. Correct?" He was asking her leading questions the same way he'd control a defense witness during a cross-examination.

"Correct."

Her shoulders had loosened up and the redness in her face had mellowed.

He continued to hold her hands and looked into her eyes. "The way I see it, whatever happens, this case isn't exactly Sacco and Vanzetti. I understand it's tough standing up in front of a jury for the first time. What about the first time you did an arraignment or argued a motion in front of a judge?"

"I was nervous."

"Do you still get the jitters when you argue a motion?"

"Nothing I can't deal with."

"Because you've gotten used to it. You realize that you know more law than some of the judges. The jury doesn't know *anything* about the law. They know even less about the facts of your case. Aside from standing up in front of a bunch of strangers, you have nothing to be nervous about."

"I'll trust you on that," she said, "because right now I feel like I'm going to throw up."

"One more tip to get you into a rhythm at the beginning of the trial: Once the judge tells me I can begin my opening, I take a deep breath and a sip of water. I stand up and slowly push my chair back in to the table." Connie demonstrated for her. "This little ritual—I know it doesn't seem like much—gives me a second to pull my thoughts together. The jury is focused on me and nothing else in that courtroom. They're watching me, and I'm performing some simple movements that I can't screw up. They see how calm and poised I am, and I haven't said a word yet."

"Eventually you have to say something. That's when I'm going to look like an idiot."

"You're not, because the next thing you're going to do is introduce yourself and tell the jurors what your role is in the trial. Now, you're talking, but you're saying something familiar. You can't mess it up. Before you know it, you're talking to the jury. From that point on it's simple: You tell them a story. You explain the facts of the case the same way you explained them to me a few minutes ago. Then you're examining witnesses, doing a closing argument and the case is over, just like that." Connie snapped his fingers. "Did you practice your opening and closing last night?"

"Yes, while I was lying in bed."

"That'll have to do for today, but from now on you should do it in front of the mirror or just stand in your apartment and imagine you're in the courtroom. Pretend the couch is the jury box and the TV is the judge, that kind of thing. Either way is good, but I think the mirror works best when you're first starting out. There's nothing tougher than watching yourself talk into a mirror."

"Now I feel like I'm going to screw up."

"You'll be fine for your opening. Just tell the story to the jury. The closing is more important. We can work on that at lunch. I'll be second-seating you, anyway, so if you run into any problems, I'll jump in. But you're not going to run into any problems, are you?"

"No," she said, smiling.

He nodded. "It's only been a couple of years since I had my first trial, so I know how hard it is. The key is to jump in there and get started, because once you're on your feet getting into *your* case—and remember, you're the one that knows every little detail of it—you won't have time to be nervous. We're like actors waiting for our stage call. Once we hit the boards, you can't hold us back."

CHAPTER 15

"Good news!" Mooney shouted in Angel's ear. Like many of the pre–cell phone generation, Mooney shouted into the phone like he was talking to someone in the next room. "I'm at New Balance in Brighton. The irregulars are called factory seconds. This is the only place in the city that sells them. They're pulling all their credit card sales for me."

"What if he paid cash?"

"Then we get nothing. I'll fax the list of names over to the office. Run their BOPs and Triple I them. Let's see if anyone has a record in-state or out."

"How far back are they going? He could have bought the sneakers months ago."

"The shoe is a model they put out last month."

"What about security cameras?" Alves asked. "Do they video the register sales?"

"Yes. But they tape over them every couple of weeks. I need you to check with McCarthy's credit card companies to see if she bought anything here. Same thing for Hayes. And call Walter McCarthy to see if he can meet me at the house again. Apologize for being such a pain in his ass. Tell him we're looking for any receipts from New Balance. Maybe that's where this guy locked onto her."

"That's a long shot, isn't it, Sarge?"

"Everything's a long shot at this point. Just fuckin' do it," Mooney snapped. "We need to look at every link we have to this guy. And tell

McCarthy I'll meet him at the house in an hour. I'll catch up with you later to see how it's going with the list."

"Got it," Alves said.

"Anything else?" Mooney asked.

"Yeah, some bad news. I heard back from the lab. There were no obvious extraneous hairs or fibers anywhere in the McCarthy house. The dryer vent didn't turn up anything either. All they found was a lot of lint that'll be impossible to sort through. No fabric or human cells on the jagged edges of the sheet-metal dryer vent cover. They're going to keep sifting through the lint, but Eunice didn't sound enthusiastic."

Mooney grunted. "I'll touch base with you later," he said.

Alves caught the edge of disappointment and urgency in his sergeant's voice. Mooney was in investigation overdrive. The man was under pressure, both from outside—the commissioner and the mayor—and from within. He seemed to be holding himself responsible for the murders. Angel thought—and not for the first time—that he would never be as driven as Mooney.

CHAPTER 16

The defense attorney was already an hour late. Connie was irritated, but he could see that the long wait in the hall outside the trial session was starting to wear on Andi. She kept adjusting her hair, flipping it back, pulling it forward over her shoulder. The defense attorney was sure to get a lecture from Judge Davis for showing up late on trial day. Good enough for him. "Stay loose." He touched her shoulder. "This could be a defense tactic to rattle you."

"Connie." He turned to see Brendan Sullivan. Brendan had been the rookie prosecutor in the office before Monica Hughes was hired. He had grown up on the streets of South Boston, a product of the D Street projects, one of the toughest public-housing developments in the city. A true Southie boy who had never left home except to go away to college. Connie admired his intelligence, his quick wit and his vicious sense of humor. And nobody put in more time working up a case than Brendan. Like everyone from Southie, Brendan was also politically connected. His influence was a direct line to the DA himself, and he made a point of letting everyone know that he couldn't lose his job unless he got caught, as he liked to say, with a dead hooker in the trunk of his car.

"What's up?" Connie said.

"You got a minute?" Brendan waved Connie away from Andi. "I've got a case with an old friend, Peter Fitzpatrick."

Connie smiled. "The state senator's son?"

"The one and only. We grew up together. Just joined his dad's law

firm. Wants to make a name for himself, impress the old man. He's trying to pressure me to take care of him on a case."

"Want me to handle it for you?" Connie asked. "I don't mind, if you
feel uncomfortable telling him to fuck off."

"I don't want you to do my job. I've been around here long enough
to handle things on my own. I just want to make sure I'm doing the
right thing."

"Go with your gut. If he was really your friend, he wouldn't put you
in this posi—"

"Hey, Sully."

Connie turned to see a tall, beefy, red-faced Peter Fitzpatrick coming out of the second session. The man's gym membership had obviously expired some time ago.

"Let him know how things work around here," Connie said under
his breath, through a forced smile of greeting. "Tell him that you don't
hand out favors." Connie could feel the muscles in his jaw tensing up.
The thought of someone using a friendship, trying to curry favor, using
political connections for personal gain—all of it went against everything
he believed in, everything the system stood for.

Brendan stepped toward Fitzpatrick to shake hands. He was just as
tall as the senator's son, but Brendan was thick with muscle, not bloat.

"C'mon, Sully, do me this one," Connie heard Fitzpatrick say.

"You know I can't do that, Pete," Brendan said. "I have to treat every
defendant the same, no matter who his lawyer is."

"It's not like that, Sully. My client's not a bad guy. If he gets a conviction, it'll end his career. He's a union carpenter. Needs his car and license to get to work. A cocaine distribution and they'll yank his license.
It's a felony conviction. Sully, he shared some coke with a friend and an
undercover saw it go down. I'm just asking you to cut him some slack
and break it down to a straight possession, a misdemeanor. Then maybe
I can get the judge to let him plead to sufficient facts. I don't want him
to end up with a guilty on his record."

The two men exchanged a few words Connie couldn't make out, and
then he heard Brendan, his voice louder, firmer. "This is a legitimate

distribution case. It doesn't matter if he sold the stuff or shared it, it's still a distribution. How can I reduce it to a possession?"

"In order to *distribute* it, he had to have *possessed* it first. It's not illogical."

"I can't believe you said that with a straight face." Brendan shook his head. "If my supervisor found out I did something like that for an old friend from Southie, she'd stick me in arraignments for a year. If the judge figured it out . . ."

Connie admired how Brendan looked directly at Peter Fitzpatrick, how he kept his hand on the man's elbow, how he sounded pained to deliver the bad news. Here was a man who knew how to avoid an ugly confrontation. Most of all, he was a man of principle.

"Sully, I've never asked you for anything before," Fitzpatrick said.

"I like it that way." Brendan let go of Fitzpatrick's elbow and took a step back.

"This guy is popular in the union." Fitzpatrick nodded his head toward his client—a tense, wiry man, uncomfortable with his combed hair and his shirt and tie—who had come out of the courtroom and was standing by the balcony glaring at them.

"Gee, I wonder why?" Brendan said sarcastically.

"It's not because of the drugs. He's not a dealer. He's a regular guy with a habit. And the union leaders like him. *They* actually hired me to help the kid out. They want him to get help. If I can get him off without a guilty, it makes me look good. The guys at the union are going to hear about what a nice job I did. Bring more work in for me and the old man."

"You're not the one that's going to lose your career."

"But it's not going to make you look bad for your boss or for the judge either. They'll think you're being reasonable."

"Sorry, Pete," Brendan said firmly. Connie could see that he felt bad saying no to a friend.

"C'mon, Brendan," Fitzpatrick said, almost begging. "Do the right thing. He's not the typical guy you see in this court. He's like you and me, just a ham-'n'-egger tryin' to make a living."

"Do the right thing?" Brendan asked, angry now.

Connie could see it in the stiffening of Brendan's back, the way his neck reddened. Their voices were edging louder. Connie imagined what would have happened if these two had met for a school yard fight. He figured that on size and strength alone, Brendan would have taken Fitzpatrick out with one punch. Andi caught Connie's attention and gestured that she was going to the water cooler. She didn't need the stress of watching two lawyers brawling in the hallway before her first trial.

"He's like you and me?" Brendan asked. "What's that supposed to mean? He's white so he deserves a break?" Brendan shot a look at the client who lounged against the wall, looking like he wanted nothing more than to light up a cigarette and toss back a beer. "I'm not giving your guy special treatment because he's white or because you represent him. I'll offer him a guilty finding with a year of probation, same thing I'd offer anyone who walked into this court."

Fitzpatrick's whole demeanor shifted. "Now I get it," he said. "All of a sudden, you're a true believer. I think maybe you forgot where you came from."

"I grew up in the projects, not in some mansion overlooking Castle Island. You don't know where the fuck I came from, so don't ever pull that shit on me. I gave you an offer. Take it or leave it."

"You can shove your offer up your ass, Brendan."

"Good. Let's pick a trial date. That is, if you have the balls to actually try a case instead of just begging for a break." Brendan turned and walked toward the courtroom.

Fitzpatrick hunkered with his client, the man gesturing wildly at the bad news.

When Connie looked back toward Andi, he saw that she'd spotted the defense attorney that'd kept them waiting. She took a few steps toward the man, her hand extended in a greeting. Good strategy. Don't show how pissed you are about the little head game of being late.

He'd have to remember to tell Brendan what a smooth job he'd done, handling Peter Fitzpatrick.

CHAPTER 17

Sergeant Mooney's silver Ford Taurus was parked on the street behind a black SUV. Angel Alves parked behind them and made his way to the back door of the McCarthy house. He stepped through the small mudroom, its walls covered in old-fashioned bead board, and directly into the kitchen. Before he found Mooney, he could hear his voice.

"Mr. McCarthy," Alves said, extending his hand to the man seated at the kitchen table with Mooney.

"Call me Walter."

"Any luck?" Alves gestured to a pile of credit card statements.

"Nothing from New Balance," Mooney said. "But we did find something strange. One of her suits is missing."

"When I got here," Walter McCarthy said, "Susan's mother was upstairs going through her stuff." The man looked as though he hadn't slept since he'd gotten the news of his ex-wife's disappearance. "She just wants to touch everything Susan wore, to smell her again." He stopped talking for a moment, trying to control his own emotions. He took a breath. "As she's going through the closet she notices that Susan's favorite blue suit is missing. It was an expensive suit that she bought in New York last fall. Susan called it her money suit."

"Are you sure it's not in the house?" Alves asked.

"I'm sure," McCarthy said. "We looked everywhere. My mother-in-law is upstairs now, taking another look." He glanced at the ceiling above them. "It's really getting to her."

"What about Fidelity?" Alves asked. "Could she have left the suit at work?"

"I checked with her supervisor," Mooney said. "She kept some clothes in a closet, but there was no suit."

"Dry cleaners?" Alves asked.

"She's gone to the same place for years. They keep track of everything by phone number. She had a few things that she dropped off on Saturday, but no suit."

"Angel, let me talk to you outside for a minute. Could you excuse us, Walter?" Mooney said.

"I'll go up and check on her." He seemed relieved to have something to do.

They walked down the stairs and into the small, fenced yard. Mooney turned to Alves. "What about the list from New Balance?"

"A few of the guys had records. Nothing significant. Mostly drug possessions and motor vehicle stuff. It might be worth going out to see them in person."

"Not now. Angel, I think our killer took the suit as a souvenir for himself. As if taking her body wasn't enough. I want you to contact Michelle Hayes's parents and see if any of her clothes are missing. I don't know what this fuckin' nut is up to, but I'm sure he did the same thing with Hayes. Call me if you need me." Mooney walked back into the house.

Alves wasn't looking forward to speaking with Michelle Hayes's parents again. Nice, solid people. He didn't want to raise their hopes. But if one of Michelle's dresses was missing, maybe they'd all have the break they were praying for.

CHAPTER 18

Andi Norton needed to clear her head. The judge had only given them a fifteen-minute recess, enough time for the lawyers and the jurors to stretch their legs and use the bathroom. She needed more time than that. Her case was falling apart.

"What the hell is wrong with you?" Connie had come up behind her.

The disappointment in his voice stung. "I'm getting my ass kicked. I can't even ask a question without that jerk objecting."

"He's playing games with you, like he did this morning by showing up late. He's trying to throw you off."

"It's working."

"No shit. He does this on every case. It's his shtick. And he's not going to let up unless you show him that it's not bothering you. Right now he smells blood. You'd better get your head out of your ass if you plan on winning."

"And how do I do that?"

"Start by showing a little confidence. What I saw in there was a person who didn't even believe in her own case. If you don't believe in it, why should the jury?"

"He keeps objecting. I can't get any kind of rhythm going."

"The thing is that you've responded to all his objections, and he's been overruled. You're winning those little battles. So the jury sees that you're not doing anything wrong. You look like the better lawyer. But he's got you rattled. If you regain your composure and keep crushing his objections you'll be fine. But you have to get fired up before it's too late."

She felt beaten down, but there was no reason for it. Connie was right, she had been doing a good job with her arguments. Maybe the defense was coming at her harder because she was a woman. Well, she had to show him that he couldn't mess with her. "Let's go kick some ass," she said as she turned back toward the courtroom.

CHAPTER 19

Alves tapped his fingers on the steering wheel as he waited for Mooney to answer his phone. Mooney picked up on the third ring. "What do you have for me?" he bellowed.

"I just left Michelle Hayes's mother. One of Michelle's dresses *is* missing. A black skirt-suit that she wore for important meetings," Alves said. "Her parents are storing all of her stuff in their attic. We went through dozens of boxes." There was a new energy running through Alves. Mooney's predawn wake-up call was forgiven. It felt good to know something new about the killer. Now they had to figure out why he took the clothing.

Alves turned the key in the ignition and pulled away from the side-walk in front of the Hayes house. Michelle Hayes's parents lived in White City, originally a couple of apartment buildings arising near Forest Hills, their pale stucco suggesting the glowing, ethereal beauty of the white buildings designed for the World's Columbian Exposition held in Chicago at the turn of the century. Alves had seen photographs in his History of Architecture class in college.

"Did he take anything else?"

"Not sure," Alves said. "Her mom didn't know everything she owned, but she had seen Michelle in the missing suit a couple of times."

"McCarthy's mother thinks the killer may have taken some of her underwear too," Mooney said. "According to her, Susan was very neat and her underwear drawer looked like it had been ransacked, but she couldn't say for sure if anything was missing."

Alves drove past Forest Hills onto South Street in Jamaica Plain. "I can't stop wondering why he's doing this." He could hear Mooney breathing on the other end. "Talking to those two families today . . . do you ever get used to it, Sarge?"

"You get numb," Mooney said, "which isn't the same thing." Then his booming voice was back, "It's been a tough couple of days, but we've finally got something. Where are you now?"

"Almost to the monument in JP."

"We need to sit down and figure out our next move."

"Sarge, it's Marcy's thirtieth birthday, remember? Her parents are having a big party for her. They've invited all our friends from the old neighborhood. I told you about it last week."

"Last week I didn't know there was a serial killer in the city. I hate to spoil your time, but you're going to have to cancel. We need to work tonight. This case is going cold quickly."

"I can't cancel. Why don't I just go for a while and catch up with you later, Sarge?" Alves was begging. Marcy was not happy with him getting called out so early on her birthday. She would be livid if he missed the party with all their friends and family. "She'll kill me if I'm not there. The kids will be crying if I don't show up."

"How are the twins doing?"

"They're fine. Angel's had a cold this week, but Iris is her usual self, bouncing off the walls."

"The kids will get over their daddy missing a party. We are working this case *together*. This isn't some assault or robbery case. It's not even your typical murder investigation. You'd better be prepared to work sixteen-hour days until we get this guy. Your family has to accept it too. Don't worry, though, I'll be sure to sign your overtime slip," Mooney said. "Marcy will be happy when she sees your paycheck next week."

"I won't be alive next week," Alves muttered. No wonder the guy's divorced, he thought.

"She did want you to make Homicide, didn't she?"

"Yeah." He knew where this was going.

"Welcome to Homicide. Do you want me to call her for you?"

"No thanks. I can handle that myself, but I appreciate your thoughtfulness."

"Don't mention it. I'll see you when you get here. And pick up some dinner for us on the way. I don't care what you get, surprise me," Mooney said.

"You hungry, Sarge?"

"As a matter of fact, I am."

"I have a great idea. How about we get some work done first. Then we can shoot over to the hall, get a quick bite and save my marriage at the same time. We have to eat anyway, and it's only five minutes from headquarters. I guarantee the food will be excellent. We won't stay more than an hour. You can be my excuse to leave, and then Marcy can be mad at you instead of me."

"What do I get out of this?"

"A free meal and a happy detective, who will show his appreciation by busting his ass for you."

CHAPTER 20

Mitch Beaulieu thumbed through a stack of booking photos from the previous days' arrests. So many black faces, so many hollow lives destroyed by poor education, drug addiction and violence. He sat at his desk while everyone packed up work to take home. He wasn't overly anxious to get to his empty apartment, the one he used to share with the woman he loved.

He'd met Sonya Jordan at Harvard Law in an advanced criminal procedure class. She was the first woman president of the Black Law Students Association and was perceived by many, especially the white males, as a militant, both for her feminist views and her opinions on racism in the United States. By the end of the first semester, Sonya had moved in with Mitch in his cramped apartment in Harvard Square. Their relationship was proof that opposites attract. Mitch had always wanted to be a prosecutor and Sonya was born to be the next great criminal-defense attorney.

Mitch was the only conservative voice on the BLSA, so he argued with Sonya over everything from affirmative action to the American criminal justice system and the prison industrial complex. They rarely agreed on anything. It was the passion in their arguments that led to the passion in their relationship. Mitch loved her. He was sure she loved him too. But in the end the philosophical differences that had brought them together tore them apart. It'd been almost six months since she'd left Boston, and he was having trouble accepting the breakup.

Looking at the booking photos served as a reminder of why Sonya had ended their relationship. She'd never bought into his view that he could help make neighborhoods safer places for people to live and raise their families. He remembered her saying that he was "persecuting his own people by helping racist cops put young black men in jail." In the end she told him she couldn't continue to live with him as long as he worked as a prosecutor.

As much as he loved her, his work was too important to give up. He did the job to make a difference. He was working for a cause greater than himself and Sonya, greater than the love they shared. It had been unfair for her to make him choose between the two things that made his life complete. He chose the job, hoping Sonya would eventually understand and come back. She never did. They hadn't spoken in months. He heard that she'd accepted a job in the DC area.

Tonight he wanted to talk, to tell her he wasn't so sure anymore. He *felt* as if he was helping his people. After all, his father had raised him well, teaching his only child what it meant to be a decent person. But his father didn't understand what it meant to be black. All through his childhood, he'd felt the stigma of being a black child adopted by a white father. And now Mitch feared his upbringing had limited his understanding of what it meant to be black.

Staring at the booking photos, he felt guilty thinking he'd had a difficult childhood. But for him it was tough growing up not knowing who his real parents were. As a teenager, he'd pictured his birth mother as an upper-class white girl with long red hair, the color of the sun setting over Chesapeake Bay, and striking gray eyes, his eyes. Mitch envisioned his father as a young black man, maybe a college student who worked summers as a laborer, who met Mitch's mother while working on her family's estate. In Mitch's young mind, his father was tall and handsome with a powerful jaw and black hair slightly darker than the color of his skin. After the two fell in love, they would sneak off into the woods surrounding the estate.

Mitch was sure his mother's parents would never have approved of the relationship, pushing her even closer to her lover. Later that summer, when her parents learned she was pregnant, she was probably sent away to a home with other unwed pregnant girls so she could give birth to her child and give it up for adoption. When she returned home, Mitch's father was gone. The two lovers never saw each other again and spent the rest of their lives dreaming of reuniting.

Mitch didn't care if his story was true. It was unrealistic and sentimental, but he clung to it because what was the alternative? Sitting around thinking his real mother hadn't wanted him?

The sky outside the courthouse was a soft pink as night began to fall on the cars, buses, and people—*his* people—passing through Dudley Square. He wished he could talk to Sonya. He needed to figure out if he was doing the right thing working as a prosecutor. As he looked down at the booking photos in front of him, then back at the people in the Square, he wondered if Sonya was right.

"Hey, Red." Connie's voice startled him. "I meant to tell you earlier. You left your gym bag in the trunk of the Response car last week. I can give it to you now or in the morning."

"Tomorrow's fine," Mitch said, distracted. Connie and Nick were walking toward the door with their briefcases. Brendan had just stood up to put on his jacket. "Hey, guys," said Mitch. "Tell me something. What do you think of when you see these mug shots every day?"

"I think they're criminals that broke the law and need to be punished," Nick said.

"What about the ones who haven't done anything all that bad?" Mitch asked.

"No matter how minor the crime, they should be held accountable," Nick said. "I believe that whole 'broken windows' philosophy. If you don't prosecute the quality-of-life crimes, you end up with drug dealing and shootings."

"That's not what I mean," Mitch said. "Focus on the *people,* not the crimes. What do you think when you see all those black faces, day after day?"

"C'mon, Mitch," Nick sighed, "don't make it a race thing. People get arrested for the crimes they commit. It's not about race."

"Jesus, Nick, you're so white-bread," Connie said, putting down his briefcase and sitting on a corner of the nearest desk. "Of course it's about race. Everything's about race in this city."

"What do you mean, I'm white-bread?"

"You're a white kid who grew up in a white neighborhood and went to all-white private schools."

"Are you calling me a racist?"

"No, but don't tell Mitch it's not about race. Most of the people arrested in this city are black. Our society has a history of persecuting *all* people of color."

Mitch nodded his head, relieved that Connie understood.

"You've had such an isolated life you can't see there's racism everywhere."

"And you're an expert?" Nick asked.

"More of an expert than you'll ever be. I went to the Boston Public Schools. I got bused all over the city. I went to an elementary school in Mattapan, where I was one of ten white kids in the whole building."

"I know what that's like," Brendan said, fixing his collar and joining the argument. "They shipped me from Southie to Roxbury. The Condon School was only a block away from our apartment, but I got assigned to a school halfway across the city. Luckily, I know how to take care of myself. But it was tough for some of the smaller kids."

For the first time Mitch realized that his educational experience was more like Nick's than it was the people in the booking photos. Aside from black skin, Mitch had nothing in common with the people in the photos or those outside in Dudley Square.

"A lot of good kids ended up with criminal records," Connie said. "They weren't bad then and they're not bad now. They're good guys who got caught up in bad situations."

"Knock it off, Connie," Nick said. "You're making excuses for them. A lot of people grow up in tough situations and don't commit crimes."

"Until you've seen the arrest photo of a kid you grew up with, you won't understand what I'm talking about. One time I picked up a case file at a pretrial, and it was one of my best friends from second grade. He had a ten-page BOP. Mostly armed robberies."

"So I've never seen a booking sheet for a kid I grew up with. So what?"

"How would you feel if a hundred Greek guys got arrested every day?"

"If they committed crimes, I'd have no problem with it."

"What if the government arresting all these Greeks was a Turkish government?"

"Wouldn't matter."

"Give me a break," Connie laughed. "If you saw booking photos of Greeks day after day in a society dominated by the Turks, you'd say that the Greeks were being persecuted and you know it."

Nick shook his head as he headed toward the door. "Screw this. I'm not going to win a three-on-one argument. I'm out of here." The door slammed behind him.

"Thanks for understanding," Mitch said.

"Don't mention it," Brendan said as he tossed a bunch of color-coordinated files in his bag. He was notorious for highlighting his notes, using different colors for different witnesses. Despite all the teasing Brendan caught, Mitch envied his organizational skills.

"You're the one that has to decide what you're going to do about it," Connie said. "Me, I think you're doing the right thing. If the system is ever going to change, it's going to change because of people like you fighting to make changes."

"But is this the best way?"

"As a prosecutor, you're in a position of power and you can change the system from the inside. If you see someone who's being persecuted, you have the power to do something about it. You can give that person a second chance and make things right."

"It's not that easy."

"Nothing's easy," Connie said. He picked up his briefcase. "You should talk to Liz. She's had to deal with the same things. She worked it out. She can help you do the same."

Connie patted Mitch on the shoulder as he and Brendan walked past him and out the door. Mitch sat staring out the window as darkness set in on the streets of Dudley Square.

CHAPTER 21

Mooney was anxious to leave as soon as he stepped into the VFW hall. The hall was decorated with pink streamers and a Happy Birthday banner printed off a home computer, and he was surrounded by people he didn't know. Parties were a waste of time, especially when there was work to be done. Sure, if it had been a party to raise money for a cop who was out injured, he wouldn't mind kicking in a few bucks, grabbing a sandwich off a deli platter and downing a couple of cold ones, but this was just a birthday party. Whoopee shit, you survived another year.

Alves led Mooney across the floor to where Marcy was sitting with some older women, probably family. "Happy Birthday, Marcy." Mooney forced a big smile. "Twenty-five, right?" He would be pleasant, for Alves's sake.

"Why do I have the feeling you guys aren't staying long?" She gave a look to her husband.

"Because we're not," Mooney shot back before Alves could say anything. "It's not Angel's fault, but we have to get back to the office. You understand, don't you?"

"No, I don't," she said, still looking at Alves. "Angel, you promised."

"I'm sorry, honey, but we'll stay for a while," Alves said. "I'll be sure to walk around and say hello to everyone."

"You'd better be quick about it," Mooney said. "I'll give you an hour tops. We've got a lot to do tonight." He could see that Marcy was angry, but she was going to have to live with it.

Mooney watched as a woman snuck up behind Marcy and covered her eyes. "Guess who." Mooney didn't care who she was, as long as she distracted Marcy.

Marcy didn't appear to be in the mood to play games. She turned her head immediately to see who it was. "Robyn." She jumped out of her chair to hug the woman. "Oh my God, Angel, it's Robyn Stokes. It's been so long," Marcy said. "You look terrific."

"So do you, Marcy. Who would guess that you're the mother of four-year-old twins?"

Alves stepped between the two women to give Robyn Stokes a hug. "You really do look great," he said. "Robyn, this is my boss, Sergeant Wayne Mooney."

"Pleasure to meet you, Sergeant Mooney."

"Likewise," Mooney managed.

"Wayne," Marcy said, "Robyn's a Mission Hill girl like me. We all grew up together."

"That's nice," Mooney said.

"She's done so well for herself. She graduated from Northeastern, top of her class."

"Marcy, you're embarrassing me," Robyn said. "How do you know all this?"

"My mother keeps me up on all the dirt from the neighborhood. Sergeant Mooney went to Northeastern too. Didn't you, Wayne?"

Mooney smiled.

"You're a Husky?" Robyn asked. "What year did you graduate?"

"A long time ago," Mooney said. Marcy was starting to sound like a used-car salesman. She was playing matchmaker and he didn't appreciate it. The last thing he needed right now was a new woman in his life. He was too busy and women always complicated things. Mooney turned to Alves. "I'm starving. Where's all that great food you promised me?"

"This way," Alves said. "I'll be right back, honey."

"Could you feed the kids too?" she asked. "They keep going over to the table, sticking their fingers in everything."

Alves nodded and smiled, leading the way to the buffet table.

"What was that?" Mooney asked. "She was trying to fix me up."

"I know. And don't think this is the end of it. She'll probably bring Robyn over while you're eating so you guys can have some nice dinner conversation. Marcy's a very smart woman."

"What does setting me up have to do with being smart?"

"Possession is nine-tenths of the law, Sarge. She has us here at the party, now she just needs to find a way to keep us here. If that means setting you up with one of her friends, so be it. If it means making me feed the kids, then I'm feeding the kids. That's why I brought you with me. If you want to do some work tonight, it's your job to get us out of here."

"Hi, Daddy," the kids ran up and hugged Alves's legs.

Alves bent down, took one of them in each arm and lifted them up. "Iris, Angel, can you guys say hello to Sergeant Mooney?"

"Hello, Uncle Wayne," they said.

"Uncle Wayne?" Mooney forced a smile for the sake of the kids. "Who told you to call me Uncle Wayne?"

"Mommy," Iris said.

"I told you she's good, Sarge," Alves laughed. "She's even got the kids in on the conspiracy. Why don't we get you a nice big plate of food so we'll be ready to make our escape?"

CHAPTER 22

"**N**ot bad, Sarge, we were only gone two hours." Alves unwrapped the piece of cake Marcy had packed for him. He usually ate healthy, but his one weakness was gold cake with white frosting. The only thing missing was a tall glass of cold milk. "You sure you don't want any of this, Sarge? It's a massive piece."

"Too full. Maybe I'll have a candy bar. I couldn't stop eating the yucca and fried plantains. That stuff must be brain food," Mooney said.

"Why's that?"

"I think I figured out what our boy's up to. He wants the bodies. I don't know why, but he wants them. Maybe he's some sick necrophiliac having sex with them. We need to check the DOC releases for all known sex offenders over the past year. This guy may have just gotten out of prison."

"I know one of the screws out in Walpole. I'll give him a call tomorrow. He'll take care of me. I'll check with the Sex Offender Registry too."

"He wants us to know the victims are dead. That's why the nine-one-one calls and the blood in the tubs. All these jackasses in the media calling him the Blood Bath Killer are falling for his little gimmick. But this blood-bath shit is just a means to an end."

"Gimmick?" Alves shoveled a piece of cake into his mouth.

"If he kills someone and keeps their body, there's no evidence of a crime. They just end up as a missing person. The case doesn't draw the same kind of attention as a murder. Angel, I'm convinced this guy has killed before. We just didn't know it. It pissed him off that we didn't know. That's when he came up with this whole blood-bath thing." Mooney shoved a stack of reports aside and pointed to a photo of a smiling Susan McCarthy on the front page of the *Globe*. "He keeps the body as a trophy and throws us a curveball and gets the attention he wants. He even gets himself a catchy nickname."

"That's not bad, Sarge," Alves said.

"It's brilliant. But what it means is that there's at least one victim out there we don't know about." Mooney took a Sky Bar out of his desk. Alves thought they tasted like they were left over from the fifties, but Mooney lived on them. The vending machines at headquarters were one of the only known sources of the relics. Mooney always broke them into four pieces, eating his least favorite—the peanut butter one— first. "Did you ever get a chance to look up the old missing-persons reports?"

Alves licked the frosting off his plastic fork. "I've got the guys from the Cold Case Squad putting together the files for me."

"We need to go back at least a year to see if anyone fits the general profile of McCarthy and Hayes. I don't think this guy started with prostitutes like a lot of serial killers. He picks his victims for a reason."

"The missing outfits might explain that. Why do you think he takes their clothes?"

"He probably can't have a normal relationship with a woman. I bet he's a professional guy who deals with professional women. He gets rejected on a regular basis by those women. This is his chance to spend some time with them without being ridiculed. Maybe he dresses them up so he can undress them. He's trying to create what he thinks is a normal relationship."

"What's next, Sarge?" Alves asked. Either he was getting a sugar rush from the cake or Mooney's enthusiasm was contagious. Whatever it was, Alves was ready to repay Mooney for letting him make an appearance at the party.

"Let's map out everything we have so far." Mooney licked his fingers, savoring the vanilla square of his candy bar. "Tomorrow we'll start looking through those old files to try and identify another vic. I'm hoping we can find his first kill. Maybe we'll catch a break and figure out how he's picking his targets."

CHAPTER 23

Dressed in his black running pants and hooded sweatshirt, Richter
stood perfectly still. He had disciplined himself to remain still for hours,
invisible to the casual observer and to anyone who might hurry by on
the distant sidewalk. While most people were afraid to go into a cemetery at night, Richter was energized by it. As a child he'd been afraid to
sleep without a light on, until his grandfather helped him to appreciate
the darkness for all its beauty.

*The old man turned off the light in the bedroom. The child was sleeping
away from home for the first time, spending some time at his grandparents'
farm. He was used to sleeping with a small night-light in his room at home.
Now, in this strange bedroom, he was terrified. Was there something under
the bed? Was there something in the closet? Could something climb in the
open first-floor window?*

"Grampa, I'm scared," the child said.

"Scared of what, boy?" the old man replied.

"I'm scared of the dark."

"There's no need to be scared of the dark. I thought you were a big boy."

"I am a big boy."

*"Big boys aren't afraid of the dark. Next you'll be telling me you wet the
bed. Now go to sleep before I give you something to really be scared of."*

"Grampa, can you just leave one light on for me so I can see?"

"Look, there's nothing to be scared of." The old man waved the child over. "Come with me. I'll prove to you that there's nothing to be scared of in the dark."

The child got out of bed and followed him down the long hallway to the kitchen. The old man opened the door to the basement and started down the stairs. The child stood at the top of the stairs, not wanting to go any farther.

"C'mon, follow me," he said. "I'm not going to bite you."

He crept down the stairs after the old man, who led him into a smaller room. This was where his grandmother stored her potatoes and turnips so they would keep longer in the cool, dark air.

"Why are we down here, Grampa?" the child asked. "What did you want to show me?" He was more frightened in the dark basement than he'd been in the bedroom. The only thing that made him feel safe was his grandfather beside him.

"This room is what I wanted to show you," the old man said. "Where you're going to sleep tonight."

"Stop kidding with me, Grampa."

"You're going to sleep where I tell you. And tonight you're going to sleep on that potato sack in the corner. You can use this empty sack as a blanket," he said, handing the child an old burlap sack.

"But, Grampa—"

"No buts, boy. You're going to sleep down here in the dark tonight. When you see that there ain't nothing going to hurt you down here, you'll understand that there's nothing to be scared of in a dark bedroom."

"I believe you! Now I know there's nothing to be scared of. I'll be a good boy and go to sleep in the bedroom upstairs."

"It's too late for that now. You go to sleep. I'll come down in the morning to get you for breakfast. You'll be fine. You'll see that there's no bogeyman in the dark."

The old man closed the battered wooden door and latched it from the outside. The room was completely dark except for the thin light that fought its way through a crack in the door. The child started to cry. He ran to the door and pounded on it.

"Grampa, let me out!" he shouted. "I'm not afraid of the dark anymore. Please let me out."

The old man didn't respond. The child heard him make his way to the top of the stairs and then the light coming through the crack in the door went out. He fell to the dirt floor. He cried himself to sleep, never making it back to the potato sack that was supposed to be his bed.

Richter opened his eyes. Now he understood what his grandfather had done for him. Richter could become one with the dark; if he stayed there long enough, he would absorb all of it and become the darkness and the shadows. He could move anywhere unnoticed. This was important because he wasn't in his own neighborhood. If spotted, he would stand out as someone who didn't belong.

He had parked his car just off Centre Street in Jamaica Plain, near a couple of busy restaurants and bars where his car would blend in with those of the patrons. From there he had walked down side streets, eventually making his way to Forest Hills Street and the entrance to Franklin Park. After he ran through the park—an area full of high school track teams and joggers by day and, by night, muggers—he jumped a fence and crossed Morton Street and slipped into the Forest Hills Cemetery. At the farthest point south in the cemetery, the land, in almost an hourglass shape, met up with Mt. Hope Cemetery and Calvary Cemetery.

He had been in his position for some time when he heard them, a bunch of teenagers moving down the street, yelling at passing cars and smashing bottles. Someone was sure to call the police. If the caller was smart enough, he'd say he heard shots fired and the cops would respond right away. If not, the response might come in an hour. That complicated things. And she was running late. She should have been home by now.

There was a little knot of tension starting up in his neck. He had to relax. He did his best work when he was relaxed. Then at the corner he spotted it, a T bus crawling along, swerving to make stops. He heard the familiar whoosh, the crank of the door and she was there, on the sidewalk right in front of him. She walked briskly up the stairs and was swallowed in the darkness.

Richter saw the lights come on. From his vantage point he studied the nurse as she moved about her snug bungalow. It was shabby, but without a man to paint and plaster, she'd probably planned to save up before she tackled the big projects. He watched as she went through her mail and then as she got ready for bed. She didn't go to sleep right away. She read a book on the couch before going to her room.

He admired her for her commitment and dedication to her work. She didn't have children or a boyfriend. Obviously, she had put aside any thoughts of a serious relationship or of raising a family so she could focus on her career. She was a nurse manager at the New England Medical Center. Maybe she had bought the house in this neighborhood thinking she'd be one of those people that would bring about change. Maybe she planned to finally clear some time in her busy day for those community groups that left flyers in her mailbox.

Richter knew that none of that was going to happen, because he was about to enter her life and change everything. Not tonight, but soon.

CHAPTER 24

Nick Costa waited in the gallery while Judge Sterling Davis prepared to send Andi Norton's jury out for a second day of deliberations. She and Connie stood at the prosecutor's table as the jury entered the room.

Nick tried to concentrate on his next case but could only think about Monica Hughes with her blond hair and toned legs. The way she was looking at him the other day, he knew she liked him too. Things started out rough with her asking about his trials the first day she'd met him. But by the end of that day he knew he'd impressed her with some of the bail arguments he'd made. And he'd made her laugh too. He needed to ask her out soon, though. He'd waited too long with Andi Norton and Connie had moved right in. But actually, that had worked out. Imagine if he'd wasted his time trying to hook up with Andi before finding out she had a kid. An instant family didn't sound like a good time to him.

But now Connie was stuck with Andi, and Nick was no longer a rookie DA. He'd been around long enough to have some war stories to impress Monica. The timing of her arrival at South Bay couldn't have been better. Maybe he'd see if she wanted to go for a walk along the Charles on Saturday and grab some lunch on Beacon Hill.

"Commonwealth versus James Watkins," the clerk called out. Nick jumped to his feet. That was his case. Andi's jury had already left the courtroom. Nick looked around for his witnesses. "Your Honor," the clerk continued, "the defendant is charged with distribution of a class B controlled substance, to wit: crack cocaine."

"Is the Commonwealth ready for trial?" Judge Davis asked.

Nick looked again for his two cops as he stepped past the bar and stood at the prosecutor's table. He was glad to see that they weren't in the courtroom. If they didn't show up, the case would get dismissed. After all, it was no big deal: just a drug case. Then he could go check on Monica in arraignments. It was her first day in there alone, a good time for him to come to her aid.

"Commonwealth?" Judge Davis shouted at Nick. "Are you ready for trial? How many witnesses?"

"Two witnesses, Your Honor. Both from the Drug Unit. I haven't seen either of them. . . ." There was a disturbance at the back of the room. Sergeant Robert Fisher and Officer Keith Hall, both in plain-clothes, walked through the room's double doors and nodded to Nick.

Shit. Now he'd have to try the case. And he hadn't done any prep beyond reading the police report. And that was late last night.

He and Fisher exchanged looks and Nick turned to Judge Davis. "The Commonwealth is ready for trial. I would ask for a brief recess so that I might have a chance to speak with the officers."

"Can we resolve this short of trial?" Judge Davis directed his question to the defense attorney. "Probation tells me that this man has no prior convictions. Why don't we take a change of plea and place him on probation?"

"Your Honor, my client doesn't want a felony conviction on his record. We're prepared to go to trial."

"Commonwealth, I'll give you ten minutes to speak with your officers and then we'll impanel a jury." Judge Davis stepped down from the bench.

Nick called both officers over. "Nice of you guys to show up."

"You're lucky we're even here," Fisher said. "We were up until four executing a search warrant. One of the busiest drug houses in the city. We had a nighttime, no-knock warrant. Had some information there were guns in the house. I didn't want my guys getting hurt."

"How'd it go?"

"Fifty grams of crack, another thirty grams of powder coke, more than five hundred packets of heroin, almost a pound of weed, two Glock 9s and a sawed-off."

"If you guys are tired, go get yourselves some big-assed coffees because we're going to trial. We only have a couple of minutes. Keith, you made the buy from this guy, right?"

"Yeah, I believe so," Hall said.

"You *believe* so. What does that mean? Look over your report and then we'll talk."

"I read the report. It's just that this happened two years ago."

"You do remember the defendant, though, right?" Nick asked. "Did you look at his booking photo?"

"I did."

"And you don't remember him?"

"His face seems familiar to me, but I don't remember buying drugs from him."

"Familiar doesn't cut it," Nick said. This could work out. Hopefully Monica was keeping a seat warm for him.

"Keith, this is the guy that sold you the drugs," Fisher said. "Look at his booking sheet. Read your report again."

"I know it *should* be him, but I can't say for sure."

"All you have to do is testify to what's in the report. Anything outside the report you can say you don't remember. You don't have to make anything up," Fisher said.

"I can't do that," Hall said. "I'd be making the whole thing up. How's that any different from lying?"

"It's not lying if you're testifying from your own report," Fisher said.

"Keith is right. He can't read off a police report. The report is to refresh his memory so that he can testify as to what he actually remembers. If he doesn't remember James Watkins selling him crack, he can't get up and state under oath that he does. In fact, I won't even call him to the stand."

"Are you fucking kidding me, Nick?" Fisher shouted. "This is the guy.

Look at the booking photo and reports. They have the same complaint number. Watkins is our guy. We can't let him off."

"If he's a bad guy, he'll be back out there selling drugs and we'll get him next time. If not, no big deal. Keith can't take the stand and testify to something he doesn't remember. How can I ethically try to prove it to a jury, when Keith doesn't believe it beyond a reasonable doubt?" Maybe bringing ethics into the argument would get Fisher to back off.

Instead Fisher turned back to Hall. "Listen, Keith, you identified him that night and we arrested him and booked him based on *your* ID."

"I know you want to win this one, Sarge," Nick said. "But no case is worth the three of us losing our credibility." He looked up at the clock. The ten minutes were up. He turned back to Hall. "Do you need another minute to look at the reports?"

"I've been looking at them all morning, Nick. I don't remember anything."

"Court, all rise," the court officer announced as Judge Davis retook the bench.

The Judge asked Nick, "Is the Commonwealth ready to proceed?"

"No, Your Honor, the Commonwealth is not ready for trial."

"Mr. Costa," Judge Davis said, "you weren't misleading the court when you told me you were ready, were you?"

"No, Your Honor. After speaking with my officers, I realize that we have insufficient evidence to proceed against this defendant."

"Could you be ready if I granted a continuance?" the judge asked.

"I don't believe so, Your Honor."

Judge Davis frowned. "Could both attorneys approach the bench?"

At the sidebar Judge Davis leaned in toward Nick. "Mr. Costa, what happened?"

Nick tried to explain, but Judge Davis cut him off. The defense attorney barely suppressed a grin.

Judge Davis turned his attention to the defendant. In a clear, stern voice he said, "Mr. Watkins, it appears that you have a guardian angel. You had better not let me see you before this court again. This matter is dismissed."

Nick was glad to be rid of the case, but he didn't want Fisher to know it. He turned, planning to commiserate with the sergeant, but only saw Fisher's back as he swung the courtroom doors open and disappeared. Hall shrugged his shoulders like a kid who's lost the game for his team but doesn't really care. He followed Fisher through the doorway.

Nick gathered up his files. On to Monica and her arraignments.

CHAPTER 25

Alves dangled the bag in front of him, and Mooney looked up from the clutter on his desk. "Thai food?" he smiled. "From The King and I? My favorite. Hope you got me a fork. I'm not eating with sticks. How can you be so good to me after I've been riding you all week?"

"This is a thank-you for letting me go to the party the other night. That saved my marriage. Besides, I'm not being that good to you," Alves said. "I dropped a bag of food off for Marcy and the kids so she wouldn't have to cook tonight. We usually do pizza on Fridays, but I figured this would be a special treat for her. Marcy wasn't happy, but she seemed to understand. Luckily she blames you for everything."

"I'll take the hit for you, as long as you keep feeding me," Mooney said. "Let me give you some money." He took his ratty old wallet, bound together with rubber bands, out of his back pocket.

"Sarge, your money is no good here," Alves said. He waved Mooney off. "And, what's with the wallet? It's falling apart. When's your birthday? I'll buy you a new one."

"There's nothing wrong with this wallet." Mooney took the white containers out of the bag and set them up on the day's edition of the *Boston Globe.* "Elastics make it harder for a pickpocket."

"So does the gun on your hip. You really think someone's going to steal a wallet from a cop?"

"You can never be too careful. Now sit down and pass the pad thai."

Alves piled some food on a plate and took a bite before flipping through some missing-persons reports. He hated not having dinner with the family, especially on pizza night. The kids loved pizza. Angel had to have pepperoni and Iris had to have extra cheese. He'd barely seen his family all week. He actually missed giving the kids their baths and arguing with them to brush their teeth and tucking them into bed. Most of all he missed the quiet time he and Marcy had together once the kids were asleep, even if it was only an hour or so before they went to bed themselves.

Alves looked at Mooney. The sergeant seemed wiped out. Five days had gone by and they were no closer to catching Susan McCarthy's killer.

"Sarge, I've gone back more than a year on the missing persons. The only one remotely close is Emily Knight. The one similarity is that she's a professional, white woman. But she's much younger, twenty-two. Never married, lots of boyfriends, nothing serious. She'd been renting an apartment in a two-family."

Mooney looked up, interested. "What's the story on her disappearance?"

"She leaves work on a Friday night last fall and never shows up for work the following Monday morning. No one reports her missing until her boss calls us."

"Did she like her job?"

"She made decent money, but a few of her co-workers said she hated the work. Apparently the stress was getting to her and she felt like she was wasting her life. Looks like she may have taken off to get away from everything."

"Did she take any of her belongings?"

"She didn't have much to take. Some old furniture she got at yard sales and the clothes she wore to work. She could be hitchhiking across the U.S. of A. for all we know. Remember those two jackass college students who took off to Florida a couple of years ago? Their parents got the police to launch a nationwide search for the two idiots. Based on what her friends and family said about her flightiness, I can see Emily Knight doing something like that."

"If you think it's a dead end, don't bother looking into it anymore." Mooney took a bite of his pad thai.

"I don't think it's going anywhere, Sarge, but right now I feel like everything's a dead end. We interviewed everyone on the list we got from New Balance and have nothing. What does it matter if Eunice can make a match to the mold if we can't find the shoe?"

"I've checked local mailmen, milkmen, garbagemen, meter readers, census takers and paperboys. You name them and I've talked to them. None of them has a record and they all seemed genuine in what they told me. If we keep at it we'll eventually make our own luck and get this guy."

"I think I've gotten everything I'm going to get out of these missing-persons files," Alves said.

"What about the sex offenders? Anything there?"

"I've got a good list of possibles, but it's a long list. I ran their records, pulled their police reports and made a file for each guy."

"We need to pay each one a visit," Mooney said. "We can start in the morning. For now, why don't you go home and get some rest?"

"Are you sure?"

"Yeah. You'll probably feel better in the morning. New day, all that shit. I'll stay here and look through those sex offender files."

Alves gulped down one last mouthful of noodles and went for the door before Mooney could change his mind. When he turned back to say good night, Mooney was looking out over the lights of Ruggles Station and Northeastern University, eating the rest of the pad thai out of the carton.

CHAPTER 26

Connie raised his glass above his head as the crew from the office gathered around him for a toast. What better way to end the week than to unwind at Doyle's? One of Boston's most historic bars, the walls were lined with pictures of famous local politicians: the Fitzgeralds, the Kennedys and former mayors Kevin White and Ray Flynn. The place was packed. The gang from the DA's office had staked out their usual corner of the bar. "To Andi Norton, the best prosecutor-who's-not-really-quite-yet-a-lawyer-but-still-managed-to-kick-some-serious-ass-in-court-this-week-by-keeping-a-jury-out-for-three-days-before-finally-getting-a-guilty-on-her-first-shot-at-putting-eight-in-the-box," Connie said without taking a breath.

The room cheered.

"You were most excellent in court today!" Brendan shouted from behind the bar. Brendan had been tending bar at Doyle's since he was hired as a prosecutor. Like all the bartenders at Doyle's, he doubled as a bouncer. A lot of young prosecutors worked second jobs—one taught Irish step dancing, another sold real estate, a couple coached high school sports.

Connie glanced at Andi. She didn't like being the center of attention, but he'd convinced her she needed to come out for a drink. She'd done a great job on her first trial and she had to let everyone congratulate her. It was tradition.

Mitch chanted "Speech! Speech! Speech!" and everyone joined in.

Andi put her glass down on the bar and stood up. "I want to thank you guys for being supportive." She was showing class, being so humble. Especially with Nick and Mitch in the room. Lately, neither one could get a conviction. She really was a nice person, and Connie admired that about her. "You have made it fun to come to work. I only won this trial because of everything you taught me. Thanks."

One more loud cheer from the group and they went back to their drinks. Andi worked her way over to Connie. He leaned in close to her and said, "I want you to know I'm proud of you. You really did a nice job. You don't need to decide right now, but I want you to second-seat me on the Jesse Wilcox trial. I need your help doing some research for the motion to suppress too."

Andi looked stunned. "Sounds great. Can we talk about it next week? I need to get going," she said. "My mom was good enough to babysit for me, but I can't leave her with Rachel all night. It's not too early for me to take off, is it?"

"Eight o'clock. You made your appearance and gave your speech. This is a perfect time to exit. Don't say good-bye to anyone except Liz. Otherwise you'll never get out of here. Nick's quite a yapper when he's had a few."

Andi laughed. "Nick's preoccupied with Monica. Haven't you noticed that he's been hitting on her all week? It looks like she might be caving in to his charm."

"I'm sure he's using his 'I do this work because I want to see justice served' line or some other bullshit to make her think he's not just trying to get up her skirt. Are you good to drive?"

"I only had one beer that I've nursed for two hours."

"Drive carefully. I'll talk to you tomorrow." He kissed her. Not a long one, more of a peck on the lips. He didn't want to make a scene or give the guys ammo, but he wanted her to know how he felt about her.

Connie turned back to the bar to look for Mitch.

"Your little protégée did a nice job."

Connie saw that Nick had come up behind him.

"She's not even a lawyer and you give her more advice than you've ever given the rest of us."

Connie didn't like the tone of Nick's voice. "I help out anyone who wants the help. Ask Mitch and Brendan how I taught them to prepare a case. It's just that some people think they already know everything and don't need any advice."

"I'm not looking for your advice."

"Then, what are you doing?" Connie moved closer to Nick, crowding him. He could smell the beer on his breath. He knew he should just step away.

"I'm just making an observation that you spend more time with Andi than anyone else. Maybe your relationship with her is getting in the way of your job. You're the senior lawyer. You should be mentoring all of us. Not just the intern you happen to be fucking this week."

Connie bumped him backward and Nick sprawled freely, barely managing to catch himself on a chair. "I'm going to ignore what you just said because you've had one too many. But if you ever say anything like that again"—Connie paused, trying to count to ten but only getting to four—"you'll be one sorry fuck. I understand you might be jealous of Andi, but that's no reason to get nasty."

"Jealous?" Nick laughed. "What the hell would I be jealous about?"

"Maybe the fact that you suck as a lawyer? Maybe the fact that you've had ten trials and have yet to convict anyone? Then Andi walks in and on her first trial hooks the guy. If you want to start winning some trials, I'd be more than glad to take on another protégé."

"Fuck you. Those cases I took to trial were dogs. I don't care what the end result was. It's not about wins and losses, it's about justice."

"Is that what you told Monica when she asked you about your record? That's your standard line, isn't it? You're right about me not mentoring enough of the younger lawyers. I'm going to start with Monica right now. I think she'd be much better off learning from me. Don't you think?"

"Stay away from her, Connie."

"I'll leave Monica alone if you stop fucking with me and Andi. Otherwise, I'll let her know what a fraud you are."

"All right, boys," Brendan interrupted them. He put a hand on each of their shoulders. "I've been watching you two for the last couple of minutes and it looks like you both have your beer balls. Nobody can win this one. The DA could stop in here any minute and you'll both be looking for jobs. Besides, I don't want to have to toss you out on your asses."

"Everything's fine. Isn't it, Nick?" Connie said. "We just had a talk and we've reached an understanding." Connie stared at Nick, who nodded his head in agreement. "See? Everything's peachy keen." Connie put his hand on Nick's back like they were old buddies.

Nick shrugged him off and angled his way through the crowd back to Monica.

Connie smiled at Brendan. "I'll have another club soda," he said.

CHAPTER 27

Richter crept down the hall of the bungalow. Ahead of him, he could see that the bedroom door was slightly ajar. The electronic melody of a cell phone being activated chimed somewhere in the darkness. She was in her bed, blankets pulled over her head. She must have heard him moving around. And now she was calling for help.

He hadn't expected her to be awake. He lunged toward her, holding her down with the full weight of his body. She tried to scream, but the sound was muffled by Richter's left hand pressing the blankets firmly over her face. Reaching under them with his right hand, he grabbed for her throat. He regretted having to wear the latex gloves. When he was sure he had a firm grip on her, Richter pulled the blankets off her face. With his free hand he ripped the phone away. No one on the other end of the line. He'd gotten to her before she made a call. He flipped it shut. For that one instant when the illuminated blue buttons on the phone lit both of their faces, Richter felt that she might have recognized who he was, but he wanted to be sure.

He scanned the room for a light and spotted a lamp on the bureau on the other side of the room. He lifted her off the bed by her neck. She struggled to push his hand away, pounding him in the chest, her feet scissoring in the air as she tried to kick him. Richter carried her across the room and turned on the small lamp. He wanted her to see him at the moment of her salvation. He wanted her to appreciate what he was doing for her. As the light came on, she saw Richter's face, and he saw a moment of recognition come into her wide eyes.

She tried to speak, her mouth sliding, opening, closing. No sound. If Richter loosened his grip, she would probably beg him to take whatever he wanted and leave her alone, promising she'd never tell anyone.

But Richter had no intention of releasing her. He'd never hear her say anything. It wouldn't have mattered anyway. He wasn't there to steal or rape. His was a nobler intention. Richter had come to her to free her from her ordinary existence.

He placed his other hand on her neck and began to squeeze firmly. The expression on her face said "Please let me live. Please spare me." Richter felt no anger or hatred. He did feel joy, even though she didn't understand what he was doing for her.

She made one last effort to elbow and kick him, but her body was already weakened, the blows ineffectual. Richter felt as if his two hands would come together. He could simply have snapped her neck, but that would've been much less meaningful. This way he could watch the life leave her body slowly. She'd have more time to see and appreciate him.

Then he saw the look of thanks in her eyes. Her struggling eased, her body sagging onto the side of the bed. Richter loosened his grip and placed her head gently down on the mattress. The pillows were on the floor and the bedding was twisted. The struggle had been more violent than he'd realized. He leaned down and felt faint puffs of air from her nose and mouth. She was still alive, but unconscious. Richter had to hurry now. He picked her up, threw her over his shoulder and carried her toward the bathroom.

Richter had a full night of work ahead.

CHAPTER 28

Mooney stepped out onto the back deck of Robyn Stokes's house. The cool air was refreshing, just what he needed. It was finally starting to feel like winter again. Winter had always been his favorite season. As a kid, the changing seasons dictated what sports he and his friends would play: baseball in the spring, basketball in the summer, football in the fall and hockey in the winter. But there was nothing like the cold winter air, chilling his lungs during a pickup ice hockey game on a frozen pond. Tonight was perfect weather for one of those games. What he'd give to be a kid again, flying around on a sheet of ice. No need to worry about women being murdered. No need to think about families being devastated. No need to feel the pressure of being the one person with the responsibility to stop the killing.

Mooney looked up into the cloudless sky, the only obstruction to his view the steam from his breath. Entranced by the crescent moon, the bright stars, he wondered how this could have happened. He'd known there would be another victim if he didn't catch this lunatic, but he hadn't expected one so soon. The 911 call had come in five days after the one placed from the McCarthy house.

Mooney had been at his desk when Operations notified him of the call. A monotone voice informed him, "I think your killer's back." A wash of darkness swept through him. "Who's our victim? What's the address? Who is the supervisor on scene?" he'd asked. Only a few hours earlier he'd sent Alves home to spend some time with his wife, maybe make up for taking him away from her birthday party.

Mooney didn't tell Alves the victim's name over the phone. He would have to tell him this one in person. He needed to keep an eye on him to make sure he could still do his job effectively. If Alves became emotionally involved, Mooney might have to take him off the case. But he didn't want to do that. Not now. They were so far into the investigation and Alves had worked too hard to be thrown aside like that.

Mooney took another deep breath of the cold air. Now he and Alves would have to tell another family, this time a friend, that their daughter, granddaughter, sister, aunt was dead; that from this moment forward their lives would never be the same. A homicide survivor had once told Mooney that losing a child was like losing a limb; that it never gets better, you just kind of get used to it not being there.

A star shot across the sky and he thought of Robyn Stokes, her soul released from her mortal body. He said a prayer for her and her family before sliding the glass door and walking back into her house.

CHAPTER 29

Alves wiped at the tears as he drove. Enough. Now he needed to be strong.

When Mooney first told him the name of the victim, Alves had tried to convince himself that it was another Robyn Stokes that had been murdered. After all, the Robyn Stokes he knew, with whom he had grown up, was from Mission Hill, not Mattapan. But he hadn't asked her where she was living when he saw her at the party. He didn't know about the house she'd bought in Mattapan. Mooney showed Alves her hospital ID photo, the pictures on the mantel, a shot of her and her mother at her nursing school graduation. This was his Robyn.

He would tell Marcy in the morning. It would be tough. But it would be nothing like telling Mrs. Stokes of her daughter's death. He'd told Mooney that he would do this alone. Mrs. Stokes deserved to learn the news from an old friend, not a stranger. Strangers had come to notify her of her husband's death years earlier. Mr. Stokes was shot during a robbery of the corner store where he worked. Angel and Robyn were kids at the time, playing catch in front of her apartment when the detectives pulled up. Even at that age, they knew what an unmarked police car was, and they also knew that the police never showed up with good news. The detectives, maybe one of them was a young Wayne Mooney, went inside and only stayed for a few minutes. After they left, Angel and Robyn went in to see what had happened. Mrs. Stokes was on the floor wailing. The sounds were so unreal that Angel first thought she was laughing.

Robyn was not the same after that day. She never wanted to come out and hang out. She stopped playing sports. She had always dreamed about being the first woman professional baseball player. She threw left-handed with a natural curve. At the time, he didn't doubt that she'd play pro ball if she wanted to.

As he pulled up in front of her mother's house, Alves could see Robyn Stokes as the young girl with the nasty curveball who was going to play for the Red Sox someday. She wore that bright smile that he never saw again after the day the detectives came to her house.

Now he was the detective coming to tear her mother's heart out. He wiped his face with his sleeve and took a deep breath before stepping from the car. It was a long climb up the five steps to the door. One more breath before ringing the bell.

He had to ring it a second time before he saw a light come on upstairs. It was a few more minutes before the door opened, and an elderly Mrs. Stokes stood before him in her bathrobe with a momentary smile of recognition. She hadn't seen him since he'd moved out of the neighborhood. "Hello, Angel," she said, sleepily. "What are you doing here? You look so handsome in that suit."

Then her expression changed as she started putting things together. He was sure she knew he was a Homicide detective now. Word travels fast in the old neighborhood, whether it's good news or bad.

Angel Alves's eyes began to well up as he stepped forward. He tried to give her a hug.

"No!" she bawled as he got close to her. She started pounding his chest with closed fists. "No. No. No." She began to sob before collapsing into his arms.

As he held the frail shivering woman close, he knew that everything had changed. This wasn't just about doing his job anymore. This was about revenge.

CHAPTER 38

The shriek from the fire alarm was deafening. Connie and Mitch followed the trickle of people laughing and chatting as they made their way down the stairs. No one ever took the drills seriously, Connie thought.

Judge Davis trained them on evacuation procedures with his unannounced drills, a response to the September 11th terrorist attacks. As if some terror group were going to target his inner-city courthouse. Word had it that someone had called in a bomb threat at nine o'clock as court was about to begin. "Probably some defendant trying to postpone his trial," Connie said. "Judge Davis will have the sessions open in an hour."

As they stepped outside into the crisp February air, Connie was surprised by the number of people who'd been evacuated from the building. With the defendants, the witnesses and courthouse personnel, there were more than two hundred people crammed in the plaza between the courthouse and the police station.

"Hey, Red, breakfast?" said Connie.

"You?" said Mitch. "Eat breakfast? Are you kidding me?"

"I eat breakfast, I just don't eat the crap you call breakfast. And I don't want to stand around freezing my ass off with people I'm going to send to jail later. We could sneak over to The Silver Slipper for some hot grits."

"Sounds good, but I'm in the jury session with Judge Davis."

"So am I. We've got plenty of time. This is a real bomb threat, which means the court officers have to evacuate the building, including all the custodies. That's a big production, getting everyone shackled up before they lead them out. We have at least an hour before the Bomb Squad clears the building."

"Let's go before someone sees us."

Connie and Mitch walked past the police station, a concrete bunker of a building that didn't fit in with the rest of the architecture of the square. The façade of the building, facing the Dudley bus terminal, reminded Connie of pictures he'd seen of the Berlin Wall. No wonder the people of Roxbury didn't trust the police.

They walked across Dudley Street into the heart of the Square. Connie liked to imagine what it was like in its heyday, when all the storefronts were open and you could hear the pitch of street vendors for a half mile outside of the Square, the old elevated Orange Line trains passing overhead with their steel wheels squealing as they made the turn from Washington Street onto Dudley Street and then back onto Washington Street. When he was a kid that slow, serpentine turn was Connie's favorite part of the ride into Downtown Boston from his family's home in West Roxbury.

But even as a child, looking down from that train, Connie had missed the opportunity to see a bustling Dudley Square. By the time he was born, this center of black culture and history had already been destroyed by years of racism and neglect. By the early 1970s many of the restaurants and stores had been boarded up and closed, the old, majestic buildings slowly decaying.

The South Bay District Court, a three-story, red-brick building designed to stand out next to surrounding granite and sandstone buildings, had been built as part of an ongoing effort to revitalize the Square. The city was trying to encourage renovation by offering subsidized loans, but it was a slow process bringing back a neighborhood that had been run-down for forty years. The new courthouse was a symbol to the black community that they had not been forgotten by the government.

Despite these efforts, the Square was still far from its original glory. The streets themselves were trash-strewn. Gangs of kids stood around harassing people, scaring away legitimate business. Many of the buildings, abandoned by fleeing merchants, had not been entered in years except by prostitutes and skinny-armed drug addicts. These same addicts spent most of their lives sitting on the benches in the Dudley MBTA bus terminal.

The Silver Slipper was one of the few places that wasn't marred with bubble-lettered graffiti; instead, the side of the building was graced with a massive mural dedicated to the history of the area. The Slipper was a fixture in the neighborhood. It had been around forever, surviving riots in the 1960s—legend had it that Malcolm X ate his breakfast at the counter—and the drug wars of the late 1980s and early 1990s.

As always, it was crowded. Connie and Mitch ordered their food at the counter, then sat at a small table.

"What'd you do this weekend?" Connie asked.

"Nothing good. Case prep."

"That's it?"

"I went out Saturday night."

"It's about time you put yourself out there again. Anyone I know?"

"Just a woman I went to law school with."

"Her name wouldn't happen to be Sonya, would it?"

"Very funny. She is friends with Sonya, though, so it's been a little awkward. We've gone out a few times. I like her and I plan on seeing her again, but I'm not rushing into another serious relationship." Mitch pulled a few napkins from the dispenser and twisted them in his hands. He looked to be lost in thought. Then he cleared his throat and sat up in his chair. "What did you do?"

"I worked at home. Andi was studying all weekend. I did get some interesting news, though. But you can't tell anyone. There was another murder this weekend."

"There's a murder every weekend."

"Let me rephrase that. The police found another bathtub full of blood early Saturday morning."

"You're fuckin' kidding me. Where?"

"Mattapan."

"Who's the victim?"

"Some woman. Robyn Stokes, I think her name was."

"How'd you find out? I didn't see anything in the papers."

"It wasn't in the papers. I talked with Alves yesterday afternoon. He knew the woman. They grew up together. He and Mooney were able to keep it quiet over the weekend, but that's not going to work for long. I'm sure 'an anonymous source familiar with the investigation' is going to leak it to the press."

"What did Alves tell you?"

"They think the guy changed his MO." Connie leaned into the table and lowered his voice. "Robyn Stokes was a professional, but she was never married, had no kids and she was black. He went from divorced white mothers to single black females with no kids. I guess Mooney's starting to wonder if the guy is just an opportunist, a thrill killer who's draining their blood to throw off his investigation."

"They still have no idea why he's doing this?"

"None."

"Did they find any evidence, any clues?"

"She did know the guy was in the house before he attacked her."

Mitch stopped twisting a paper napkin from the dispenser and looked at Connie.

"It looks like she might have tried to call for help from her cell. The crime lab took the phone to be fumed for prints." Mitch was a great audience. "They're hoping maybe he grabbed it from her."

Mitch dropped the twisted paper. "You said Alves knew this woman."

"He grew up with her. He had to tell her mother the bad news. I feel sorry for this guy if Alves gets to him."

"There you are." Nick stood in the restaurant's door, calling across the crowded room. Right behind him, Connie could see, was Monica, looking irritated. "Thanks for inviting us to breakfast."

Connie gave Mitch a dip of the head, letting him know the conversation was over, and Mitch nodded.

"Your invitation must have been lost in the mail."

The waitress deftly slid a plate with a stack of pancakes and cheese grits toward Mitch. "Is this for you or the whole table?" she asked Connie as she put down a serving-sized bowl of grits. "How on earth are you going to eat all that, son?"

Connie offered a smile. "I can handle it. Thanks."

"What'll it be for you all?" she said, turning to Nick and Monica.

"Thanks, we'll eat at the counter," Nick said.

Monica stood there for a moment, then shrugged her shoulders before following Nick.

Connie winked at Mitch then picked up his spoon and started in on his mountain of grits.

CHAPTER 31

Going out for breakfast had broken up their morning routine. Now Connie and Mitch were taking turns answering on their cases in Judge Davis's session.

Connie admired Judge Davis. He treated everyone with respect. Even more important, he cared about the people in Roxbury. Judge Davis referred to his courthouse as a "beacon of hope for the people of Roxbury." He had shown his commitment by staying in the community, even after he'd become a successful attorney and then a judge. Born and raised in Roxbury, he had every intention of dying there. From the comments he made from the bench it was clear that he believed that the person sitting in judgment of the many black defendants should himself be black.

Some of the old-timer Jewish defense attorneys said that he was a man who had true *rachmanas,* the Yiddish word for mercy. They knew that Judge Davis was never afraid to give someone a second chance, regardless of any criticism he might take from the public or the media. He wanted people to feel that they could come to his court and find true justice. But if he gave someone that second chance and they made him look bad by committing another crime, he wasn't shy about sending that person to jail.

"Commonwealth versus Isaac McCreary," the clerk called out.

"Good morning, Your Honor." Connie stood up and looked toward the defense attorney as she approached the bar with her client, a sad sack of a man in a print shirt his wife had probably pressed for him that morning. He looked around the courtroom as though he'd been dropped there from another planet.

Connie checked his watch and saw that it was 12:40 P.M. "I'm sorry, Your Honor, good *afternoon,* Conrad Darget for the Commonwealth. The Commonwealth is answering not ready for trial on this matter." Connie felt like a parrot repeating the same words for the eighth time that day. He had summoned the civilian witnesses on all of his cases, but none of them had shown up for court. Typical.

The only witnesses who did show up were the police on two drug possession cases. Both defendants pled guilty and were placed on probation. Every other case was "dismissed for want of prosecution." This case was Connie's last DWOP of the day and he wanted to get it over with. He tried to get at least one trial a week and eight DWOPs on Monday was a bad way to start the week.

"Mr. Darget," Judge Davis said, "why has the Commonwealth answered not ready on so many cases this morning?"

"I'm not sure, Your Honor, but I do apologize to the court," Connie said. "All of the civilian witnesses I summoned for this morning chose to ignore their subpoenas."

"Mr. Darget, I can issue *capias writs* to have them brought before the court in custody. Is that what you'd like?"

"No, Your Honor. These cases have all been relatively minor misdemeanors. The case against Mr. McCreary is a dispute between neighbors that ended in a shoving match. Mr. McCreary is charged with assault and battery. The defendant is forty-five years old, has no prior criminal record and the alleged victim has since moved to a new apartment in another neighborhood."

"I understand, Mr. Darget. This case is dismissed. What else do we have on the docket?" Judge Davis asked his clerk as Connie stepped back and resumed his seat at the table with Mitch.

"What a waste of time," Connie whispered to Mitch. "What do you have left, Red?"

"One more case, but I don't think it's going. The guy's charged with selling crack in a school zone. He's looking at the mandatory two. I'm hoping he'll take a plea with a little bit of jail time if I dismiss the zone. Stick around and see what happens, then we'll go upstairs."

"Commonwealth versus Anthony Furr," the clerk called the case as Mitch, the defense attorney and the defendant stood up.

"Mitchum Beaulieu for the Commonwealth," Mitch said as he approached the bench.

"Attorney Norman Woodrum for the defendant, Anthony Furr," the defense attorney said. He and the defendant, a youngish man with an athletic build and a defiant look permanently fixed to his handsome features, approached the bench. Woodrum was a man trapped in the sixties. He had long gray hair pulled back in a ponytail that looked like it hadn't been washed in a week. If he wasn't wearing a cheap wrinkled suit, you'd think he'd just jumped out of his Volkswagen bus after returning from Woodstock. But he was much respected as an advocate for his clients. He was a true believer who never trusted the government and fought like a pit bull to give his clients a fair trial. He felt the system was biased against the indigent and against young black men in particular.

"All right, gentlemen," Judge Davis said. "Are we ready for trial or is this going to be a plea? What's your pleasure?"

"Your Honor," Mr. Woodrum started, "my client is willing to change his plea to guilty if the court would place him on probation. Mr. Furr is twenty-eight years old and has no criminal record prior to this arrest. He has always held a regular job as a construction laborer and is married with a young daughter. He was laid off several months ago and foolishly started selling drugs to support his family. His first day on the street he sold to an undercover cop and was arrested. This is his first run-in with the law in his twenty-eight years. He certainly does not deserve to go to jail for two years."

"Thank you, Mr. Woodrum," Judge Davis said. "I understand your position and I would love to place your client on probation. Unfortunately, Mr. Furr sold drugs within a school zone and I have no discretion in what sentence he receives. Mr. Beaulieu and the Commonwealth hold all of the cards here. If the Commonwealth doesn't move to dismiss the school zone charge, your client has to serve the two years in jail, unless, of course, he goes to trial and is acquitted."

Connie caught the implication of the judge's words. He was sure it wasn't lost on Mitch either. Judge Davis was trying to pressure Mitch into dismissing the school zone charge. The prosecutors didn't mind giving a man a break, but any leniency should still involve some jail time. The defendant had to be punished for selling the drugs that were ruining lives.

"Your Honor," Mitch began. "I appreciate Mr. Woodrum's argument, but the law is the law and the defendant was selling crack cocaine within a thousand feet of a school, in a neighborhood that's been plagued with drugs and violence. The Commonwealth would be willing to dismiss the school zone if the defendant would plead guilty to the distribution and take a six-month term in jail, followed by two years of probation."

"This is the problem I have with the school zone law," Woodrum argued. "Mr. Beaulieu talks about my client selling drugs near a school, knowing that you can't go anywhere in this city without being within a thousand feet of a school. Every black kid that gets caught with drugs in the city is looking at a mandatory two years in jail, while kids in the lily white suburbs get a slap on the wrist and sent home to Mommy and Daddy. It's a racist law. And I don't see how Mr. Beaulieu can pretend it is not."

"I'll tell you how," Anthony Furr said. "He's a fuckin' sellout. A pawn for the white man."

"That's enough, Mr. Furr. I won't have language like that in my courtroom," Judge Davis said.

Furr turned to stare at Mitch. "Remember one thing, my brother. You're not white, and the day you realize that, it'll be too late. You'll have sold your soul to these white devils."

Connie watched as the judge raised his eyebrow to the court officer, warning her to be on alert.

The court officer took her time rising from her chair and approached Furr from behind.

"And the devils will turn their backs on you. You'll face your sins alone. There won't be any brothers left to stand with you, Mr. Beaulieu, because you've destroyed their lives."

Mitch stood motionless.

"Mr. Furr," Judge Davis said, "that's no way to speak to the man who holds the key to your freedom. I suggest you let your attorney do the talking for you, and please be more respectful to this man if you plan on walking out of this building without handcuffs and shackles."

"That's just it, Judge. Based on what Mr. Beaulieu has said to my attorney, I'm not walking out of this courtroom of my own free will. I've sat in here all day," Furr said as he turned to face the gallery of seats behind him and continued around to face the judge after a complete pirouette, "and I have watched one black defendant after another stand before this court and get no justice. It's clear to me. I'm going to be taken into custody by this here court officer," he said as he pointed to the fifty-something-year-old, heavyset woman standing behind him studying her manicure. "And I'm not going to be led off to jail without first giving Mr. Beaulieu a piece of my mind."

Connie turned in his chair to face the court officer. He tried discreetly to get her attention. He'd seen Furr perform his little spin move a moment earlier. Furr had become cagey since he'd first approached the judge. Connie could see that he was checking the number of court officers when he turned toward the gallery. But the court officer was oblivious.

"I've never broken the law," Furr continued. "Not even a speeding ticket. Then just once, I do something stupid to put food on the table and this man wants to send me to jail. Well, Judge, I can't go to jail. I made a mistake. I'm sorry for what I did. Mr. Beaulieu, no matter how hard you try, you will never wash my blood off your hands. And, Mr. Woodrum, please tell my wife and daughter that I love them."

Anthony Furr turned toward the gallery, this time with no intention of turning back toward the court, and made a break for the door. The court officer struggled to grab hold of him. Instinctively, Connie stood up and started after Furr. Behind him, he heard the officer calling for backup. Connie was hoping to catch him before he made it to the stairs.

But Furr wasn't trying to make it to the stairs. As they closed in on the balcony that looked down on the main foyer to the courthouse twenty feet below, Connie realized that Furr was heading straight for the railing at a full sprint, with no intention of stopping. Connie saw two court officers from another session trying to get to Furr, but all of them were too late.

Seeing how gracefully he jumped over the balcony rail, tucking his arms by his sides and crashing headfirst into the marble floor below, Connie thought that Furr must have been on the diving team in high school. He never uttered a sound as his body fell. It was a beautiful, perfect dive that led to a horrible, messy death.

As Connie reached the balcony he looked down and saw Anthony Furr, lifeless, lying on his back, his eyes open, staring up at the domed ceiling of the courthouse. A massive pool of blood began to rapidly expand outward from his crushed skull, like a thick red halo. As Connie turned away, he found Mitch standing next to him. His light brown skin was ashen.

"So what do you think, Mr. Beaulieu?" Woodrum said as he walked up to them and looked over the balcony at his dead client. "Do you think Boston is a safer place now that you permanently removed Anthony Furr, a father, a husband, a hard-working man, from its streets?"

"Leave him alone," Connie said. He could see how shaken Mitch was. "You know Mitch was just doing his job. Your client is dead. You can knock off the act."

"May God forgive you for what you've done, Mitch Beaulieu," Woodrum said as he walked toward the stairs leading down to the foyer.

Mitch sank to his knees. Connie put a hand on his shoulder and lifted Mitch off the floor by his jacket as people from the other courtrooms were drawn out by the commotion, gathering around the balcony.

"Mitch, get up," Connie said. "You can't let people see you like this."

"Connie, I . . . shit, Connie, I just killed that man."

"Shut the fuck up. You didn't kill anyone," Connie said. He put his arm around Mitch's back and hurried him toward the stairs. "Let's get up to the office." Mitch was silent, barely dragging his feet. "I'm not going to let people see you like this, Red," Connie said.

CHAPTER 32

The Whittier Street Housing Development was spitting distance from One Schroeder Plaza. It was also the current residence of Michael Sampson, a convicted rapist and home invader who had been paroled from MCI–Shirley Prison six months earlier. Convicted rapists weren't supposed to be living in public housing complexes, but Sampson wasn't on the lease. He was living with his mother, the way he had his entire adult life—when he wasn't being housed in a prison.

Angel Alves rang every doorbell in the building except for one. It took less than a minute for someone to buzz him and Mooney in. Alves propped the door open with a large rock, a trick he had learned as a rookie cop, just in case they needed to call for backup. Any delay in getting help could mean the difference between life and death.

Alves looked around the first-floor hallway, making sure they were alone, before following Mooney to the third floor. They stood on either side of the door to apartment 301 as Mooney knocked on the door. They listened for sounds inside the apartment. Nothing.

Then Alves knocked on the door, this time much harder than Mooney. "Boston Police," he said in a loud voice.

Now there was movement. At first they heard someone walking around, but no one came to the door.

A third knock, this time from Mooney and a sterner announcement of police presence in the building.

Much quicker movement in the apartment now, too quick to be Michael Sampson's elderly mother. Alves removed his gun from its holster and took a few steps back before launching his body into the door. He heard it crack. He stepped back again and hit it with more force. The doorjamb split open. One hard kick and they were in the apartment.

"Not bad for a little guy," Mooney said.

Alves was already moving through the apartment, clearing each room before moving on to the next. One room left: the bathroom at the end of the hall. Alves heard the toilet flush and tried the door. Locked. "Boston Police!" he shouted, more of a courtesy than anything else, before kicking the door open.

"Don't shoot," Michael Sampson said, his hands over his head, "please don't shoot me." Water was flowing out of the toilet onto the floor as he tried to flush away a half pound plastic bag of weed.

"Shithead, pull that out of there before you flood the building," Alves said.

Sampson reached into the toilet and pulled out a large Ziploc bag.

"Now get out here." Alves grabbed Sampson by the back of his shirt and threw him down the hall toward the living room.

"What do you guys want? I didn't do nothing."

Mooney laughed. "You didn't do nothing? You think your PO will be cool with you having all that weed?"

Sampson didn't respond.

"I didn't think so," Alves said. "We have some questions for you and, unless you feel like going back to Shirley on a parole violation, I expect your complete cooperation. *¿Comprende?*"

Sampson nodded.

"Where were you Friday night? And it better be the fucking truth."

CHAPTER 33

Connie tended to Mitch the way a paramedic might treat a person with a concussion, trying to keep him awake and alert. Mitch was staring down at the table in front of him, eyes unblinking, face covered in sweat. Connie expected Mitch would be throwing up soon.

Even behind the closed door, Connie could hear the muted sounds of the commotion below. The two of them wouldn't be alone for long. Mitch still hadn't said a word. Now he made a low moaning sound, and Connie rubbed the back of his neck in an effort to comfort him.

Then the door swung open and Liz Moore came into the conference room. "What's going on downstairs?" she asked. "The front of the building's closed off by cops and EMTs."

"One of the defendants in the trial session jumped off the second-floor balcony," Connie said. "Killed himself."

She glanced at Mitch and back at Connie. "Who?"

"One of Mitch's defendants. We thought he was going to plead guilty. Next thing you know, Woodrum plays the race card. The defendant flips out on Mitch, calling him a sellout. Then he makes a break for it. Lands a perfect ten on a swan dive off the balcony."

"What was his name?"

"Anthony Furr," Connie said.

A look came over Liz's face. Disappointment? Barely controlled anger? Connie wasn't sure.

"Woodrum talked to me about this case last week," she said. "He said Furr wasn't a real drug dealer, that he'd never been arrested before and he wouldn't survive in jail. I told him there was nothing I could do for him. Woodrum's going to raise holy hell. I'd better call the DA before he does." She looked over at Mitch. His skin was still ashen gray. "Mitch," she said. "How are you doing?" He stared down at the table. "Bring him into my office," she said as she stepped out of the conference room.

Once they were in Liz's office, Connie propped Mitch up in an upholstered armchair. Connie didn't know if he should leave them alone, but Liz didn't say anything, didn't really look at him, so he stood by Mitch's chair.

"I know what you're thinking," Liz said, "but you didn't do anything wrong. When someone brings up race with one of the white guys, they feel like they're being labeled a racist. When they do it to you, they make you feel like Judas. You're not. You're a good prosecutor. You were doing your job, and you did it well. Furr got caught selling drugs. He's responsible for what he did. He couldn't face the penalty for his actions."

Something in her words seemed to strike Mitch. "Anthony Furr was a decent man who made a mistake. And I stood there selling the company line: If you do the crime, you do the time. I should have listened to his story. Felt some compassion for his circumstances. I never talked to you about the case. Maybe there was something we could have done for him."

"Would it really have mattered?" she asked. "You know office policy. Even if we reduce the charge, the defendant has to do some jail time."

"But maybe Furr should have been the exception to the rule. Maybe I showed no compassion toward him because he was black. If that's the case, then my actions are inexcusable."

"What are you talking about?"

"Would I have done more for him if he were a *white* man with no record? Did I assume that he'd be able to survive in jail because he was black? I don't *think* that's what I did. Now I'm not so sure."

"Listen to me. I've supervised you long enough to know that's not how you think. I've watched you in court and the way you handle pleas. You treat everyone with respect and professionalism, no matter what their race. You witnessed something tragic today. But it wasn't your fault."

Liz stood up. "Let me tell you a story. My first day on the job, I was excited just to be standing in a courtroom, doing something for the community. I'm preparing a stack of thirty or so arraignments, thinking I'm the good guy and everyone's going to admire what I'm doing for them. Then the first defendant I'm about to arraign calls me a 'sellout bitch' in open court. I look out over the faces in the gallery and can tell they think the same thing. It hurt. I knew that a lot of people in the black community didn't trust the police or prosecutors, but I believed it would be different for me. As a black woman, I thought I'd have some credibility with witnesses and defendants in the courtroom, that people would see me as a fair prosecutor. I was wrong. But I didn't let that stop me from doing my job."

"I took this job for the same reasons. Now I'm not so sure—"

"There *are* people who appreciate what you do every day. Unfortunately, you don't get a chance to meet them. All you see in the courthouse are angry defendants and reluctant witnesses who don't want to be labeled as snitches. But most people in this community want to live in a neighborhood where their children can play outside without the constant fear of gunfire."

Mitch sat up straighter, his long fingers relaxing on the chair's arms. Liz was starting to get through to him in a way that Connie could not.

"Mitch, those are the people who respect you and appreciate what you do. You'll probably never meet them because they're busy working two jobs and don't have time to hang around a courthouse and thank you for the work you do."

Liz moved back toward her desk. "See those two Norman Rockwell prints?" she said, pointing to the wall behind her. There were two gold-framed prints, one of a little black girl in pigtails and a white dress; the other an illustration of parents, circa 1943, lovingly tucking their kids into bed, the father holding a newspaper with a headline of wartime bombing. Connie wanted to get that same Rockwell print of the bedtime scene—after all, *Freedom from Fear* was the only one of the four freedoms they had control of as prosecutors.

"Those aren't up there because they're pretty," Liz was saying to Mitch. "They're up there to remind me every morning why I do this job. They help keep me strong in my mission. The print of the little girl is called *The Problem We All Live With.*"

"That's the little girl," Mitch said, "Ruby Bridges, who had to walk the gauntlet every day, escorted by federal marshals, just to go to her desegregated school in New Orleans."

Liz nodded. "Do you think that six-year-old girl had someone telling her that they appreciated what she was doing for every black child in America? Do you think anyone in that mob told her how much they respected her as they called her 'nigger' and threw rotten fruit at her?"

Mitch's eyes were fixed on the print.

"I'm not nearly as brave as Ruby Bridges," she continued. "I keep her picture there to remind me of what *she* did for me, to help me keep fighting for the next generation of children out there. Are you familiar with the other print?"

Mitch nodded. He wiped at his face with his shirtsleeve.

"Our job as prosecutors is to try to make every parent in this city feel that safe about their kids, whether they're tucking them in bed at night or dropping them off at the park to play. Until we reach that goal, our work isn't complete."

Mitch stood up from his chair. "Thanks, Liz. I've taken up enough of your time."

"My door's always open," she said.

Connie glanced at Liz as Mitch stood up and walked unsteadily out of her office.

"You think he'll be all right?" Connie asked, looking after him.

She shrugged. "No one has ever killed himself because of me doing my job. My guess is, right now it doesn't matter what we say. He has to work things out for himself and decide if he really wants to be a prosecutor. Being a prosecutor is a tough job. We have incredible power over other people's lives."

CHAPTER 34

Mitch stared at his computer screen saver with its simulation of fast-moving stars. He imagined himself floating through space, dreaming he was someone other than Mitchum Beaulieu, the person responsible for another man's death.

He wished he were a young kid again, back in Laurel, Maryland, where he'd been raised by his adoptive father, a wealthy, eccentric widower, Marshall Beaulieu. Marshall's young wife, Christina, had died giving birth to their stillborn child.

Marshall had sworn that he would never love another woman, but he had always wanted a son to carry the Beaulieu name. His father told him how sometime after Christina's death he'd decided to adopt a child. He traveled to the Sisters of Hope orphanage in Baltimore to find a son. All of the children looked the same to him with their fair skin, blond hair and blue eyes.

Then Marshall Beaulieu saw a young boy, no more than two years old, sitting alone on one side of the room coloring on a piece of white construction paper. "You were always different," his father told him. The other children wouldn't play with him and he didn't seem to care. "You were all alone in the world, like I was."

The boy had light brown skin and a full head of reddish-brown hair. He had gray eyes, a shade of gray that Marshall was familiar with, the color of a storm cloud on a hot August afternoon, the color of

Christina's eyes. And as though he were watching that storm cloud fast approaching in the summer heat, Marshall anticipated the relief that rain would bring.

When his father approached him, Mitch stopped coloring and looked up. Marshall tried to coax him over for a hug, but he got frightened and started to cry. He was the most handsome child in the room, even when he was crying, his father told him, and Marshall knew right then that this child would be his son.

Mitch closed his eyes and imagined himself back in that room, getting hugged by his father. It had been so long since he had seen his father, touched him, spoken with him, smelled his distinctive smell of sweet pipe tobacco and peppermint. He missed him, especially at a time like this when he needed his support and advice. He realized he had no one in his life now. Everything around him was shattered. He needed someone to help him make it through.

A punch in the arm startled Mitch from his thoughts. "Hey, Red, are you going to come get a workout or what?" Connie stood beside him, his suit jacket slung over his shoulder.

"I think I might stay here and try to get some work done," Mitch said, trying to focus on his computer screen.

"You might stay and do some work?" He sounded like a parent questioning a child who'd refused to do his chores. "A workout will help clear your head. Come with me."

"But I really don't feel like—"

"I don't care if you pedal around on an exercise bike or walk on the treadmill, you're not going to stay here alone and think about what happened today. It'll burn off some stress and you'll feel better."

"I don't want to stay long. And I don't feel like lifting any weights."

"Fine," Connie said. "No lifting—even though nothing relieves stress better than pumping iron. You don't even need to break a sweat. I just want you to get up and do something."

Mitch could see Connie wasn't going away. He turned off his computer.

"Great," Connie said. "Let me just say good night to Andi. She and Rachel are going to dinner with her parents tonight."

Mitch stood and started to pack his briefcase. He wasn't going to get any work done anyway, so he snapped the case shut and slipped it under his desk. He was putting on his suit jacket when Connie came back.

"Let's go," Connie said.

Mitch followed Connie down the stairs, shuffling after him like a little kid tagging along behind his big brother.

CHAPTER 35

Alves focused on the road in front of him. **"Who's next on the list,** Sarge?"

"Whoever you want. We've got guys in West Roxbury, Eastie, Brighton. Take your pick. They're all the same. Psycho losers who live with their mothers and run around attacking any woman they come in contact with."

"Let's go to Eastie. I've got a good feeling about the other side of the harbor."

"You want to grab a coffee first?"

"I'm all set."

"I'm not. Stop at the next Dunkies."

Alves was frustrated by the day they had put in, questioning six of the worst sex offenders from their list. None of them seemed to be their man, but he felt as if they were on the right track. At least they were out of the office, shaking people down, trying to make something happen. A couple of his old drug informants had mentioned some of the same people from their list as possible suspects. If they kept at it, he was sure they would catch the bad guy.

Alves stopped at a Dunkin' Donuts on Boylston Street. Mooney didn't get out of the car. He sat there, staring at Alves, examining his face, something he had done a couple of times during the day.

Alves looked straight out the windshield, refusing to look over at Mooney.

"You okay, Angel?"

"Yeah." Alves didn't turn his head.

Mooney was patient. He was good at what he did, not the least bit bothered by the uncomfortable silence in the car. Mooney seemed to be waiting for Alves to turn toward him. Alves wasn't about to lose this test of wills.

Finally Mooney said, "I want to get this guy as much as you, but you've got to slow down a little. Don't put so much pressure on yourself."

"I'm not putting—"

"Yes, you are, and that's okay. That's what makes a good Homicide detective. But I can see that you're personally affected by this case. And that's *not* okay. I like the drive you've been showing the last couple of days, but you can't let this eat you up. Even when he's behind bars, it isn't going to take away the pain that he's caused. Robyn's mom has been destroyed and she'll be fucked up for life. All we can do now is keep this guy from hurting anyone else."

Mooney opened his door. "You sure you don't want a coffee?"

Alves shook his head.

Mooney nodded and slammed the door shut.

CHAPTER 36

Andi Norton had trouble inserting the key into the knob. The hallway was poorly lit, several bulbs burned out in the chandelier. She heard a noise on the first floor and waited to see if anyone was following her up the stairs. Everything was silent. She opened the door to her condo with one hand, holding Rachel up over her shoulder with the other. Rachel had fallen asleep during the ten minutes it took to go from Newbury Street in the Back Bay to their condominium in Southie. Her own place was a reward from her parents for getting into law school. They were pretty cool, choosing to give their only daughter some of her inheritance while they were still alive.

Without turning on any lights, Andi moved quietly down the front hall, through the living room and into Rachel's bedroom. Andi felt Rachel's regular breaths on her neck. She was sleeping soundly. Andi pulled the quilt back and gently placed Rachel on the bed, her blond hair forming a halo around her head as it spread out on the pillow. She slipped off Rachel's jacket and her shoes. She could sleep in her leggings and jersey. No need to wake her up. Pulling the covers up, Andi kissed Rachel on the forehead. "Sweet dreams, princess."

Back in the living room, the answering machine was blinking. One message. It was Connie. "Hi, Andi. Just me. I'm still out with Mitch. We're at Kilronan's. Just checking in to see how dinner went. Miss you. Talk to you tomorrow."

A muted rustling sound just outside her door. Was someone in the hallway? Her door was at the end of the hall. It couldn't be Connie. He was at Kilronan's. Had she locked the door? The dead bolt? She moved toward the door. Don't run. No need to panic. Then she heard the noise again. Someone fooling with a doorknob? She turned the dead bolt and leaned against the door, trying to relax. She took a breath and turned to look out the peephole. Down the hall was her neighbor, balancing grocery bags and fooling with her keys in the dark hallway just as Andi had done a few minutes before.

She needed a drink.

Andi went into the kitchen and poured herself a glass of merlot. On the couch, in the dark, she sipped the wine. She tried to think positive thoughts. Connie. She'd been seeing him for only a few months, but she was starting to care for him. He seemed to understand her situation as a single parent, how she wanted to take things slowly for Rachel's sake. It was important that she not have a bunch of men walking in and out of her daughter's life.

Andi needed a man that wasn't just out for sex, someone who was mature enough to realize that there was a child involved in the relationship. Conrad Darget was starting to look like that man. But she needed to be sure. She took another sip of wine. He respected her responsibilities. During the time they'd dated, he'd never tried to do more than kiss her. A perfect gentleman. He'd told her that they could take their time until *she* was ready, and he had kept his promise.

Andi couldn't believe she cared so much about a man she'd never slept with, or maybe what she couldn't believe was that she hadn't slept with a man she cared so much about. Connie had been very patient. Too patient? A nagging thought crept into her daydream. What if she *was* being played? What if this *was* his way of getting to her?

No. It was the wine, the late hour, too many bad dates talking. He'd done so much for her at work, and he wasn't showering Rachel with gifts and attention to win her over. Andi moved into her bedroom without turning on the lights.

CHAPTER 37

Mitch stayed at the table while Connie went to the bar for another round of Murphy's Irish Stout. He felt miserable, but grateful that Connie had made him go out. The workout had helped take his mind off things and now the beers were working their magic, helping him forget a little. Hanging out with a friend was much better than sitting all alone in that empty apartment, thinking about how Sonya was right.

It was Connie's idea to go for a beer at Kilronan's in Mission Hill, a Boston neighborhood made famous by Charles Stuart. Stuart shot and killed his pregnant wife before making a frantic 911 call. He accused a black man of the shooting, bringing the city to the verge of a race war as the police engaged in an aggressive manhunt for the killer. The police eventually turned their attention back toward Stuart, but the damage to the black community had been done. In the end, Stuart took his own life by jumping off the Tobin Bridge into the Mystic River.

Kilronan's was about a mile from the courthouse and right around the corner from where Stuart had killed his wife and unborn son. Tonight, there were only a couple of other people in the pub, all sitting at the bar, while the two of them huddled at a table in a dark corner.

"Hey, buddy," Connie said as he returned with the beers, "you're not getting depressed on me again, are you?"

"No."

"Good, because if we're going to survive in this business, we have to get used to making tough decisions. Once we get up to superior court the stakes will be even higher."

"Connie, I killed a man today. Could the stakes be much higher?"

"You only did your job. You were given a set of facts and presented those facts to a judge. And, like you said in court, the law is the law, no matter what Woodrum says."

"But what if I am a sellout? I feel like the Judas that Furr accused me of being." That quickly, Mitch felt dangerously close to breaking down again. "Connie, my sole purpose in life is sending young black men to jail. I don't know if I can do it anymore."

"You're anything but a sellout. It would be easier for you to become a defense attorney like Woodrum and get up on your soapbox and talk about oppression. Instead, you're a role model to the young kids growing up in the city who want to make their neighborhood a safer place to live. You're the one trying to eliminate the drugs that are destroying the black community. You should be proud of yourself and what you do. What happened today was tragic. But we're not responsible for the choices a man makes."

"What would you do if you were in that situation? You're a law-abiding citizen your whole life. Then one day you make a mistake that's going to send you to jail for a couple of years. Would you be able to tough it out or would you kill yourself?"

Connie thought for a moment and said, "I think I'd be able to do the time."

"I couldn't make it through a single day being caged. I'd probably kill myself the same way Furr did. Quick, easy and painless."

Mitch remembered his own father, who had struggled for so long with the loss of his wife, Christina. Around the time Mitch was going off to college he finally realized that his father had adopted him to fill the void left by her death. It was during his sophomore year in college, just after the Christmas break, that Mitch had received the call that his father had killed himself. Apparently Marshall Beaulieu had felt he was losing Mitch and couldn't stand the thought of being alone again.

"Furr's death was messy," Connie said, "but you're right about it being quick and painless. I don't think I could ever kill myself. I think it would be harder to kill yourself than to survive in jail. If nothing else, the man had balls."

"I'll drink to that," Mitch said as they both downed the last of their beers.

Mitch thought about how jumping off a balcony took a lot of guts, but it was nothing like the meticulous time and effort employed by his father to hang himself, with his hands tied behind his back. Mitch never figured out how he'd done it, but it certainly took nerve and commitment to go through all that and not change his mind. Mitch wished that his father had called him first. Maybe hearing Mitch's voice, thinking of Mitch being alone, would have changed his mind.

Mitch had inherited the entire Beaulieu estate, but it wasn't financial security that he needed. He needed his father for guidance and counsel. He no longer had Sonya to help him work things out. The only one he could talk to, the only one he trusted now, was Connie.

"Blood Bath Killer Strikes Again!" Nick Costa poked his head into the conference room as he pointed to the Tuesday morning headline in the *Herald*. "This guy is really on a tear."

Connie felt the temperature in the room drop by a few degrees. He'd just been updating Liz on the most recent murder. And she wasn't pleased. The television and print media had picked up on Robyn Stokes's death. The BPD was taking shit for burying the story. They were also being accused of recklessly creating a public safety risk.

"That's not funny," Liz said.

"Doesn't anyone have a sense of humor around here?"

Liz was biting down on her lower lip to control her anger. Nick had made a big mistake with this one. Best to stay out of it.

"A young woman was killed over the weekend," Liz started. "She's the third woman murdered in the last few months, the second in the past week, and you think there's something funny about that?" Liz raised her hand to stop Nick from responding. "And, correct me if I'm wrong," she said turning to Connie, "but I don't think the police have any leads."

"They don't," Connie said. "I talked with Alves ten minutes ago. They're getting a lot of heat, but they're no closer to catching this guy than they were after the first murder."

Liz focused back on Nick. "Which means more innocent victims may lose their lives."

Nick tucked the newspaper under his arm.

"Alves sounded pretty concerned." Connie was enjoying this.

"As well he should," Liz said. "We should all be concerned, especially since we work for the district attorney, the city's chief law enforcement official. If you think there's something humorous here"—she gave Nick a withering look—"please let me in on it. Maybe we can give the DA a call and share the joke with him."

Nick looked defeated. After a few seconds of silence he said, "I'm sorry. I shouldn't have been kidding around."

"No more jokes. No more trying to scare people in the parking lot at night. This isn't high school. You're a lawyer. Start acting like one."

Nick turned and silently left the conference room.

"I don't have time for his bullshit. Nick's prank in the parking lot got me thinking. We need a plan to ensure our own safety coming and going late at night and early in the mornings."

"Maybe we should have a staff meeting to set up a protocol," Connie suggested. "All these women were killed at home, but Alves said that doesn't mean he won't attack somewhere else. They haven't figured out his pattern yet. He could be stalking women and waiting to attack, or he could just be an opportunist, killing women he's never seen before."

"Do they have an idea as to the common thread linking the victims?" she asked.

"It could be anything. He might be watching them as they leave work, go grocery shopping or to the cleaners. Alves thinks that women should be vigilant at all times, keeping an eye out for anyone who could be watching or following them. You're right, nobody should walk out to the parking lot alone at night. Anyone who works late should call next door for a police escort to their car."

"That's good," she said. "We'll have a meeting so we can discuss different safety options."

"If you want, I'll call a community service officer and see if she can get rape whistles for the women."

"Do you think you can get ahold of her this morning?"

Connie looked at her, surprised by the request's immediacy, and thought he saw a shadow of fear cross her face.

CHAPTER 39

The crisp sheets felt cool against Richter's skin, the ceiling fan whirring above his bed. He had just finished with Robyn Stokes, allowing him some time to reflect on all he had accomplished. The past week had been eventful. He would have to slow down a little to keep the detectives off balance. He would pick up his pace when the time was right, but for now Richter would simply take pleasure in his achievement.

He could take a life without feeling any anger or hatred. It was a skill he had worked on for many years. There had been times when he had acted on his emotions, but those were in the past. Richter knew that killing out of anger would eventually get him caught, because anger is a motive. That was the beauty of his current work. No one would ever realize that Richter was killing anyone, because he had no motive to kill anyone.

Looking up at the ceiling fan, he remembered the first time he had wanted to kill. At that time, the desire arose from anger. He was young and he had not yet harnessed his rage.

Richter never took his eyes off Pam Brown's tight pink panties as she ran to get the Ouija board out of the closet. They had just finished playing a game of strip poker and Richter had called for a vote to decide if they should play with the Ouija board before getting dressed. It was, in theory, a democratic vote. Unfortunately for the girls they were outnumbered three to two, so everyone had to stay in their underwear a little longer.

It was ninety degrees and humid, with only the ceiling fan to cool the room. At sixteen, Richter was the youngest of the group, but he was bigger than the other boys, almost six feet tall.

Frank and Brian Jansen, twin brothers whom Richter had nicknamed the Smurfs because they were short, chubby and looked exactly alike, sat on one end of the couch across from him. Pam strutted around in her pink panties and bra, enjoying the attention from the boys. Luz Perez had taken over the other end of the couch, trying to cover herself using her yellow midriff T-shirt as a blanket. She wasn't her usual flirty self. Stripping her down to her underwear had exposed her as a tease.

Luz was curled up on the couch with her knees clamped together and pulled up to her chest. Her face was flushed and she looked as if she was ready to cry. It was obvious that she had no intention of playing any more games.

Richter stared down toward her feet and said, "Luz, your epidermis is showing."

She looked up and saw where his eyes were focused. She tried to close her legs tighter together and lower the shirt.

"It's still showing," he said, this time staring at her chest.

She put her arms across her chest.

"I can still see it, Luz."

"No you can't. You can't see anything, you liar."

"You have no idea what your epidermis is, do you?"

"Yes I do."

"What is it, then?"

She was silent. Richter could have told her right away, but he enjoyed watching her embarrassment as everyone waited for her answer. He let it go on for a few seconds before he said, "It's your skin, stupid. Your epidermis is your skin." The boys all laughed.

Luz started to cry and Pam went over to comfort her. "Jesus, you know she's upset, so stop picking on her."

Richter looked at Luz and said, "I'm sorry. I was just teasing."

"Fuck you. Don't even talk to me."

He shrugged. The truth was that he'd enjoyed making her cry.

Pam set up the Ouija board, trying to break the tension. "The board is ready. Let's ask it some questions."

Luz didn't move. Frank Jansen stayed where he was on the couch too. He hated it when they played Ouija. Frank was terrified that the devil made the planchette move across the board. Anything that might involve the devil scared him to death.

Richter, Pam and Brian huddled close to the Ouija board. They touched their fingers lightly to the planchette and Pam asked the first question, "Am I going to be married someday?"

Their hands slid across the board to the word "Yes" and Pam smiled. Richter had been interested in Pam and thought she looked great in her scanty outfit. But he couldn't resist the chance to have a little fun with her too, so when she asked who she was going to marry he moved the planchette to the L, the U, then the Z.

"Real funny, you jerks," she said, taking her hands off the planchette. "Who did that?"

"Not me," Richter and Brian said in unison.

"Yeah, right."

"Now it's my turn," Richter said. He waited for the others to put their hands back on the game piece. "Is there anyone in this room who has a crush on me?" Richter slowly moved the planchette toward the "Yes."

"Who is it?" he asked. Before he could move the planchette to spell out Pam's name, it started toward the letter S, then A, T, A and N. Now Pam laughed with Brian and Luz joining in. Luz laughed extra loud.

Frank didn't think it was funny at all. "I told you that thing is evil," he said.

For a moment Richter was stunned by what had happened. How could the Ouija spell out "Satan" when he was trying to make it spell Pam's name? Then, with everyone laughing at him, he realized Pam or Brian had done it. But which one? Brian wasn't smart enough. It must have been Pam. He watched her face as she continued her forced laughter. She didn't seem so cute anymore.

"Who did that?"

"Not me," Pam said in a sarcastic voice, mimicking what he'd said to her a few minutes earlier.

It wasn't funny. He fixed his eyes on Pam's. Richter could see that Pam was starting to feel uncomfortable. She forced out another burst of laughter. He clenched his teeth, the way he did when he was angry. His eyes didn't waver. He wanted to whack her on the head. Then he thought of a better way to spoil her fun.

He walked over and stood above her. "Come clean and I'll forget it happened."

"Hey, buddy," Brian said, "chill out. We're just having a little fun."

"I'm not your buddy," he said without looking away from Pam.

"I didn't do anything," she said.

Richter held both of Pam's arms and pinned them against the sides of her body. "Admit you did it."

"Let go of me. You're hurting me, you maniac," she said as she twisted and turned her body, trying to break free from his grip.

"I'm a maniac, am I? I'll show you maniac," he said, calmly lifting her off the floor.

He looked up and saw that they were directly beneath the ceiling fan that had kept them cool all afternoon. He lifted her higher so she could hear the hum of the motor and her hair began whipping around. Richter never took his focus off her eyes. They showed how frightened she was at the thought of what he might do to her. She couldn't move her arms. He had perfect control of her until he felt the paralyzing pain in his groin, so intense it reached his head instantly. Even in agony he maintained his grip on her. He felt her stiffen in fear once she realized her kick had only served to anger him even more. "Somebody stop him," she begged the others. "He's crazy. He's trying to kill me."

But they were all just as afraid of him as she was. He was bigger and stronger than any of them and he was sure that none of them wanted to switch places with her. "Listen to me, Pam," Richter said. "I don't like people who cheat. We have rules for a reason. When people break those rules, they need to be punished. That's why I teased Luz, as punishment for being a tease. Your sentence is going to be a little harsher, and more permanent, if you don't admit what you did."

"All right, you made your point. Now, why don't you let her down before you hurt her?" Brian tried to intervene.

Richter ignored him. When Brian started toward them, Richter said, "Step the fuck back or her head gets chopped off. She needs to confess her sins." He looked up into her eyes and said, "So what's it going to be?"

"I didn't do it," she pleaded. "I swear to God I didn't."

Richter slowly lifted her closer to the fan whizzing above her head. They all looked up and saw the gap between the blades and her head start to narrow. Her long blond hair was getting sucked up toward the blades. She tried to struggle but he was too strong. She made one more attempt to kick him in the groin, but he blocked it this time. She started sobbing, begging him to let her go.

When the fan caught a few strands of her hair and pulled them out of her scalp she let out a scream.

Richter smiled. "You're running out of time, Pam. You know I don't mind doing this." He loved being in control of her fate. He felt like God.

The look on her face let him know that everything had changed between them. It didn't matter that she liked him or that she thought he was handsome.

"I'm sorry I moved the Ouija," she said, gasping for air.

"See, it wasn't that difficult, was it?" Richter put her down. She collapsed to the floor, scrambling toward the others. Luz took her into the kitchen to try to comfort her.

"What the fuck was that all about?" Brian shouted.

"I was just messing with her," Richter said. "I wanted to spoil her little joke."

"You were going to cut her head off just to spoil her fun? Are you fucking crazy?"

"Relax. I wasn't really going to do it, but I had to get her to admit what she'd done."

"That's sick."

"Yeah, well, maybe Satan made me do it." He laughed, as he looked down at the Ouija board with the planchette still pointing to the letter N. He felt no regret for what he had done. Pam had broken the rules and she needed to be punished.

PART TWO

. . . .

What is good?—Whatever augments
the feeling of power, the will to
power, power itself, in man.
What is evil?—Whatever springs
from weakness.
What is happiness?—The feeling
that power increases—that
resistance is overcome.

—FRIEDRICH NIETZSCHE,
The Antichrist

CHAPTER 40

It was almost seven o'clock when Connie turned off the television. There was nothing on the news about the murders. The police had kept such a tight lid on their investigation, or what little there was to it, that there was nothing new for the media to report.

Earlier that day Connie had spoken with Angel Alves. Over the past few weeks, the detectives had tried the ploy of setting up Mooney as a "super-cop," plastering his face on every evening newscast, hoping to draw the killer out by challenging him. If the killer sent a taunting letter to Mooney, there might be DNA evidence on the envelope flap. The killer might reveal a detail of the crime not released in the media. The BTK killer had been caught when he left a computer disk for detectives to find.

Alves had mentioned that Mooney suspected the killer might be in custody on an unrelated charge. That would explain why it had been so long since he had killed. If that were the case, the detectives knew the hiatus wouldn't last.

Connie went into his bedroom and changed into shorts and a T-shirt. He sat doing his stretches before putting on his running shoes. There were times when he would sit and meditate. This was not one of those times. He finished his stretches and stood up, ready to go for a run through the streets of Hyde Park, a neighborhood that looked more like a suburb than an actual section of the city. Connie ran through its quiet streets a couple of nights a week to clear his head.

The early spring air felt good on his face as he stepped out of the house. He looked around and saw that the street was empty, but the individual houses were full of life. Most people were home from work—eating their dinners, helping their children with homework, watching the evening news or maybe reading a book. They felt safe, safe from the outside world, safe from any harm.

This was Connie's favorite time to run. Watching people in the evening presented a clear picture of what their lives were really like. The sky was dark and the homes were well lit. It gave him the opportunity to look into this little window to people's lives, a snapshot of the absolute normalcy of their everyday existence. Through his work, Connie had seen how abruptly everything could be turned upside down by the actions of a single person.

He shivered as he thought how easy it would be for a killer to enter any of these houses and change the families forever.

Connie got a rush thinking about his responsibility as a prosecutor to keep them safe. As he continued on his five-mile run, looking in the windows of every house he passed, he felt as though he was the protector of all these people.

CHAPTER 41

Angel Alves watched the tape, frame by frame, studying each of the faces in the crowd. He compared them to the still photos scattered across the conference-room table.

"Angel!" Mooney's voice startled him. "Marcy's on the phone. Main line."

Alves hadn't heard the phone ringing. How late was it? He looked at his watch. Ten o'clock. "Tell her I'm in a meeting, Sarge. I'll call her back."

"I'm not selling her that bullshit. You tell her. She's hysterical. Says you never stay out this late without calling. You haven't called her all day."

"I can't talk to her. She's just going to tell me to come home, that I need to get some rest. I don't need that pressure right now. I've got too much to do."

"What exactly are you doing? I didn't even know you were still here."

"Comparing the TV footage from the McCarthy scene to the stills the guys from ID took of the crowd outside Robyn Stokes's house. See if anyone showed up at both scenes. We talked about this, how these guys like to come by and see their handiwork."

"Any luck?"

"Not yet."

"Keep at it." Good sign. At least the boss didn't think it was a bad idea. Mooney pointed to the blinking red light on the phone in the center of the table. "Talk to your wife, first. I don't mind working you hard and putting a little strain on your marriage. That's fun. But I'm not going to be responsible for your divorce."

Alves picked up the phone. Marcy was crying.

CHAPTER 42

Wayne Mooney opened the door to his apartment and flipped the light switch. Something brushed against his ankle. Biggie. Good thing his Maine coon cat didn't hold grudges. If not for the automatic cat food dispenser and a toilet full of water, Biggie wouldn't have survived the past month of neglect. The cat led Mooney into the kitchen, looking for something better than the dry kibble he'd been surviving on. Mooney opened a can of tuna, a special treat, and dumped it on a dish before grabbing a couple of beers for himself.

Sitting on the couch in the living room, Mooney popped open a sixteen-ounce can of Schlitz and guzzled half. It was tough to find Schlitz anymore, but Mooney knew a source that helped him keep his fridge stocked. Biggie jumped onto his lap, needing to be petted more than he wanted his tuna.

The apartment was a true bachelor pad. Mooney's father, God rest his soul, would have told him it needed a woman's touch. There were no window treatments beyond the pull-down shades that were in the apartment when he moved in. There was a couch, a coffee table and a television with a built-in VCR, but nothing else. No pictures on the wall, no other accessories.

It had been weeks since he'd had a chance to sit on the couch and watch television. He actually missed the activity, if that's what you'd call it, which had been part of his usual routine every night for a year after the divorce. That was the only good thing that came out of the recent killings. They helped him get off his ass and back to doing his job, the job that was the main reason for the divorce. Today would have been their tenth anniversary. They had eloped to Las Vegas and were married at Caesars Palace on the 15th, the Ides of March. They had known they were testing the fates, but they'd both thought it was funny at the time.

The divorce was much less eventful. It was her Christmas gift to him a little more than a year ago. She ended up with the house and the car; he got Biggie and this apartment in Adams Village. The Dorchester boy had finally come home. Pretty sad, but that's all there was after nine years of marriage. Beware the Ides of March.

He took a second gulp from his beer and it was gone. He found the remote between the couch cushions and turned on the TV before opening the other beer. It was going to take more than a couple of drinks to relieve the pressure of this case. Almost three months had passed since Michelle Hayes's murder in December, and he and Alves were no closer to finding the killer. They'd had the McCarthy and Stokes murders, and nothing since. He saw no pattern to what the killer was doing, no significance to the dates he chose. No common thread between the victims.

And where were the bodies?

What was the sick bastard doing with the bodies? How could three women disappear without a trace? Did he bury them somewhere? Shallow graves that were formed not by digging but eventually by the passage of time—dead leaves in fall, new growth in spring? New England still offered acre after acre of thick woodland. Would their bones turn up months later, the soft flesh they needed to determine cause of death already gone?

It was only a matter of time before there would be another homicide. And there was nothing he could do about it.

He started flipping through the channels when he remembered seeing a commercial for a pro wrestling on-demand channel, where you could order some of the old matches, the classics. It took him a few tries, but he found the match he was looking for.

For Mooney, nothing tapped into the human struggle between good and evil better than professional wrestling. And it did it in very basic terms. You simply had a good guy, or "baby face," versus a "heel," the bad guy. In pro wrestling, like all other forms of entertainment in the television age, the good guys might lose a battle here and there, but they always won in the end.

What fascinated Mooney was how effortlessly a wrestling promoter could turn a popular baby face into a despised heel, further proof that the masses were like sheep that could be easily manipulated. The most beloved wrestler could become public enemy number one by simply pulling some underhanded stunt on his opponent, like a thumb to the eye or a cheap-shot knee to the groin. But the worst thing a baby face could do was betray a friend.

That was exactly what wrestling fans thought André the Giant did to Hulk Hogan. The main event from Wrestlemania III in 1987 pitted a 7′ 4″, 540-pound André, one of the most popular wrestlers of all time, against a young Hogan, the world champion. In the months leading up to the match, André had been turned into a heel. André's transformation was founded on his jealousy of Hogan and his desire to win the championship belt that had been denied him throughout his career. The script called for André the Giant, "The Eighth Wonder of the World," to get body slammed and pinned for the first and only time in his career.

It was a difficult match for Mooney to watch. André had put in all those years as a fan favorite who had never lost a match, and now, at the end of his career, he was going out as a despised villain, disgraced by a new hero who would go on to carry pro wrestling on his shoulders. As big as André was, he and the rest of the world had learned that night that he wasn't bigger than the wrestling industry.

Mooney began thinking about the killer. He knew that the real world wasn't like pro wrestling, that the good guys were the good guys and the bad guys were *real* bad guys. There was no middle ground. The roles could not be reversed, and the good guys didn't always win.

Mooney watched as the big man was lifted and then slammed helplessly to the mat. He was sickened by the sight of André the Giant, the wrestling legend, pinned to end the match, stripped of his pride and dignity at the end of his career. Mooney turned the television off and sat quietly drinking his beer, petting Biggie, the silence broken only by the sound of the cat's loud purring.

CHAPTER 43

Richter military-pressed the *giryas* over his head for the twentieth rep. The burn he felt in his lats, traps and triceps was incredible. He slammed the giryas back down on the rubber-matted floor. Leave it to the Russians to come up with a simple piece of equipment—a cast-iron cannonball with an attached handle—that gave you the ultimate work-out. Americans called them kettlebells, but Richter preferred the Russian name, *girya.* It was their invention; they had the right to name it. Working out with the giryas maintained the kind of strength he'd developed working on his grandfather's farm during his summers as a kid.

He didn't mind going to the gym a couple of nights a week, but when he wanted a real workout he would go home and use his own equipment, especially the giryas.

Richter first started using them in college, and they'd played a big role in his success as an All American wrestler. The first pair he bought only weighed about thirty-five pounds each. They were meant for be-ginners, but they gave him an incredible workout. In almost no time his overall weight increased while his body fat virtually disappeared. Now he only used the eighty-eight pounders, which most people couldn't lift off the ground with two hands. The key to mastering the giryas was de-veloping the correct swing to ensure that your body was properly bal-anced during the workout.

He liked doing the double military presses, lifting them straight up from his shoulders toward the ceiling. But the toughest workout was the one-armed snatches, the ideal exercise. Lifting the weight from the floor toward the ceiling worked every muscle in his body. Nothing made him feel more powerful. Doing the snatches gave him an escape from everyday life. They took him from being a schlep who went to his job every morning, and turned him into an animal, a beast, a man with extraordinary strength.

His other weight-lifting equipment was organized neatly in the corner. Each piece of equipment served its purpose, but if left alone on a deserted island all he would really need to maintain his physical prowess and his spiritual well-being would be the giryas. As he reached down to lift them up for another set, he felt as if he *was* alone on an island—and perfectly happy to be there. Richter preferred to be alone when lifting weights. That way he didn't have to deal with those who weren't serious about getting a workout. It bothered him that people didn't take conditioning as seriously as he did. He thought back to an incident that had occurred when he was in high school.

Richter's friend bent down into the squat position, his face turning purple as he struggled to stand back up with the 405-pound barbell balanced across his shoulders. Richter was close behind with his hands under his friend's arms, spotting him to make sure he didn't lose control of the weight. As they stepped forward to lower the barbell onto the squat rack, some loser bumped into the bar. It was the slightest contact, but it was enough to throw Richter's friend off. He staggered backward. Richter stepped forward and reached under his friend's arms, hugging his chest and using all his strength to steady him. Together, they regained control of the weight and stepped forward, lowering the weight back onto the steel rack.

As his friend was nodding that he was okay, Richter heard a girl stretching out nearby tell the same guy to watch where he was going. The guy laughed and told her to fuck off. Richter had never seen him before. He must have been new to the gym, but he was big, taller and heavier than Richter. He had the puffy muscles and pinhead of a steroid user. When Richter caught up with him, the guy was busy hitting on a girl in a thong leotard.

Jerks who treated the weight room like a singles club didn't belong in a gym. Weight lifting was a religion and, even as a teenager, this was Richter's house of worship. He didn't appreciate some 'roid-head being disrespectful in his sacred place. He walked up behind the guy and tapped him on the shoulder. "Excuse me," Richter said in a pleasant voice. "Don't I know you?"

"I don't think so," the guy said. He seemed annoyed by Richter's interruption. He turned back to the woman.

Richter tapped his shoulder again and politely asked if he was sure.

"Yeah, I'm sure!" the guy shouted. "And don't touch me again."

"But I swear I've seen you someplace before."

"You haven't, so why don't you fuck off?"

"What's your name?" Richter asked.

"None of your fucking business."

Before the guy could say another word, Richter grabbed his left hand, bending it back into an unnatural position. Once he had him in a solid wristlock, he pushed him facedown into a weight bench. Now he could twist the guy's wrist with one hand and push his head into the bench with the other. "Well, Mr. None-of-Your-Fucking-Business, do you realize what you just did?" The guy struggled to get away from Richter, but he was locked up tight. Richter could see that the guy was doing everything not to scream in pain. "You bumped into that barbell while my friend was finishing his reps."

The guy tried to twist away, but Richter was too strong. He turned his head to the left, looking at Richter from the corner of his eye.

"You could have hurt someone because you weren't paying attention." Richter applied more pressure to the wrist as the guy struggled. "This is a weight room, not a pickup joint. You want to meet women, go somewhere else. Be thankful I'm not really angry and that my buddy over there seems okay."

The guy struggled to breathe with the pressure Richter was putting on the back of his head, pushing him into the bench with all his weight. He gave a feeble nod of his head.

"I want you to go over and tell my friend you're sorry for being such a fucking idiot."

Richter released his grip. The young woman had watched the little wrestling match with interest. Most of the women in the gym were constantly being hit on by guys like this loser, so they didn't seem to mind watching one of them get dressed down.

The guy got to his feet, shaking his wrist and rubbing his neck, trying to get the blood flowing again. He glanced around at the small crowd that had gathered. He must have figured it was best to do what Richter had told him to. He walked over to Richter's friend and said, "I'm sorry for being such a fucking idiot." With as much dignity as a busted man could muster, he picked up his towel and headed for the showers.

The woman flashed Richter a smile. The group of guys, hoping for a fight, started to move apart. "So," Richter asked his friend, "you ready for your next set?"

CHAPTER 44

Professor Roger Olsen reached into his briefcase, took out a pair of aviator goggles and put them on. Flipping his necktie over his shoulder, he announced, "Fasten your seat belts, boys and girls. Today we're going to fly."

Outside the second-floor window of the New England School of Law lecture hall, a drizzling rain fell on the city. Looking out, Andi Norton knew that April showers would bring something good in May, but she couldn't remember what. It was almost the end of her final semester, and she was pressured, tired and overworked. She hadn't been keeping up with her studies because of the long hours she'd been putting in at the courthouse. She'd originally planned to work eight hours a week. One day. The eight hours had turned into sixteen and sometimes twenty-four. She was in court at least two days a week, but last week she had gone in every day because she'd had her second jury trial, another guilty verdict. It was a great experience, well worth the backlog she was trying to clean up at school.

Professor Olsen had flipped the goggles back onto his gray hair, his eyes blazing with intensity. "Okay, people, you should all remember this case from Criminal Procedure. A young girl has been abducted from a YMCA in Des Moines, Iowa. She's believed to have been kidnapped, possibly murdered. The suspect was apprehended two days later in Davenport, Iowa, roughly one hundred sixty miles east of Des Moines. His attorney in Des Moines had him turn himself in to the police,"

Olsen continued, "on the condition that his client not be interrogated. On the long ride back to Des Moines, the detective did not interrogate him."

"That's open to debate. You're talking about the Christian Burial case, right?" Andi said. She had read it recently while getting ready for a motion to suppress, but she couldn't remember the actual case name.

"Someone remembers the case," Professor Olsen smiled. "Why is it open to debate, Ms. Norton?"

"The detective did not interrogate him per se, but the statements made by the detective could easily be seen as rising to the level of interrogation. Although not actual questions, the statements were designed to elicit a response from the suspect."

"Can anyone follow up on Ms. Norton's observation?"

A voice, Andi couldn't see whose, from the other side of the class said, "The detective talked to the suspect about the approaching snowstorm and that, if they were going past the location of the girl's body, they should stop and find her now so she could get a proper Christian burial. If they waited until morning, after the suspect talked with his lawyer, they might not be able to find the girl's body. As a result of the conversation, the suspect felt guilty and led the detective to the body."

"Good," Professor Olsen said. "Now, what are the issues here? Which, if any, of the constitutional rights of the prisoner were violated?"

While the class launched into a discussion of constitutional law, Andi thought about the motion to suppress she had to argue the next day on a real case, not some law school hypothetical. And she had to argue it in front of a real judge, in a real courtroom, with a real defense attorney trying to rattle her by objecting to every question she asked her witnesses. She wasn't worried, but she knew she had to do some more work on the case to be properly prepared. Sitting in this classroom listening as other aspiring lawyers tried to make brownie points with Professor Olsen wasn't helping her.

Hers was a drug case where the cops had done a nice job of building a strong drug distribution case against the defendant. It was what they did after the arrest in order to get the defendant to make a statement and lead them to the rest of his stash that concerned her. She kept re-playing the facts, trying to figure out a way to argue that the police had acted within the law, and that the defendant's statements and the stash of drugs should not be suppressed from evidence.

"All right, people, please stow your snack trays and return your seat backs to their upright position," Professor Olsen said as he took off his goggles and tossed them into his briefcase. Everyone in the class started to close their laptops and pack their books as Olsen drew his tie back over his shoulder and smoothed it down over his blue oxford shirt. "This flight is over but we'll continue with Miranda issues next time."

Andi looked down at her watch. It was 2:30 and class was over. She had missed the entire class discussion. She glanced at Professor Olsen, accidentally making eye contact. He knew she'd spaced out during the whole class. She could tell from the look on his face. He gave a fake smile and motioned with his head toward the door. He wanted to see her in his office. Shit. She could point out that she'd started the discussion. That obviously didn't matter to him, though. She should have skipped class altogether. She could have done some work on her motion and she wouldn't be in trouble with her favorite professor. But she couldn't skip his class today because she'd missed it all last week. She wasn't looking forward to this meeting.

CHAPTER 45

Connie sat still as Judge Catherine Ring read her findings on Jesse Wilcox's motion to suppress. Her decision was staggering and Connie felt his jaw tightening. Behind him in the gallery, Jesse Wilcox stifled a laugh. Judge Ring had allowed the defense attorney's motion and suppressed all of the drugs in his apartment. Luckily she couldn't suppress the drugs and gun that Wilcox threw out the window into the neighbor's yard or Connie would have had to dismiss the case.

Connie waited until Judge Ring was off the bench before he made a move for the exit. He shoved the courtroom door open with both hands.

Alves caught up with him. "Calm down, Connie," he said, following a few steps behind.

"What the hell was that all about?" Connie said, his voice edging toward a shout.

"I'm as mad as you are," Alves said. "She's a liberal judge. We both knew that going in."

"This has nothing to do with being liberal on the law. This has to do with your credibility. She's saying that you lied, that you just busted into that apartment with no lawful purpose. She knows you went to that apartment for a domestic call. Shit, I even played the nine-one-one for her. You get there. You hear a woman screaming. A baby crying. You break the door in. What were you supposed to do?"

"I did everything the right way."

"I tried to tell her that, but she didn't listen," Connie said. "Then she suppresses all the drugs he had in the house, including the crack he tried to hide in the baby's diaper. The kid not more than a year old with a diaper full of jums. What's wrong with that bitch?"

"She's a Dukakis appointment. Remember the Massachusetts Miracle?" Alves was trying to calm him down. "The only miracle is that none of the guys she's let out of jail have killed anyone yet. Maybe we can try to impeach her."

Connie shook his head. "She's rich and her husband's too powerful. She never set foot in Roxbury before becoming a judge. I heard she got lost trying to find the courthouse on her first day. She thinks she's doing the inner city a favor by setting criminals free. She doesn't care if they're gangbangers or drug dealers. What's it to her? She's going home to her big house in Weston at the end of the day."

"What about taking her up on appeal?" Alves asked.

"I don't think so. She was smart enough to make her decision based on credibility, not on an issue of law.. She basically said that she didn't believe that you heard any noise coming from the apartment. And since Wilcox's girlfriend took the stand and said there was nothing going on, Judge Ring had conflicting testimony to justify her ruling. Appellate courts never question a motion judge's credibility determinations. Besides, Wilcox's got a private attorney. If we take it up and lose, my office has to pay for his attorney's fees. That ain't happening. Basically she believed a coke whore over a BPD Homicide detective."

"What's next?"

"Our only option is to go to trial with the stuff he threw out the window and hope we win. We don't have a date yet. We're looking at late May or early June."

"Well, let's hope we don't draw her as a judge." Alves shook Connie's hand and headed for the stairs.

It bothered Connie to see Alves's credibility hurt in court. Alves was a man of integrity. This wasn't just a game to him. He took his job seriously.

"Hey, Mr. Darget. Better luck next time."

Connie turned to see Jesse Wilcox smiling as he stepped out of the courtroom with his lawyer. Wilcox was sporting a loud, thick-striped shirt—yellow and lime green—probably from the Pink store downtown, with baggy jeans and brand-new Timberland boots. The vein near Connie's temple throbbed. He wanted to kick the punk's ass, and he knew he could, but he had to remind himself that they were in the courthouse hallway and he was a prosecutor. Wilcox knew he'd knocked Angel Alves's reputation around. And Connie didn't like it. "This one's not over yet, Jesse," Connie said.

"It was over before it started." Wilcox laughed.

"What does that mean?" Connie took measured steps toward Wilcox.

"Shut up, Jesse," his lawyer said. He grabbed Wilcox's arm, leading him toward the stairs. "Let's go."

"Sorry, Mr. Darget, my lawyer says I gotsta go."

Connie had done the right thing staying calm, but Jesse Wilcox was a little too happy and a little too cocky.

CHAPTER 46

Andi Norton poked her head into Professor Roger Olsen's office. He was on the phone but gestured for her to take a seat.

It was hard to say how old Professor Olsen was, his closely cropped hair the color of galvanized nails. His skin was dusty-looking, his hands elegant with their long fingers—piano fingers, as Andi's mother would say. He had the habit of adjusting his steel-rimmed glasses—tight to his face, if he was pleased, down toward the end of his long nose, if he was not. Right now his glasses were so far toward the end of his nose Andi couldn't figure out how they were clinging to his face. Professor Olsen had become her mentor since she'd taken his Criminal Procedure class her first year of law school. The last thing she wanted to do was disappoint him.

"Hello, Andi. How are you doing?" he said as he hung up the phone.

"I'm doing fine." She could tell he was trying to exchange pleasantries before getting into what he really wanted to talk about.

"How's Rachel?" he said. He was one of the few people at school who knew about her daughter. Outside of a small circle, her private life was private.

"Fine," she said. "She's a handful."

"How old is she now?"

"Three."

"That's great. I remember when my Ally was that age. It's a wonderful age."

"Look, Professor, I know you didn't call me in here to talk about my daughter and how things are going for me at home. So feel free to get to the real reason you wanted to see me."

"I didn't mean to upset you by asking about Rachel," he said, leaning forward in his chair, "but I assure you, my concern for her is genuine. Are you all right, Andi? You sound stressed."

"I'm fine. And I didn't mean to snap at you, but I know there's another reason you called me up here."

"You're right, Andi. I want to know what's been going on with you lately."

"I apologize for not getting involved in class today, but I was thinking about a motion I have coming up in court."

"Your lack of involvement in today's class discussion is the least of my concerns. After your initial comment, you weren't even paying attention. Be thankful I didn't call on you and embarrass you. You're lucky I know you well enough to recognize that your recent behavior is out of character."

"I'm sorry, Professor, but I've been busy with the DA's office. It's exciting getting a chance to handle my own cases."

"That's great, but you're not a lawyer yet. And if you flunk out of law school, you'll never become one. I wouldn't be making such a big deal out of it if your performance in class today was an isolated incident, but this isn't the first time it's happened this semester. Last week you never made it to class."

"I was held on a jury trial all week. The jury was out deliberating for three days."

"You mean you missed *all* your classes last week?"

"Yes, but I had a jury trial and I won."

"You can't just stop coming to school. You're about to graduate."

"But they keep asking me to do more work. I don't want to say no to anything. I want them to know how much I love the work. I'm hoping to get hired after I graduate."

"First of all, if you don't start coming to school and paying attention in class, you're not going to graduate. Secondly, the DA's office isn't going to hire you just because you graduated from law school. You still have to pass the bar exam. And finally, I told you before that the people you're working with now aren't going to be making any hiring decisions in that office. The district attorney is a politician and his decisions are politically motivated. I'm glad that you're doing a good job over there, and that will certainly help when the DA asks his people about you, but his final decision will come down to *who* you know rather than *what* you know."

"I still don't want to disappoint the people I'm working with. I don't want them to think I'm not a team player."

"I understand that too, but when it comes time for me to make some phone calls on your behalf to my friends up on Beacon Hill, it would help if you had decent grades to complement your work experience in the DA's office. What about the young lawyer you told me about? The one you've been seeing. What was his name again?"

"Connie. Conrad Darget."

"Yes, Conrad Darget. He seems to be supportive. Hasn't he told you to focus on your studies?"

"I think he assumes that I'm doing my schoolwork. He's been a big help to me on my cases, always taking time to make sure I'm prepared for court. He's letting me second-seat him on a big trial in June."

"He needs to make sure that you're prepared for class. You can tell him I said that. Now, I don't want to belabor the point, I just want you to know that I'm concerned about your grades slipping. I expect this to be a wake-up call. Understood?"

"Yes, Professor."

"Now that we have that out of the way, why don't you tell me about the motion that kept you from paying attention in class?"

"It's a drug case where the police arrested a guy selling heroin to an undercover officer in a school playground. When he was arrested he only had two glassine bags of heroin left in his sock. The officers read him his Miranda rights and asked him where the rest of his stash was. He already had an attorney from a previous drug case, so he asked to speak to that attorney."

"You know that the officers had to stop questioning him?"

"Right. Because I'm familiar with the Christian Burial case."

"But they didn't stop questioning him, did they?"

"They didn't really ask any questions. One of the officers said, 'It would be a shame if a five-year-old kid got ahold of those heroin packets and put some of that poison in his mouth.' The defendant sat and thought about it for a few minutes before he told the officers that they'd find the stash in a fence pipe near the edge of the playground."

"Now, I know you weren't paying attention in class today, but you do know that the police officer's statement, although not a question, was meant to elicit a response from the defendant after he had already asked for a lawyer. You know that you're going to lose the motion, don't you?"

"I did think it was a tough one to win. I planned to argue that there was no interrogation and even if the judge did find there was an interrogation, I'd argue that the drugs would have eventually been found because the officers knew the area well."

"Andi, whenever a judge hears the 'inevitable discovery' argument from a prosecutor, they know it's an argument of last resort. It sets off bells, telling the judge you don't have a solid legal argument. Don't fight too hard with the judge on that one, because you'll lose your credibility with the court."

"But I have to make the argument. I'm not going to concede the fact that the police violated the defendant's rights. Then I'll lose my credibility with the cops."

"You're right," he said as he tilted back in his chair and pushed his glasses up on the bridge of his nose. "But think, Andi. Even if the stash of drugs is suppressed, you still have a very strong case of illegal distribution of heroin, which is the original offense the defendant was arrested for, right?"

"Yeah." Andi felt her face flush. She had overlooked the obvious. The defendant sold to an undercover cop. It's tough to get a case any stronger than that. She smiled, more a sign of relief than happiness. "So even if the drugs in the fence pipe are suppressed, I still have a case against the defendant and he doesn't get off scot-free."

"Exactly," he said.

"I still wish that they hadn't gotten sloppy by asking him a question after he'd asked to speak to his lawyer."

Professor Olsen took off his glasses. "That wasn't sloppy. It wasn't just a line to get him to talk. It was good police work. What if a child did find the heroin, and took it or handed it out to his friends? The police officer had to make a split-second decision and he decided it was better to have drugs possibly get suppressed than to lose a child's life."

"I hadn't thought of it like that."

"It's easy for lawyers and judges to sit in courtrooms surrounded by court officers, metal detectors and security guards and criticize the work of police officers. But those officers are the ones on the street that have to make the tough decisions. As a prosecutor, it's your job to fight to defend their behavior. Not in every case, but certainly in a case like this, where the police had a genuine concern for public safety. You're probably going to lose, but that doesn't mean you shouldn't fight. Make it clear that, regardless of what the court finds, the officers would not change their actions if presented with the same situation again."

Professor Olsen was right. Her motion wasn't a chess match with a clear winner and loser. Decisions and actions were more complex than that, some outcomes more important than a win-loss record.

CHAPTER 47

Angel Alves sat in the shadows of the last pew. Saint Margaret's Church in Jamaica Plain was almost empty early on a weekday afternoon. The only other figure was a small woman dressed in black, the light through the stained-glass windows creating an aura of blue as she moved toward the side of the altar.

He watched as Mrs. Stokes lit one of the candles. The small glass holder flickered with a red flame he could see even from his position at the back of the church. As he watched her kneel at the altar to pray, he knew what she was asking God for. The woman accepted that her daughter was dead. She knew it in her mother's heart. All she could pray for now was that Robyn's body would be found and she could give her child a proper burial. With the trust that older people have in authority, Mrs. Stokes believed that the police would find her daughter's body. That *he* would bring her little girl home.

Alves blessed himself and headed out the heavy oak doors into the bright spring sun.

CHAPTER 48

Mitch Beaulieu stood next to a stool in his apartment's small living room. It was just after noon, and the Red Sox were closing in on another victory. The Sox played an early game every Patriots' Day, Boston Marathon Monday. Mitch wasn't much into watching sports, but Connie had convinced him to have the guys over. It would help take his mind off work. He had spent most of the weekend cleaning the apartment, which he'd let go for months.

Lying down with a throw pillow as his headrest, Connie took up most of the couch. Across the room, Brendan was sprawled in a La-Z-Boy chair. Nick was relaxing on a chaise longue Mitch had taken from his father's house. As a child it had been his favorite reading seat.

Mitch was trying to enjoy the company, but he was just too nerved up that someone was going to accidentally break a family heirloom or put a drink down on his father's antique coffee table. He needed to stop obsessing. If he would just let himself relax, he could have fun with this sports party. They were happy with pizza and a fridge full of beer.

"Hey, Mitch," Connie said. "Why don't you have a seat? You're making me nervous."

"I'd rather stand and stretch my legs." He wanted to be ready in case he needed to make a quick move with a coaster or extra napkins for the greasy pizza.

"We're not going to break anything," Connie said. "Haven't we all been on good behavior?"

"I'm not nervous about that. I just feel like standing."

Brendan turned to Mitch, holding an empty bottle. "If you're just going to stand there you may as well make yourself useful and grab me another beer."

"What do I look like, your girlfriend?" Mitch joked.

"She'd be more than glad to get me a beer. C'mon, man. You're already up, and you are the host." Brendan laughed.

"Miller or Bud?"

"The High Life, of course. The Champagne of Beers. It was the first beer I ever drank as a kid in Southie. We used to sit on the rocks out by Castle Island and share a six-pack and get totally trashed. Those were the days. Hanging out with you guys reminds me of those summer nights, when the biggest concern was getting caught drunk by my mom or throwing up from the bed spins."

"From what I've seen, you still get trashed from two beers," Nick said.

"The Greek kid from Rozzie is going to talk to me about drinking. I tell you what, why don't you go have a couple of shots of Metaxa and shut the hell up?"

"How does an Irish guy from Southie even know what Metaxa is? Oh, never mind. Liquor is the one thing the Irish *do* know about."

"That's the best you could come up with?" said Brendan. "Another Irish alcohol joke? You need some new material, buddy." Brendan stood up as Mitch handed him a beer. "This is a great apartment, Mitch. What's your rent, if you don't mind me asking?"

"Eight hundred."

"You're kidding. For an apartment in Harvard Square?"

"Welcome to the People's Republic of Cambridge." Mitch smiled. "I got this place when I was in law school. I don't think I'll ever move out."

Brendan walked over and tapped a door that was off to the right of the television. "What's back here?"

"My bedroom. I wouldn't go in there if I were you. It's a mess. I cleaned up by throwing half my shit in there."

Brendan opened the door and looked in the room. "Bedroom? I can't even see a bed."

"I told you. Now, get out of there."

"Whew! It stinks worse than a locker room." Brendan pulled his shirt up and held it over his nose. "You need to do the laundry before that stuff comes to life."

"Close the door. I'm serious."

"Okay. Don't get your bloomers in a twist. What about this room?" Brendan reached for another door at the foot of the couch, where Connie was sitting. "What's with the dead bolt?"

"That room's really off-limits," Mitch said. "I've got personal family stuff in there." He suddenly realized that this was what he was worried about: someone trying to intrude on his private life. Having people over was one thing, but having them pry into his secrets was another. He wasn't sure what their reaction would be if they saw what was in the room, but he was certain they wouldn't understand it. That room was the one sanctuary he had in his life. It was the place he could go to when he wanted to be alone, but not feel alone.

Nick stood up, nudging Brendan away from the door. "It looks like we're onto something here. Wouldn't you all love to know what's behind door number one?"

"The door's locked, Nick." Mitch began to gnaw at his fingernails. It was a bad habit he usually managed to control. "Don't even think about going in there."

"Maybe you forgot to lock it. Let's see. It must be something good." Nick reached for the knob.

Mitch moved quickly and knocked Nick's hand away, sliding himself between Nick and the door. He could feel the anxiety rising in his chest. He never should have invited them over. He didn't want them to see him lose his temper. He needed to defuse the situation without making himself look like a nut.

"I was right, guys," Nick smiled. "We're onto something here." He tried to reach around Mitch to get to the knob again.

"That's it." Mitch grabbed the smaller man in a headlock and started grinding his knuckle into Nick's scalp. "You want a noogie, is that it? I'll give you a noogie, if that's what you're looking for."

Connie and Brendan started laughing as Nick struggled to get out of his grasp. He managed to free his head after a couple of seconds.

"Hey, that hurt." Nick backed away from the door, rubbing his head. "All right, I get it. You don't want me going into that room."

"That's right. Try it again and you get an atomic wedgie," Mitch said.

"I was just kidding around. I didn't see you jumping down Brendan's throat for going in the bedroom."

"Brendan weighs, what, fifty pounds more than me? I'm not stupid enough to try and noogie him."

"Have a seat, Nick, before you get your ass kicked again," Connie said.

"I would like to see what's in that room, though."

"Don't push your luck," Mitch said.

"Fine." Nick started back to his seat, then made another quick lunge toward the door. "I almost had you there." Nick laughed before taking his seat on the chaise.

Mitch sat at the end of the couch near the door so he could guard it. He had played it off pretty well, making a joke out of it. But he was sure they were all curious now about what was in the room. He never should have invited them over.

CHAPTER 49

Alves watched Mooney step through the tall French doors into the entrance hall of the old mansion, now broken up into a handful of up-scale condominiums. It was four in the morning. Mooney didn't appear to be fully awake, his eyes half open, his face devoid of color. He wore a clean, newly pressed suit with a starched white shirt. They never knew if they'd be caught on camera, so they always looked professional.

"What's her name?" Mooney asked.

"Jill Twomey. An investment banker."

"Was it him?" Mooney asked.

Alves nodded. "The call came in about a half hour ago. Never said a word. Left the phone on the kitchen counter. No signs of forced entry. Our man either got out of lockup somewhere or he got bored."

"Where's her unit?"

"Down the hall, on the right. The bathroom is just off the bedroom," Alves said, leading Mooney to the entrance of her condominium.

A uniformed officer was looking around the living room as Mooney and Alves arrived at the front door. Behind him was a guy wearing tan khakis, a button-down oxford shirt, tasseled loafers with no socks and sunglasses flipped up and balanced on his gelled hair. A regular Joe Cool.

"What the fuck are you doing?" Mooney asked.

The young cop spun around to face them, offering a thin smile. Joe Cool hesitated for a second and then tried to take control of the situation. He reached into his pocket and took out his credentials. "Richard Wahl. I'm with the district attorney's office. I work out of the East Boston Court."

"I'm sorry. That's why I've never seen you before," Mooney said, now with a pleasant voice. Alves recognized that Mooney was ready to explode on the young lawyer. "Is this your first night being on call?" Mooney asked.

"First week. I actually went out to a shooting Saturday night and a sudden death last night—"

"Gee, Dick, that's great," Mooney cut him off. He put his hand on his shoulder and led him toward the door. "There's just a few things you probably want to remember when you go out to a call."

"What's that?" Joe Cool asked, nonchalantly, sauntering along toward the door, not suspecting a thing.

Alves could see Mooney's knuckles turning white as he tightened his grip on the back of Mr. Cool's neck, almost bringing him to his knees. "Don't you ever walk into another one of my crime scenes. Now, get the fuck out of here, Dick." Mooney shoved him through the door and turned to the young patrolman, who still hadn't said a word. "Your job is to make sure no one comes in here, including yourself, without my permission."

"Yes, sir. I'm sorry," he said as he hurried into the hallway and disappeared.

Alves would have felt bad for the two of them if Joe Cool hadn't been such a cocky bastard. Mooney had taught them never to compromise a murder investigation.

Mooney turned back to Alves as if nothing had happened. "Angel, where are the guys from the crime lab?"

"They should be here any minute. I talked with Eunice. She's coming out too."

"We have to make sure we don't miss anything. Any thoughts on how he got in?"

"I checked around the back of the house before you got here. It's pretty dark back there. And there's an overgrown rhododendron blocking her windows. He could have gotten in that way. Nobody would have seen him."

"Put a couple of uniforms back there to make sure no one goes near those windows until the crime lab gets here."

"Already done," Alves said. "I told them to keep everyone away from the house so they don't mess up any possible shoe prints."

"Then I want that whole area around the windows fumed for finger-prints, inside and out. Have them set up a tent ten feet in all directions. Same for the inside. If they can't do it with a tent, remove the windows and take them back to the lab for processing. Cut the whole wall out with a Sawzall if you have to."

"I'll talk to Eunice about the best method."

"I have to call the commissioner. He wants constant updates. I wish I had more for him. The only thing we know for sure is that this guy likes to kill on weekends and holidays. He might be holding down a reg-ular job, and these are the only times he can squeeze his murders in. I don't see any other pattern. Fuck, I even checked if he's working on a lunar cycle."

Alves felt sick about it, but he was grateful to have a run at another crime scene. Now, at least, they had the possibility that the killer might have made a mistake and left them something. How else could he find Robyn?

CHAPTER 50

Richter sat in the darkness, meditating. His work was not yet complete but soon, God willing, it would be. If God willed it, then God would continue to provide Richter with the necessary opportunities. He always had.

Richter grew closer to God with each of his achievements. When he was a child, a woman, maybe a teacher at school, had told him that "cleanliness is next to godliness." She couldn't have been more wrong. The only thing that was close to godliness was power, absolute power over others.

Richter thrived on the power he achieved by saving the chosen few. There was no greater feeling than controlling, and then taking, the life of another. Most people, ordinary people, spent their lives trying to increase the amount of power and influence they had over others. Foolishly, their main goal was to use this power for financial gain, popularity, fame. They were not seeking true power.

Richter received his greatest satisfaction watching the lifeblood slowly leave a person's body at his hands. He understood that there was no greater way to influence someone's life than to take it away from them, and then watch the domino effect of how that death altered the lives of those around them. This was absolute power, the ability to affect the lives of others against their will and in a way that could never be reversed.

But exerting this power had never been Richter's real reason for killing. He was making a serious sacrifice for the people he had killed. Each time, he was risking his own life, his own liberty.

He took these ordinary people and gave them something more. He showed them that there was something greater. People cried for them, prayed for them, created small shrines by hand. No one had done this for them when they were going about their everyday existence. Before, they were sheep. Now they were immortal.

Once they overcame their initial fears and realized that it was futile to struggle, they had all accepted their deaths willingly, quietly slipping into a peaceful slumber. He could have killed them more easily, and perhaps less painfully, but it was important for them to see their savior as they breathed their last breaths. Richter was comforted knowing that even if they felt any pain, it was brief. Now they would never have to experience pain again. Once they became a part of his creation they would appreciate all he had done for them.

Richter stood and walked over to his DVD collection. The darkness felt cool against his naked skin. He inserted a disk and sat back on the couch before pushing the play button on the remote control.

This was his tribute to Jill Twomey. Only two days had passed since her death and Richter had plenty of television footage. It started with a television reporter standing in the street outside Jill's home talking about the tragedy that "had rocked this quiet neighborhood in Jamaica Plain." Jill lived on Moss Hill, an exclusive area where the mayor of Boston also lived.

The reporter spoke with one neighbor after another about what a nice woman Jill Twomey had been and how they could not believe something so horrible had happened to her. One woman talked of playing tennis with her every Sunday morning and the mayor, although he did not know her personally, talked about seeing her running past his house a couple of times a week.

The mayor promised to put as many officers as possible on the case. He announced, his face intense with the graveness of the situation, that he'd get the FBI involved in the investigation. Jill Twomey was the fourth woman murdered in less than six months and the police still didn't have a single suspect or any viable leads.

Richter began to get aroused as he watched. He always did. Even that first time in Arizona. But he couldn't allow it. He wasn't weak like the others. Many of them would deny that there was anything sexual about their killings, but it was always about sex with them. He could control his urges. He was above that.

The image switched to a news anchorwoman talking about the tragedy of Jill Twomey's death. Behind the anchorwoman was a still photograph, probably taken from Jill's college yearbook. There she was, with her big 1980s hairdo that was probably held up by half a can of Aqua Net hair spray, ready to take on the world. Maybe she'd hoped to be famous someday. If only she knew how famous Richter had made her, she'd be thanking him now. The story then cut to a field reporter who spoke with some of Jill's work friends, all of them crying.

This was all building up to his favorite part. One of the syndicated tabloid news shows had gotten hold of a tape of Jill at a company cook-out. She looked good in her cutoff jeans and tight white T-shirt. She was making silly faces at the camera as several men tried to put the moves on her.

Richter hit the rewind button and watched the footage a second time. This was the real Jill Twomey. She wasn't sitting in a stiff, uncomfortable pose for a yearbook photo.

Richter watched as Jill walked toward the camera, acting sexy, arching her back, sticking out her chest and shaking her hips. She looked to be a little drunk, trying to put on a show for the cameraman as she danced toward him. She caressed her hands up and down her body from her hips to her breasts, with the men watching her every move. Wolves closing in around Richter's innocent little lamb.

Jill Twomey would never have to worry about the wolves again. Richter shivered knowing that he had saved her.

CHAPTER 51

Not a good sign. Four empty coffee cups scattered in front of Mooney and it wasn't even lunchtime. Mooney started talking before Alves got through the doorway.

"In case you didn't know this already," he said, his feet propped up on his desk, "you can never trust the feds." Behind Mooney's head, filling almost the entire wall, was his dry-erase board with columns written in different color markers. There was a column for each victim, listing leads, evidence recovered and connections among the cases. There was a lot of white space on the board.

Angel Alves had only had one experience working with the FBI and it wasn't a good one. It was before he'd made it to Homicide. He and the BPD Drug Control Unit had been working a case for months with DEA agents. As they were getting ready to wrap up the investigation, the FBI got involved in the takedown of the big dealers and ended up taking credit for the whole operation. "I hate those guys as much as anyone," Alves said, "but I don't think we have any choice."

"After the mayor goes on TV and makes the announcement, there's nothing we can do."

"What do we know about the people they're sending?" Alves asked.

"They'll be here tomorrow. The commissioner told me they're from the Behavioral Analysis Unit in Quantico. They probably have less street smarts than a fifteen-year-old kid from Dorchester."

Alves recognized the beginning of a familiar rant. If no one interrupted him, Mooney would go on for hours.

"The commissioner wants us to share all our files. They're supposed to be two of the bureau's top profilers. They're going to fill us in on the general characteristics of our killer and give us some investigation tips. Then we'll be in a better position to catch the guy." Alves detected the sarcasm tinting Mooney's voice. "Bullshit. Profiler or no profiler, it's going take hard work and luck on our part. A mistake by the bad guy wouldn't hurt either." Mooney gestured for Alves to take a seat. "Profiles are just common sense. I've already come up with my own. It's the same one that they have for most serial killers. I guarantee you it's what these guys from Quantico will come up with. I'll bet you two slices and a Coke, if you'll take my action," Mooney stuck his hand out toward Alves.

"No thanks, Sarge. I'll take your word for it."

"White male, age twenty-five to thirty-five, lives with his mother or alone, doesn't have many friends, has a history of arson and/or animal abuse as a child, commits organized and planned killings, may have lost his job or a promotion to a woman due to affirmative action, has had difficulty dating but may currently have a girlfriend, although there is a strong likelihood that he doesn't have sexual relations with her and he may actually be impotent."

Alves smiled. Not much different from the profiles the experts always came up with on the crime shows Marcy watched. But Mooney was rolling. Let him go with it.

"Say I were to come up with a profile of a drug dealer in a largely black neighborhood like Roxbury or Mattapan, he would be a young black male wearing loose-fitting, dark clothing, possibly riding a bike. That could describe almost every kid in that neighborhood. He would also come from a poor background. He's not interested in school and sees that he can make money easily by selling drugs.

"I could come up with the same profile for every other neighborhood in the city. In Brighton the kid would be white or Asian, in East Boston he'd be Hispanic, and in Southie he'd be white. We can't go around arresting every kid who fits the description. That's why police departments get sued for profiling. Once our guy makes a mistake, we can use our profile to build a case against him. But we still need to have evidence that he committed the crime."

Alves snuck a glance at his watch. Enough with the profile lecture. He wanted to get back to work, anything to feel like he was *doing* something besides sitting in Mooney's office, a captive audience.

"This isn't hard science. Our guy might not fit this profile at all. He could be black, Asian or Hispanic. He could be forty-five years old and have ten girlfriends and a great job. Just like the drug dealer in Dudley Square might be white. It's not as likely, but it certainly is possible."

"It's possible that he could be a little green man from Mars too, but he's not."

"As for the feds," Mooney ignored Alves's little dig and continued with his spiel. "I don't mind them coming in here telling me about their profile. They'd just better not think they're going to take over my investigation."

Alves heard the hum of Mooney's pager. Salvation.

CHAPTER 52

Connie looked up to see Angel Alves walking toward his desk. "Do I know you?"

"Don't get excited," Alves said. "I'm heading right back out."

"What do you mean? We're supposed to do case prep."

"Not today."

"Angel, if we're not ready for trial we're going to get our asses handed to us. And Jesse's going to walk again. We have a ton of work to do. The trial is only a month away."

"Connie, the Jill Twomey murder has changed everything. We've got the FBI up here and Mooney's on a rampage. Forget about prep. I'll be lucky if I can get here for the trial."

"Are you insane? You know how long I've been trying to put Jesse away. He's dangerous."

"Not as dangerous as the Blood Bath Killer. We work on his case and nothing else. Orders from the commissioner. Not that I needed the order. I want to catch this fucker. And I'm going to."

"Do me a favor before I lose you for good?"

"What?"

"Just pull all the FIOs on Wilcox. I want to know who he's been hanging around with. It'll help me on cross if any of his friends show up as surprise witnesses for the defense."

"I'll bring them by tomorrow. Then you won't see me for a while. I have to get going. Sarge will be wondering what happened to me."

"How's he doing? I haven't seen him since the McCarthy scene."

"Grumpy as ever." Alves walked toward the back stairs. Then he turned suddenly and stopped. "I almost forgot the most important thing. I learned something today that really pissed me off. Jesse Wilcox's lawyer is a former law partner of Judge Catherine Ring."

Connie could feel his jaw tightening up.

"From the look on your face I'd have to say you didn't know that tidbit of information. How's that for justice?"

Connie watched as Alves disappeared down the backstairs. He felt a terrific surge of anger. He thought back to what Jesse Wilcox had said to him after the motion, that it was all over before it started.

CHAPTER 53

Coming toward him down the corridor from the Homicide Unit were the two FBI agents that Alves had met a few days earlier. He couldn't get their names straight so he just thought of them as Smith and Jones, Smith being the taller one who seemed to do all the talking. He could tell both men were angry.

"What's wrong, guys?" Alves asked.

"Sergeant Mooney doesn't want us involved in *his* investigation. You've been good to us, but we can't work with him. We're heading back to DC this afternoon. I know he doesn't believe us, but we were trying to help."

Alves stood silently as the two agents headed toward the elevators. What the hell was Sarge thinking? He was asking for trouble going against the mayor.

"And, Detective"—Smith turned back to him—"FYI, I don't believe this guy's a sexual predator. You're wasting your time with that one. I could be wrong, but there doesn't seem to be anything sexual about what he's doing."

"Why's that?"

"Nothing to suggest he's committed sexual assaults at any of the crime scenes. Not while the victims are conscious, unconscious or deceased. He attacks them, incapacitates them, drains their blood, takes them away. A sexual predator wouldn't be able to control himself like that. If he's looking to act out a sexual fantasy, he would definitely want to act it out in the victim's house, in her bed, on her couch. He wouldn't miss the opportunity to act it all out while he's alone with her in her house. Nothing would be more gratifying to him."

"So what's he doing?"

"Sergeant Mooney just gave us his *Reader's Digest* profile. Actually not bad for a miserable old-timer. He's right about the blood bath being a way of telling you that the person's dead without leaving you the body. Draining them of their blood is an important part of his ritual. The bathtubs themselves are just convenient. It's the logical place to do something like that. And the warm bath expedites the bloodletting. I'm not sure what he's doing from there. If he's keeping the bodies, he has to be doing something to preserve them. You may want to check to see if there have been any chemical thefts from local funeral homes in the last year. Or maybe he's a trained mortician himself. And then again, he may be dumping the bodies somewhere."

"I hadn't thought of the mortician angle."

"Detective Alves," Smith said, looking Alves in the eyes, letting him know that he wanted to help, "serial killers don't stop killing. They don't slow down. They kill more frequently. They kill until someone stops them." Smith turned toward Jones who was holding the elevator for him. "Feel free to call if you ever need us."

CHAPTER 54

Alves entered the Homicide Unit looking for Mooney. "Sarge, what did you do?"

"I fired those two sons-o'-bitches, trying to poach my case."

Alves was sure Mooney had lost his mind. "You can't fire them, they don't work for you. But *you're* going to get yourself fired once the mayor and commissioner hear about this. What happened?"

"Those two *profilers* spent three days reviewing *our* case files, visiting *our* crime scenes and re-interviewing *our* witnesses. This morning I get a call from Jill Twomey's mother, hysterical, asking why these two men from the FBI want to go through her daughter's condo again. I can take a lot of shit, Angel, but I'm not going to let some kid with a BA in psychology damage my reputation with the family of a homicide victim."

Mooney's face was mottled red as he leaned in toward Alves. Alves was glad he hadn't been in the room when Mooney went at it with the two agents.

"I catch a load of shit from Mrs. Twomey," Mooney said, "then our friends from the FBI show up with their *profile*. Let's just say you're lucky you didn't make that bet with me. It was the same profile I gave you. Then they give me their *tips* for bagging a serial killer: Review footage of spectators at the crime scenes and family press conferences; pursue those losers who volunteer to help with the investigation. I told them we had gone so far as to set up hidden cameras at the memorial services and community-safety meetings to look for familiar faces. They reminded me that as a rule the killer wants to stay close to the investigation. I really appreciate them coming up here to enlighten us."

Angel settled in, content not to say anything until Mooney finished.

"Besides causing me some unnecessary headaches, it's been a waste of time. One thing led to another. Now we no longer have to deal with those two clowns."

"Sarge, as far as the feds go, they weren't all that bad. They're just doing what they were told to do."

"They were wasting our time. No, they weren't just wasting our time—they were actually setting us back. Poor Mrs. Twomey. Bad enough that her daughter was murdered, now she thinks the detectives handling the investigation are a couple of boobs."

"They did have some interesting thoughts."

"Like what?"

"They don't think he's a sexual predator."

"That remains to be seen."

"They also suggested that we check for any chemical thefts at area funeral homes. If he's keeping the bodies he has to be preserving them somehow."

"That's assuming he's keeping the bodies. We don't know what he's doing with the bodies."

"Come on, Sarge, you have to admit it's not a bad idea."

"All right. Do it. But I think we would have heard if there were any break-ins like that."

"Why?"

"You know what they do with that stuff?"

"No."

"I thought you were a drug cop before you came up here. Back in the seventies we had some funeral home breaks. Kids were using the formaldehyde-based embalming fluids to make angel dust."

"Our profilers also threw out the possibility that he might actually be a mortician."

"Or a taxidermist." Mooney laughed. "You can look into that too, Angel."

"Sarge, what are you going to do about the bosses? They're going to flip out when they hear what you did to those guys."

"They might chew my ass out, but they're not going to take us off the case. We know the evidence better than anyone. It would take weeks for someone else to get up to speed. They'll be mad for a couple of days. Once we catch this guy all will be forgotten."

"For your sake, I hope so."

CHAPTER 55

As Connie finished his baked potato and drank the last of his skim milk, Angel Alves pushed open the conference room door, balancing a cup of coffee and a stack of reports. "I can't stay and visit," he said. "Connie, these are the FIOs you asked for."

"Sweet."

"What's an FIO?" Monica asked, sipping her mug of tomato soup.

"Field Interrogation and Observation report," Connie said. "Every time the Youth Violence and the Anti-Crime guys see someone they know hanging out on a corner, they take down all their information, name, DOB, address, who they're with. Then they enter all that info into a report."

"Connie wanted to know what our boy Jesse's been up to, so I ran his name and came up with this," Alves said, waving the reports in front of him. "Wait till you see the rapscallions he's been hanging with."

"Jesse who?" Monica asked.

"Wilcox," Connie said.

"Connie's white whale." Mitch was wrapping up the rest of his sandwich.

"Be careful with this guy. You don't want him thinking it's personal," Brendan said.

"Don't worry about me."

"He already beat you on the motion," Nick said. "He's halfway to another acquittal."

"I have faith in Connie." Alves slipped the FIO reports onto the table.

"Anything new in the Blood Bath case?" Connie knew everyone was interested in the topic, but he knew Alves well enough to ask.

"Nothing specific. Checking known sex offenders, recent DOC and jail releases. Even halfway houses. Mooney's still considering them possibly sex-related. I'm not so sure anymore."

"Makes sense to see if he just got out of lockup," Connie said. "He's probably some scumbag that's walked through the system a million times and keeps getting off with a wrist slap. Our system is such a joke."

"What are you talking about?" Brendan said, his mouth full with the last bite of his Italian sub from Spinale's. "You think you'd be more than happy with the way you've been banging out guilty verdicts lately."

"Who cares about guilties?" Connie said. "I'm talking about a system where we end up with uneducated people deciding the fates of criminal defendants who are facing the loss of their precious liberty. I think it's fucked up."

Nick put down his burger, wiped his mouth with a napkin, and straightened up in his chair. "What's so fucked up about it?" he asked. "The right to a fair trial by a jury of our peers is the heart of our legal system. It's one of our most fundamental rights guaranteed by the Constitution."

Connie laughed. "The only thing the system does is guarantee that every person with a brain is too busy to serve on a jury, leaving us with jurors that belong in that *Star Wars* bar."

"The Cantina?" Brendan interrupted.

Mitch laughed, nearly choking as he sipped from his thermos cup of black tea.

Connie said, "What we need in this country are panels of judges or professional jurors with a certain level of intelligence. Then we'd be guaranteed true and just verdicts."

"You don't think we get just verdicts?" Monica asked.

"All we have is a game where the defense attorneys try to get a bunch of half-wits on the jury so they can trick them into finding a reasonable doubt. I've had success over the past year because I've learned how to play the game better. Why should I care about getting a true verdict if no one else does?"

"Have you forgotten that you're a prosecutor?" Nick asked indignantly. "You're not supposed to blindly advocate for convictions. You're supposed to uphold the law and try to do justice. You can't look at this like it's a game you're trying to win. That's unethical."

"Don't give me that *unethical* shit. The reason we have to play these games is this ass-backward jury system. We need a system where professionals who are well schooled in the law determine the facts of the case and then mete out punishment."

"You mean like Richters?" Mitch said.

"What?" Nick asked.

"In Germany they use panels of judges instead of jurors. They're called Richters. One of the useless facts I remember from Crim Pro."

"I like that word," Brendan said. "When I grow up I want to be a Richter."

"Who the hell wants to live in a society where a select group acts as judge, jury and executioner?" Nick asked.

"I do," Brendan said.

Nick shook his head. "What are you, a Nazi?"

"Here we go. Calling me a Nazi to attack my credibility is an argument *ad hominem*," Brendan said.

"I don't know anything about *hominems*, but I don't think that the Germans have historically been fair in the way they hand out justice," Nick said.

"I'm with Brendan on this one," Connie said.

"Me too," Mitch chimed in.

"Ditto." Alves hadn't said much. He seemed ready to leave at any moment but looked to be enjoying himself. "If you had panels of judges, you'd be less likely to end up with bag jobs like the one Connie and I just got hit with on the Wilcox case."

Connie turned to Monica. "You're still new, so you should learn this now, before you're led astray by defense-attorneys-in-training like Nick.

The first day I walked into this courthouse Liz told me that none of this was on the level. I didn't know what she meant at the time, but I figured it out soon enough. If you follow my lead, you're definitely going to win some trials, unlike Nick, who's lost all ten of his trials."

"Low blow." Brendan laughed.

Monica turned toward Nick in disbelief. "You've lost ten trials in a row."

Nick looked down at the table.

"I don't mean that as an insult to you," Connie said. "You're the one who thinks this isn't about winning and losing. It's about justice being served, right? Maybe justice prevailed at each of your trials. Maybe those defendants were innocent. All we can do is take the facts we're given, then paint them in the light most favorable to our cause. If that's not a game, I don't know what is."

"It's not a game," Nick said. "I don't prosecute someone unless I truly believe they committed the crime. I need to believe it beyond a reasonable doubt before I try to convince a jury beyond a reasonable doubt."

"You can believe it beyond all doubt, but you still don't know what happened. Everything really starts with jury selection. You need to figure out which jurors are going to connect with you and trust you. Otherwise you'll never win."

"It always comes back to winning and losing with you," Nick said. Monica was still glaring at Nick, but he wasn't looking back. "Maybe it does bother me that all of my trials have been not guilties. But maybe those defendants *were* all innocent and justice did prevail."

"Let me tell you something about justice," Connie said. "Everyone we prosecute is judged to be guilty or not guilty. Nobody is found innocent, because nobody is innocent. Today's victim is tomorrow's defendant. Justice does come down to winning and losing. If I think a defendant is guilty, the only justice I'm looking for is a win and a guilty verdict."

"You need to change the way you look at things. I don't expect you to be totally idealistic, but it would help if you had some faith in the system you've chosen to work in."

"You misunderstand me." Connie stood up from the table. "I have absolute faith in the system. I have faith that jurors are stupid and gullible. I have faith that I know how to manipulate them. And I know I am going to launch Jesse Wilcox, even without the evidence Judge Ring stole from us."

"That's what I like to hear," Alves said.

CHAPTER 56

"I think that went well, don't you?" Mooney said.

Alves couldn't even look at Mooney as they closed the door to the commissioner's office behind them. "My career is over," Alves said. "I just made Homicide. Everything was going so well. Now it's over."

"I'm not going to let you get hurt," Mooney said. "I took the hit. He knows I'm the one who shit-canned our friends from Quantico. I'll be sure to tell the mayor too."

"You saw him, Sarge. He blames us both. He thinks I should have stopped you."

"Don't worry, Angel. I'm the one that's going to get screwed when this investigation ends. At least we've still got the case. That was the plan all along."

"Sarge, he said he's going to ship you to Evidence Management in Hyde Park." Alves pictured the aluminum building that resembled a cavernous storage shed stuck on a tired street at the edge of Boston's city limits.

"Yeah, but he won't do it until we close the case. By then, all will be forgiven. He'll assign me out there for six months just to send a message, then he'll put me somewhere else."

"Back on Homicide?"

"I don't think so. He's pretty pissed. I made him look bad with the feds and he's one of the biggest FBI suck-ups around. He's a member of the National Academy Associates."

"I thought that pin on his lapel said NRA."

"I wish. He took the NA course with the FBI back when he first made sergeant twenty years ago. He wears that pin every day. Civilians don't realize what it is. I mean, what high standards! They even make you get a high school diploma, *or its equivalent,* before they let you in!"

"All that matters is that the guy wearing that pin is going to ruin our careers."

"*My* career," Mooney corrected him. "Stop crying about it and tell me what you've come up with on that funeral home angle."

Maybe Mooney was right. No one was going to get in their way while they were working the case; and once it was solved they would be heroes. They just needed to focus on their work and they would be fine. "Nothing yet. But I'm looking into every one of them. If there's anything there, I'll find it."

CHAPTER 57

The mayor, flanked by the DA, and the Boston Police Commissioner, was having his usual difficulties saying exactly what he meant. Speaking without notes as he did, the man had a tendency to ramble and say too much. Halfway through a press conference updating the media on the progress of the investigation, the mayor announced that "The FBI profilers called in to assist on this case believe the killer has committed similar crimes, maybe in another city."

"Good luck with that lead," Richter said to the images on the television screen. The Tucson police had had no reason to focus their investigation on him. How would the police in Boston ever link him to what had happened so many years ago?

Sunday night, the end of spring break, but Richter hadn't gone away because he needed to study for midterms.

Richter's eyes were sore and his brain was pudding from reading all day. A trip to the men's room, a splash of water on his face and neck, a quick lap around the University of Arizona's main library and he'd be ready to focus again.

The floor seemed deserted. Then he spotted a young woman sitting at one of the long tables. She looked up and gave him a nod as he walked past. Maybe she needed a break too. A good discussion to get the blood flowing. Richter twisted his head awkwardly to see the title of the small book she was holding. A treatise on anarchy.

"I am the chairwoman of the Anarchists Club." She smiled at him.

"The Anarchists Club?" he asked. "An organization for people who don't believe in organizations and their rules—isn't that an oxymoron?"

"Up to the Os in your vocabulary builder?" she sniped. Richter couldn't tell how tall she was because of the way she was sitting. She had dark hair and brown eyes. If she lost the glasses she would have been pretty. She half smiled at him, as if to say she was tolerating his comment, certainly not closing the door to the conversation. "It's not that we don't believe in organizations, per se. It's all forms of government that we oppose, because governments, by their very nature, are oppressive. We examine the androcentric derivation of the rules and strictures that shape our lives in traditional forms of government."

"Androcentric? Up to the As in your vocabulary builder?" he asked. She smiled.

"Look," he said, pulling a chair from another table and sitting with his chest against the chair back, "men may have formed the governments and laws, but those laws are there to protect women as well."

"We women have to stop thinking of ourselves as victims who need to be given structure in our lives by those who oppress us."

She took off her reading glasses and looked at him more closely. She really was pretty. As she used her glasses to punctuate her points, Richter saw that her nails were bitten to the quick.

"So you're not so much against rules as you are against government forced on you by men. You're more feminist than anarchist."

"The whole concept of government is a male idea, so feminism and anarchism go hand in hand," she said. "I don't believe we need laws, because people in their natural state are good."

"John Locke, right? I'm more of a Thomas Hobbes fan, myself. Life in a society without laws would be 'solitary, nasty, brutish and short.' " Richter smiled. "All you need is one person like Hitler and that throws off your whole system."

"Hitler was able to do what he did because of androcentric concepts like nation, race and superiority. Without those prevailing ideas, he never could've thrived."

Richter was pleased to see that she wasn't a pushover. She liked to argue *and didn't let her emotions get in the way of reason. A young philosopher in training. "What about Nietzsche and his notion of superiority, that a superman could make the decision as to whether another should live or die? Without our laws, what would prevent an intelligent, logical, rational person from coming to the conclusion that less valuable members of society are dispensable?"*

"Again, you're falling back on your male paradigms."

"Unless you're going to have an all-female society," he said, "you're going to have male influences. And if you've got males, you need laws to control their violent impulses. Let me ask you a question: Do you think it's wrong to kill another human being?"

"Excellent question," she said. "This is one of my basic problems with government. Sometimes killing is sanctioned—executions, times of war. Other times it's punishable by death or imprisonment. There's no consistency in the application of your laws."

"If you want consistency, then you should be able to answer my question. Should we never be able to kill or always be able to kill?"

Her dark eyes and long brown hair, which fell down past her shoulders, were a nice change from the countless blondes on campus. "For starters," she said, "if we had no television, no violent movies, no pornography, no men brought up with football mentalities, we might have a shot at living our lives in peace without the restrictions placed on our civil liberties by a government."

"Plato never watched television and never played football. He wrote in The Republic, *'Mankind censures injustice fearing that they may be the victims of it, and not because they shrink from committing it.' You still haven't answered my question," he said.*

"Of course it's wrong to kill."

"Is it inherently wrong, or have our laws just made it illegal?"

"Inherently wrong."

"Perfect. You believe it's inherently wrong, but what if I don't? Without laws, government, police, prosecutors, what would stop me from killing?" He suddenly realized how loud his voice had gotten. They both stopped to see if they were disturbing anyone, but their section of the library was deserted.

"I'm with Plato. The only reason it's wrong to kill is because we don't want others killing us."

"So you really don't think it's wrong to kill?" she leaned toward him intently and asked in a voice just above a whisper.

"I'm not saying it shouldn't be illegal to kill. I'm trying to make a distinction between something being morally wrong and its being illegal. Our society is becoming devoid of any sense of morality, so why hold on to this hollow belief that there is something morally wrong with killing another person? You said it yourself, sometimes we sanction killing of humans and sometimes we condemn it. I think we should be consistent."

"We couldn't exist as a society if we said it was okay to go around killing one another."

"Of course it has to be illegal to kill people, but it's no more wrong than killing any other living creature. I eat meat every day. We as a society have massive factories where we kill animals on an assembly line and package the meat neatly so we can eat it at our convenience." Richter had made these same arguments in his philosophy class and easily converted half the class to his view.

"But those are just animals. It's different with human beings. Human life is more valuable than farm animals or even pets."

"Life is life. Let's say I have a loyal dog that loves me so much he runs to me and jumps on me, licking my face every time he sees me. He brings so much joy into my life. Is my life any more valuable than his? Should someone be able to arbitrarily take that dog's life?" Richter kept his voice low, but he could feel the anger building. He couldn't allow that. He needed to control himself, not let emotion influence his argument.

"I see your point with pets, but as much as I love animals, we have to place a greater value on human life. How can any society, male or female, exist if people don't have the basic right to live? Look at early human civilizations," she said, frustration shading her voice. "These would be situations where killing for territory, family or self-preservation would be accepted. Such societies were based on aggressive male tendencies. The androcentric creations of nationalism and race are just extensions of those ideals."

"So you think that if we had a society run by women we wouldn't need laws to govern us?" he asked. "Let's assume for a second that I'm living in that society. Without laws and the fear of being punished, what would stop me from getting up out of this chair"—he stood up—"walking over to you, and putting my hands around your neck?"

When Richter's hands first touched her cool skin he meant only to demonstrate how easy it would be to kill someone, shattering the naïve fiction that people are good and don't need laws to control them. But it felt so good, better than he had imagined. He was pleased at how thin and supple her neck was, his hands wrapping around it neatly, tightening his grip around her throat almost instinctively. She looked shocked at first, then hopeful he was just trying to make a point and not really hurt her.

He could feel her vulnerability as she strained to talk, to scream, to breathe. Her legs bumped under the table and she went after his fingers, trying to bend them back, but he was too strong. He felt her neck swelling, the blood backing into her chest and heart, trying to force its way to her brain.

It was incredible, holding life in his hands. How many times had he dreamt of this moment, never knowing if he would have the will to actually do it? But could he go through with it? He could simply pull away and she would live. It was too late for that. She was staring into his face. And it felt good to watch her life slip away, knowing that he was in control of the decision to kill her or let her live. He kept his grip on her as she struggled and fought until her body slid back into the chair.

People always thought about killing others when they were angry, but they seldom meant it. Richter had actually followed through on his desire, not out of anger, but simply because he chose to do it. He had wanted to know what it would be like to take someone's life. The actual feeling was far more exhilarating than he had ever expected.

He stood there for some time, overcome by this feeling of power. Suddenly he remembered that he was still in the library. Stupid. What was he thinking? He spun around to see if there was anyone behind him. He walked up and down the adjacent corridor. The book stacks were clear. They were alone.

He started to walk away, and then stopped to look at her one more time. The pretty anarchist's body was slouched in the chair with her head tilted back. Her eyes were open and bulging out of their sockets. The last thing they had seen was Richter. Her tongue was sticking out, her soft brown hair strewn across her face. It was a shame that she was going to look like such a mess when somebody found her. It seemed as though, in addition to losing her life, she had lost some of her dignity. For that he was sorry. He hurried back over to her, straightened her up in the chair and fixed her hair by brushing it off her face with the back of his hand.

She still looked terrible. He rested her arms on the table and placed her head down as if she were sleeping. That was better. She looked peaceful as long as you couldn't see her face.

A flash of panic raced through him. Had anyone seen his face? Was the anarchist alone or was someone on the way right now to meet her for dinner? What about all the surfaces he had touched? He needed to stop, relax, think. He walked back into the men's room and wet some paper towels. He wiped down everything he could think of, from the doors to the tables and the fixtures in the men's room. As far as he was concerned he had never been anywhere near this woman, even if someone said they saw him with her.

Richter knew what he had done was impulsive, foolish, but he didn't regret killing her, although he never should have done it in such a public place. For now he simply needed to make sure that he didn't get caught. Should he leave the library? No. He'd be seen leaving the building around the time of her death and immediately become a suspect. His best course of action would be no action. He would go back to the carrel where he'd been studying and continue as if nothing had happened.

The police would be called when her body was found and Richter would say he was in another part of the library. The police would never expect the killer to stay in the library. Even if they did suspect him, it wouldn't matter. As long as he stuck to his story, they would have no evidence against him. Never admit to anything. The best part was that he didn't even know her name. If he didn't know her, then he would have no reason to kill her. No motive. The perfect crime.

He took a final glance at her. As he studied her he realized that only a few minutes earlier he'd been talking and arguing with this woman. She'd possessed intelligence, feelings, beliefs and beauty. She'd had classmates, friends and family. Now he'd touched all of their lives as well. Richter, a person they would never meet, had made a massive, lasting impact on their lives and they didn't even know it yet.

CHAPTER 58

"You may proceed with your opening statement, Mr. Darget," Judge Sterling Davis said from the bench. The jury had just been sworn in. Connie had studied them as the clerk administered their oath: "Do you swear that you shall well and truly try the issues between the Commonwealth and the defendant according to the evidence, so help you God?"

"Thank you, Your Honor." Connie poured some water into a cup. He intended to put his evidence in quickly and efficiently, to get the jurors to focus on him rather than Judge Davis, who had spent the last two hours directing them through the impanelment process. Now it was Connie's turn to let the jurors know that they were in *his* courtroom.

Connie rose from his chair. Mitch, Brendan and Andi were in the back of the courtroom watching his opening, and in a way he was performing for them as much as for the jury. He wanted to convey to the jury that they were the most important people in the courtroom. There was an implicit deal that he struck with his juries through his mannerisms and the intonation in his voice: He was going to offer them his undivided attention in return for theirs.

Connie stepped behind his chair and pushed it in. He had to show a concerned expression, a look that told the jurors he was so troubled by this case that he didn't know where to begin.

Once he felt that they were all watching him, and there was absolute silence in the courtroom, Connie looked up at the jury and scanned the panel, making eye contact with each of them before speaking.

"Good morning, ladies and gentlemen, my name is Conrad Darget and I represent the Commonwealth in this case. During this trial you'll hear testimony that this man, Victor Carrasquillo," he said as he stood in front of the defendant, pointing his finger at his sullen, defiant face, "sold crack cocaine while in possession of a firearm. You will hear testimony from several police officers that they observed the defendant sell drugs to a known drug user and that when they placed the defendant under arrest he had a loaded nine-millimeter firearm in his waistband."

Then Connie explained the facts of his case and what he expected the evidence to be, making sure the jury felt that he was fair and unbiased toward the defendant, even while he advocated for a conviction. Connie could make the jury believe it was the evidence itself, not him, arguing and proving the defendant's guilt.

Until eight months ago, Connie had lost most of his trials. Last September Judge Samuels had pulled him aside and critiqued his performance after one of those losses. It was the last time Connie had taken Jesse Wilcox to trial.

The door to Judge Nathan Samuels's chambers was open. Connie rapped gently on the door frame. He wasn't in the mood for any words of encouragement. He'd done such a pathetic job that even the judge felt bad for him. And not just any judge, but Judge Samuels, one of the toughest judges in the city.

"Good evening, Mr. Darget," Judge Samuels said. "Come on in." When they'd built the new courthouse, the legislature made sure the judges were taken care of with lavish surroundings. The walls in Judge Samuels's chambers were paneled with solid mahogany. The judge was an imposing figure behind his antique oak desk.

"Your Honor, I know what you're going to say. 'Hey kid, don't be down on yourself. You did a great job, but you had a typical Suffolk County jury. They never trust the police—'"

"You think I called you in here to show you pity?" Judge Samuels asked. His usual stoic appearance changed to annoyance. "Young man, I brought you in here to inform you that you lost that trial before it ever started."

Connie was stunned.

"You have no concept of how to pick a jury. I've presided over your last three trials, all acquittals. You never use your peremptory challenges to strike jurors."

"I like to assume that all jurors will honor their oath to decide the case according to the evidence."

"That's your first mistake," Samuels said curtly. "Jurors in this city come in here looking for reasons to acquit defendants. You need to convince the jury that there's no way they could possibly find him not guilty."

"But, Your Honor, I thought I picked the ideal jury this time, with the perfect foreperson."

"That is precisely the problem, Mr. Darget. You picked an inadequate jury, especially the foreperson. She was barely out of college and working her first real job. That girl had no life experience to apply toward making a decision in a criminal case where a man faced imprisonment."

"I hadn't thought of that." Connie felt like a fool.

"You also left three college students on your jury. Mr. Darget, I'm going to let you in on a secret. Students don't know shit from apple butter. They can't decide what classes they're going to take next semester. How do you expect them to decide on a man's fate? The easier decision for jurors is always to let the accused go free and then convince themselves that the Commonwealth failed to prove guilt beyond a reasonable doubt."

"Judge Samuels, I always try to select younger jurors. I think I can connect better with people closer to my age."

"Mr. Darget, your thinking is flawed. Young people don't have anything invested in this community. They come here to go to school and stay on for a few years to work and party before going back home. The people who have a stake in keeping crime down and sending guilty people to jail are the middle-aged and elderly homeowners."

"You think I would have won this case if I'd picked a better jury?"

"Maybe, maybe not. But you need to pick better juries if you're going to have a chance. You can't just pick pretty young women you enjoy looking at.

They distract you. And the men on your jury aren't paying attention to the evidence."

Judge Samuels was right. Connie stood up, deep in thought, and started to wander out of the judge's chambers.

"You're welcome, Mr. Darget," Judge Samuels said.

"I'm sorry, Your Honor. Thanks for the advice. I was just trying to figure out how to connect with older jurors once I've got them seated."

"By being yourself. Don't try copying what other people do in the courtroom. Develop your own presence. Don't be discouraged, Mr. Darget. Keep practicing and you'll see improvement. Remember the only way to practice is by trying cases in front of real juries."

Connie later learned that Judge Samuels made it a point to summon each of the young lawyers in the DA's office to his chambers for his critiques. The judge seemed to feel that it was his responsibility to act as a mentor. For Connie, the meeting was a watershed event in his career, leading him to a revelation about how to better prepare for trial and connect with jurors. He began to practice his openings and closings at home. He allowed his personality to come through so jurors would like him, trust him and convict the defendants he was prosecuting. Like small-time pusher Victor Carrasquillo.

"All the testimony you hear in this case will come from this witness stand." Connie walked over and placed his hand on the rail in front of the stand. "These witnesses will tell you about what they observed on the day in question. They will tell you about the transaction they saw this defendant engage in with another individual. They will tell you about the drugs they recovered from this other individual. Finally they will tell you about the gun they recovered from the person of Victor Carrasquillo."

Connie moved to the center of the courtroom, directly in front of the jury box, scanning the jurors. "But these witnesses aren't ordinary witnesses. They aren't just people off the street who have never seen a drug transaction before. The witnesses you will hear from in this case are all experienced officers who specialize in drug investigations. You will have the opportunity to see and hear them testify so that you can judge the credibility of their testimony."

After losing so many trials early on, there had been times when Connie didn't want to stand before another jury. Now things were different. He'd had more trials than any other prosecutor in the courthouse. Whenever there was a difficult case others were afraid to try, Connie would throw eight in the box and go. If he kept trying the tough cases, he knew that he would eventually achieve his dream of becoming one of the top prosecutors in the district attorney's office.

CHAPTER 59

Using his fork, Angel Alves pushed the black beans on his plate, creating a small hill surrounded by a moat of yellow saffron rice, a chicken drumstick acting as a bridge across the moat.

He tried to avoid looking at Marcy. She seemed more sad than angry. She couldn't be angry with him. She had lost an old friend too. Alves was sure she wanted him to do everything he could to catch the killer. But now she was losing her husband to the investigation. She'd made an attempt at conversation, telling him how Iris and Angel had done at gymnastics, but it was forced. All he could think about was how old Mrs. Stokes had looked the last time he saw her.

He had spent endless days calling funeral homes in the region, checking to see if they were missing embalming fluids and running the criminal records of all their employees.

One local place of interest was the boarded-up Jones Funeral Home in Mattapan. The business had been run into the ground by the son of the original owner. There was something about that fairly new lock to the basement and the way the son couldn't find the key that nagged at Alves. Once they broke the lock and got in, they found a decent stock of dusty chemicals. Things looked pretty much undisturbed. But since the records were either damaged or lacking altogether, there was no way to tell if anything was missing.

Marcy started to clear the dishes. Alves felt guilty for not commenting on the meal or asking Marcy about her day. But he knew that it would lead to complaints about her getting stuck with the kids' activities. Then she would feel selfish, knowing that he was doing this for Mrs. Stokes and for Robyn.

"I'm taking the kids in town tomorrow after school." Marcy broke the silence. "We're going to the aquarium."

"That sounds like fun," Alves said to the kids, trying to be festive.

"Daddy, can you come?" Iris looked up at him with her little smile. She was going to be beautiful like her mother.

"I'm sorry, sweetie, but Daddy has to work tomorrow."

"But you work every day," Angel pleaded. "Why can't you come with us tomorrow?"

"I just can't, buddy. Once Daddy finishes working on this big case, he'll take you guys somewhere fun."

"Promise?" Iris asked.

"Cross my heart." Alves caught Marcy's eye as she sponged the table. "I'll call the captain down at District 1 and see if he'll let you park out front. Save some money."

"We're taking the train. I hate driving in traffic and the T is faster."

Alves didn't like the idea of her bundling up the twins and all they needed for a day at the aquarium onto the subway. He was all too familiar with the characters you found on the trains. And on their way home they'd have to deal with the rowdy teenagers getting out of school. But what else can you do?

It was so obvious that he was shocked they hadn't thought of it before. People who live in the city take the T to work. They don't waste time fighting traffic, finding a place to park. They relax and read the paper.

"Marcy, that's it."

"That's what?"

"Angel, Iris, why don't you guys go upstairs and play? Mommy and I will be up in a few minutes to get you ready for bed." He waited until the two of them started up the stairs. He stood up and took out his cell phone. "That's where he's finding his victims. It has to be. All of the victims have been professional women who took the T into work every day. He didn't meet them out at New Balance. If he did we'd probably have victims outside the city. He's choosing his victims while they're riding a train or a bus, oblivious that some psycho is watching them. Then he's following them home so he can stalk them at his leisure before killing them."

"My God." Marcy gasped. "If this is true, you need to warn people."

Alves hit the speed dial on his phone. "That's why I'm calling Sarge."

CHAPTER 60

Richter watched with disgust as Richard Speck pranced around his prison cell with his shirt off, flabby chest and stomach flopping around. He was showing off for the camera.

The documentary started with footage of the crime Speck had committed, murdering eight student nurses in their South Chicago town house. Initially, Speck had entered their apartment to commit a burglary, forcing his way in with a gun and a knife. He found six women in the house and, over the next hour, three others returned home. He had planned to tie them up and rob them, but once he had them under his control he decided to rape, strangle and stab them too. He killed all of the women except for the one who had answered the door when he forced his way in. She had somehow managed to hide under a bed and Speck lost track of her. She later identified him by the tattoo on his forearm that read "Born to Raise Hell."

Richter was especially bothered by the crime because Speck killed the women for no reason. For one moment in his sorry life, Speck found himself in a position of power, and he abused that power. He hadn't killed the women for the good of society. He did it for pure self-gratification, and for that he deserved to rot in hell.

Speck had clearly developed a hatred for society. Now, sentenced to spend the rest of his life in jail, he acted for the cameras as if he were enjoying himself, as if he *wanted* to be the bitch of his very large prison cell mate. But his eyes told a different story. His laughter couldn't hide the regret he must have felt for giving up his life for one night of squan-dered power. Now he had no power over anyone's life, not even his own. All he could do was smile for the cameras in a final, pathetic attempt to hurt the families of the women he'd killed.

Speck had been aptly named, for he was nothing more than a small spot or particle, an insignificant dot. He was a person who had never done anything important.

Richter, on the other hand, had done so much to help others, to help them escape their worthless lives. More than that, he was helping to make the world a better place. From the moment he and Emily Knight conceived of the plan, Richter had acted for the benefit of all men, for the greater good, for society as a whole. He would continue with his work until it was complete, knowing that whatever he did, he would never end up like Richard Speck.

CHAPTER 61

It was eight o'clock when Richter stepped off the bus, wishing he never had to ride the T again. He needed to be alone, not on a crowded bus. He wanted to get home so he could sit in the dark and collect his thoughts.

Then she tapped him on the shoulder. "Excuse me, sir."

Richter wasn't in the mood to talk with anyone, to be nice to them. He didn't have the patience for it. He turned to face her. The juror. He couldn't remember her name, but she was a juror from a trial he'd lost several weeks earlier. His favorite juror, or so he'd thought. What did she want?

"Can I help you?" Richter asked, acting confused, as though he didn't know who she was.

"Don't you remember me? I sat on your jury a while back."

"Ah, yes." Richter thought about the case. The defendant was one of the major dealers in Grove Hall. "How are you doing?" he said in a forced, pleasant voice. Then he thought, maybe it was fate that had brought the two of them together. This was his chance to find out what they'd been thinking when they'd voted to acquit. "What was your name again?" Richter asked.

"Emily. Emily Knight."

"Nice to see you again, Ms. Knight."

"Do you mind if I walk with you?" she asked.

"As long as you don't mind cutting through the woods."

"Not if I'm with you," she said, smiling. "I usually walk all the way around them. They give me the creeps."

"Don't worry, I'll protect you." He'd spent weeks preparing for that trial to make sure he'd get a conviction. She and her fellow jurors had acquitted the defendant after only fifteen minutes of deliberation.

As they entered the woods Richter understood why she would think they were creepy, especially at night. The darkness and the leaves on the trees and thick shrubs made it difficult to see more than a few feet ahead. They walked carefully along an asphalt path. There was no light except that provided by the moon.

"I'm glad I ran into you tonight," the juror said. "I wanted to speak with you about the trial. I feel really bad about what happened. You did such a nice job. I could tell you'd put a lot of work into it. You were so upset when you heard our verdict. I waited to see you afterward, but you never came out of the courtroom."

"I took the back stairs right up to my office." Richter felt the first twinges of anger. She'd put a violent criminal back on the street.

"I wanted to let you know how we reached our verdict," she said. "The other five jurors didn't believe the police officers had actually seen the defendant hand the drugs to the other man. I believed it, though."

Richter's anger fanned out and turned hot in his stomach. All along he had thought that none of the jurors, including Emily Knight, believed the officers. "Why did you vote to acquit him if you believed he did it?"

"I held out as long as I could. Then I gave in to the pressure from the others."

"You held out as long as you could?" His anger and frustration erupted. "You deliberated for fifteen minutes before lunch arrived and you had a verdict as soon as you finished eating. What did you do, vote to acquit once you found out they weren't serving dessert?"

"That's not fair," she said, her voice cracking as if she was going to cry. "You don't know how hard it was being the only one who thought he was guilty while everyone else was convinced that the police were lying. It didn't help that there were no fingerprints or DNA linking him to the drugs."

"No fingerprints or DNA, in a street-level drug case? You actually

*thought we should have submitted the drugs for DNA testing?" He was
dumbfounded.*

*"That can happen. I've seen it on TV," she said. "People always leave
some biological or trace evidence when they commit a crime."*

"I can't believe people watch so much television that it's come to this."

*"Nobody's blaming you. It's not your job to test the evidence. And besides,
what's the big deal? All he did was sell one bag of heroin. It's not like he hurt
anyone."*

*"It's not like he hurt anyone?" Richter asked. Her eyes were wide with
fright.*

*"I'm sorry," she said, trying to calm him down. "I didn't mean to upset
you. He's just a poor inner-city kid trying to make a living."*

*She looked ahead, probably to see how far it was to the edge of the woods.
Richter knew there was nothing but a long dark path.*

*"What if I told you that that 'poor inner-city kid' raped and killed a
woman when he was sixteen years old just for shits and giggles? And what if I
told you he only went to jail until he turned twenty-one?" He moved closer to
her. "And what if I told you that he's the main suspect in the murders of two
of his competitors in the drug trade, but no one will come forward to testify
because everyone's terrified of him? And what if I told you that a drug
conviction was the only way we were going to get him off the streets, at least
for a couple of years?" Richter was now within inches of her face.*

*"You're scaring me. I'm sorry, but I didn't know he'd hurt anyone before,
none of us did. If we'd known all that we would have convicted him."*

*"You're not supposed to know that. You were supposed to do your job.
You knew he sold those drugs, but you let him get away with it because you
were too lazy to do your job. You stupid bitch, you let a murderer go free."*

*He could see terror in her eyes. She must have known she couldn't calm
him down. She turned away from him and stumbled down the path. She'd
taken only a couple of steps before Richter caught her by the hair and dragged
her backward. She started to scream. His first impulse was just to shut her up
with a chin lock. Instinctively he spun her around and took ahold of her neck.*

*Richter lifted her in the air as she pounded at his arms. He held her tight.
She was trying to speak, to beg or maybe to scream for help. But no words*

came. Richter watched her face as she struggled to breathe, but she was losing her strength. Finally her body relaxed.

He had to decide what to do with her. He sat her on the ground with her back against a tree, the moon lighting up her face. Her milky white skin glowed in the moonlight. She had a pretty face, not beautiful, but certainly pretty. He touched her skin. So smooth. So young. Richter couldn't just leave her in the woods. She deserved better than that.

CHAPTER 62

Richter went to the back of the car and popped the trunk. *"What are you staring at?" he asked Emily Knight. Her eyes were fixed open, gazing up at him. "It was your fault I had to kill you and you're looking at me like I'm to blame. You're lucky I came back for you."*

He took her by the belt and jacket collar, lifting her out of the trunk like the bales of hay he used to haul on his grandfather's farm. Emily seemed heavier than the hay, and she was more awkward.

Richter was careful not to hit Emily's head on anything. He carried her through the kitchen without turning on any lights.

Richter placed Emily on the couch and sat next to her, looking into her eyes, blank and cold. "I can't begin to tell you how disappointed I am in you," he said.

Richter stood up and began pacing in front of the couch. "Do you realize how much aggravation you're causing me? I need to figure out what to do with you. I didn't want to leave you in the woods, but I can't just bury you in the backyard either. If you had just done your job and followed the evidence, neither of us would be in this situation."

But then Richter realized what he would do with Emily Knight. He would arrange it so that Emily would never let him down again. Richter lifted her up and placed her in his empty refrigerator. She would be fine in there while he made the arrangements.

But he needed to take his time and do things right.

PART THREE

. . . .

The man of knowledge must be able
not only to love his enemies, but
also to hate his friends.

—FRIEDRICH NIETZSCHE,
Thus Spoke Zarathustra

CHAPTER 63

The late-spring light filtered in through the tall windows facing Huntington Avenue. The annual pottery sale at the Massachusetts College of Art was bustling with shoppers. Andi Norton browsed around from table to table hoping to find a gift for Connie. Andi and Monica Hughes had snuck out for some shopping on their lunch hour. Andi watched as Monica, two tables ahead of her, bought an oversized mug that came complete with hot herbal tea. Andi caught up with her and picked up a piece at the end of the table. "What do you think about this one?"

Monica studied it, taking a cautious sip of her tea. The mug was so big Andi lost sight of her face for a second. "What is it?"

"I don't know, a pencil holder, a coffee mug, a soup bowl. It's whatever you want it to be."

"Is Connie going to like it?"

"I hope so. It's handmade by a real artist. Who wouldn't like it?"

"Connie."

"Right. What the hell am I going to get him?"

"I don't know, but whatever it is, I don't think you're going to find it here. Why are you getting him a gift? Is it his birthday?"

"No. I just thought I'd get him something to thank him for all he's done to help me. He's given me two trials. And I'll be second-seating him on the Jesse Wilcox trial." At the next table, students were selling massive bowls full of homemade chili. "Who could eat all that?" Andi asked. "It's the size of a serving bowl."

"Connie could probably eat it, if he ate anything but those disgusting lunches he brings every day."

"That's it. I'll get him one of these bowls. Without the chili."

"What's someone like Connie going to do with a beautiful piece of pottery?"

"Eat his family-sized servings of oatmeal. This is the perfect size." Andi paid for the bowl and the young art student began carefully wrapping it in old newspaper. "You put aside that tough-guy image and he's a big teddy bear," Andi said as they waited for the young woman.

"I hope it works out for you."

"What's the deal with Nick? He seems to be stalking you."

"I think he's cute."

"Are you serious? He's ridiculous, following you everywhere."

"I don't mind him. He keeps asking me out and I keep putting him off. One of us will eventually get promoted or transferred. Then I'll give him a shot."

"What are you thinking? He isn't ready for a serious relationship."

"What makes you think I'm looking for a serious relationship?" Monica winked.

"You're crazy." Andi laughed. "What about Brendan? He's a nice guy."

"Not my type. Besides, he already has a girlfriend."

"Allegedly."

They both laughed.

The student placed the wrapped bowl in a used plastic supermarket bag and handed it to Andi. "We'd better get going. We've already been gone for an hour. Nick might have a panic attack if he's away from you too long."

CHAPTER 64

Richter's headache had dulled, but it was still there, lingering behind his eyes. The stiffness in his neck was there too. He never should have agreed to take *her* out for a day of shopping. Too domestic. Big mistake. That must have been what got her talking about their long-term plans together. Now she wanted to go away for a long weekend in Maine. Soon she'd be talking about moving in together. He couldn't let that happen. Not now. He was too close. Richter needed her, but he didn't want things to get too complicated. He had agreed with her weekend getaway plan just to shut her up. He would come up with an excuse to get out of it later. He needed to put up with her a little while longer. Then he could get rid of her.

Richter put his window down as soon as he started the car. They had just left a discount women's clothing warehouse and were headed for a store that specialized in knickknacks and home accessories. Both stores were always packed with women looking for bargains. All the different perfumes in the air were overwhelming. Throw in some potpourri, scented candles and poorly ventilated stores, and his headache would be raging again.

He only went to places like this when forced by a woman. He remembered being led into a communal dressing room as a child. There he was, staring up at the crotches of overweight, scary women who undressed in front of him as if he weren't even there. He would feel dirty for hours afterward.

Richter was glad they were driving now. The cool air filled the car as they drove on the highway. It was almost June and the weather still hadn't warmed up consistently. It had been eighty degrees two days earlier, when a cold front came in from Canada, bringing with it a steady downpour of rain. Richter leaned his head toward the open window, allowing the rain to cool him off.

"Could you close your window, please?" the woman asked. "It's freezing in here and my bags are getting wet in the backseat."

"Sorry. I've got this terrible headache and the cool air helps." Richter had to put up with her. She was very important, after all. He suspected the police profile would be of a loner, a man who had difficulty forming relationships with women. Richter had to prove that he was at least involved with someone.

"Why didn't you tell me you weren't feeling well?" the woman said. She seemed genuinely concerned. "Let's just go home. I can go shopping some other time."

"Don't be silly. We only have one stop left. Then I can go home and take it easy."

"But if you don't feel good—"

"I'm fine. I'll check to see if they have aspirin while you shop. We're almost there anyway."

"Are you sure? I won't be upset if you want to go home."

"Really, I'll be okay."

They drove the rest of the way in silence. As he parked the car she said, "You can stay out here if you want."

"I'll come in. If I start to feel worse I'll go back out."

The air inside the crammed store was stifling in contrast to the crisp air outside. Richter scanned the store. There were women, kids and shopping carts everywhere. "I'm going to go look for the aspirin," he told her. "I'll meet back up with you."

She was already engrossed in a picture frame rimmed with buttons. It would probably be a half hour before she'd even notice that he wasn't with her.

Richter cut across toward the middle of the store. A woman was walking in front of him with a cart full of junk and three crying kids, with a fourth one just waiting to plop out of her swollen belly. She had pale white skin with blotchy red cheeks that she'd tried to cover with powder. Her hair stuck straight up with hair spray and she repeatedly snapped the gum in her mouth. The garish red lipstick and nail polish added the finishing touches.

He felt a sharp pain behind his eyes as he caught a whiff of her perfume. Richter tried to make his way around her cart, but it was taking up the whole aisle. He should have thought to leave his jacket in the car. He would probably knock over a display if he tried to take it off in the narrow aisle.

He took a right turn down the next aisle to see if he could get ahead of her. His path was blocked by another pregnant woman. Barely squeezing past, he was confronted by a different family coming down the aisle.

All of their odors joined to form one stench. The smell seemed to have gotten stronger. Richter looked at the shelves to see that he had stumbled into the scented candles and potpourri section.

He was getting hotter. He had to get out of that aisle. He edged his way past the family and found himself at the back of the store, surrounded by a group of women in the gift-bag aisle. They were wearing way too much spandex. He closed his eyes for a moment. Their conversations about sales and bargains, and this looking cute and that smelling nice, were running together to make one inescapable sound. He finally took off his jacket and turned back the way he had come.

Richter thought about a passage in Jonathan Swift's *Gulliver's Travels*. It was so well written that when Richter read it he had felt as though he was right there with Gulliver, seeing, hearing and smelling everything that Gulliver had.

Gulliver was in the land called Brobdingnag, inhabited by people sixty feet tall. He had been stripped naked and placed on the breasts of naked women. Their skin appeared "coarse and uneven" with "a mole here and there as broad as a trench, and hairs hanging from it thicker than pack threads." Gulliver was disgusted by this whole experience. Jonathan Swift's mother must surely have taken him into the women's dressing room as a child.

He was still hot, even with his jacket off, and thinking of Gulliver's trip didn't help at all. It was like imagining himself on a long cruise in a rocky boat in an effort to cure himself of motion sickness in a car.

There was the front entrance to the store. He walked toward it quickly. He'd told the woman that he would see her outside, hadn't he? The cool air hit his face. He kept his jacket off as he looked up to the sky. The rain on his face was a soothing relief.

CHAPTER 65

Connie and Alves made their way up the stairs of the old triple-decker, each step creaking as they moved. It was the last week of May, six months since Michelle Hayes had been murdered.

"You look like shit," Alves said.

"It's three o'clock in the morning. What do you expect?"

"I expect you to wake up before coming to a crime scene." Alves laughed.

"What's her name?" Connie changed the subject.

"*His* name was Edwin Ramos," Alves said as the two men entered the third-floor apartment.

Connie stopped walking and grabbed Alves's arm. "It's a guy?"

"Yes."

"What the . . . Are you sure it's the same killer?"

"The MO is there, everything's identical, right down to the nine-one-one call. Public still doesn't know about the calls."

"Now he's killing men? What does that mean?"

"We don't know. He fucked with our heads when he killed Robyn Stokes, because she was the first vic that wasn't white. Then he goes and kills Jill Twomey, another white woman. Now he kills a Puerto Rican dude. He's all over the place."

"What does Sarge think?"

"He's frustrated and angry. So am I. We can't figure out any pattern, not as to when he strikes or who he's going to pick as his next victim.

Nothing. We were hoping the warnings we put out for people to be careful riding the T, to watch for strangers following them home, would slow this guy down. Now he goes and kills a guy. Men aren't as likely to be worried about being followed. That could be how this guy ended up dead."

"Ramos live alone?" Connie asked.

Alves nodded.

"Who else lives in the building?"

"Nobody. He owns the house. Bought it a few months ago. Fixing it up. I guess his plan was to fix up all three units, live in one of them and rent out the other two. He finished this apartment and was living here while he worked on the other ones." Alves scanned the apartment. "Judging the quality of the work, I'd say he was quite a handyman."

"Poor bastard," Connie said.

"Hey! Don't touch that." Alves's attention was on a young lab tech who was about to pick a couch cushion off the floor and put it back on the couch. "Don't move a fucking thing until ID gets pictures of the whole room. I want them taking full panoramic shots so we have a virtual crime scene."

"Yes, sir."

Alves joined Connie as he walked down the hall toward Mooney, who was kneeling outside the bedroom. On Mooney's right ankle Connie spotted a holster holding a small revolver, probably a .22 or .25 caliber. Mooney was so old school, if the department would allow it, he'd probably be carrying a big revolver on his waist instead of the standard-issue 9mm Glock. "Hey, Sarge, how's it going?" Connie called out.

"I've been better," Mooney said. "Don't go fucking with my crime scene like that last DA."

"Sorry about that. You won't see Richard Wahl again. He got booted off Response."

"Joe Cool got shit-canned?" Alves laughed.

"You're going to get shit-canned too if you don't do some fucking work."

"I guess that's my cue," Alves said, walking back toward the front of the apartment. "He's very subtle."

"I've noticed that about him."

Mooney went back to supervising the collection of evidence in Ramos's bedroom. He also had two techs from the Identification Unit dusting for latent prints on every surface in the house. Smaller items like a lamp and a watch had been collected and bagged. Mooney even had them remove some of the doors to be fumed for prints back at headquarters.

"Sarge, can I check out the bathroom?" Connie asked.

"From the hallway," Mooney barked, "but don't go in any of the rooms, don't touch anything and don't get in my way."

"Whatever you say, boss." Connie crept down the hall. He could see the tub just as he got to the threshold of the bathroom.

The tub reminded him of a scene from an old horror movie, where some sexy, naked woman pops up out of the blood and scares the hell out of the viewer. But this was no movie. The deep red created a stunning contrast to the white enamel of the old cast-iron claw-footed tub. Connie could smell the blood in the air, salty and metallic.

He felt invigorated being back at a crime scene with Mooney and Alves.

There were several white bath towels on the floor next to the tub with a bloody imprint of a human body. More blood-soaked towels were tossed in the corner. Just like the other crime scenes. Connie was fascinated by the image and the story it told. He wondered if the police would ever figure out what it all meant.

CHAPTER 66

Richter smiled at the juror. Linda Bagwell wasn't the most attractive woman he'd ever seen. Her longish brown hair was pulled back in a bun. She was wearing no makeup. She had small breasts and wore a blouse that was too tight. Her skirt made her look bottom heavy, like a pear.

Yet Richter knew she'd do just fine. He had seen her confidential juror questionnaire, making a mental note of her personal information. She lived downtown. At the age of thirty-three she was still single with no children. She had her MBA and JD and was working at a boutique consulting firm downtown. She must have been very bright if they'd hired her despite her physical shortcomings. Although she was obviously successful, he could tell she had never really enjoyed herself. He could see it in her eyes. She wasn't happy with her life.

Richter pictured her as one of the nameless, faceless sheep he saw every day on their way to work. They were herded into their high-rise buildings for the day, then set free long enough to eat and sleep before being herded back in the following morning. The juror was a well-paid sheep, nothing more, nothing less.

Richter would change all of that. He got that warm feeling inside that most people get when they give toys to a charity at Christmastime or give a dollar to a homeless person.

Richter was going to give the juror a much greater gift. He sent her another little smile as she sat in the jury box. This time she actually smiled back.

She was perfect.

CHAPTER 67

Richter gazed out the window at the Back Bay skyline. The setting sun reflecting off the John Hancock and Prudential towers in the distance created a postcard image of the city.

Friday night. Only a few people were still in the office. The weekend weather was supposed to be warm, so most of the others had left early. Richter watched Nick in his cubicle, muddling through paperwork.

In the half-lit, silent office, nagging thoughts of his last trial edged out all other concerns. His jury had deliberated a little too long. The women, he knew, had been enthralled. But the men he wasn't so sure about. This potential weakness grew in his mind until all he could think about was how to establish that bond of trust with every juror.

"Hey, buddy," Nick interrupted his thoughts. The city outside the windows was blanketed in darkness now, the streetlights were on.

"Yeah?" Richter looked up, rubbing his eyes.

"It's getting late. You want to get a bite? We can grab some Chinese from the Golden Temple."

"Best egg rolls in America." Maybe there was a simple solution to his dilemma. "We can eat at my house. Have a couple of beers. Watch the Sox."

"I could use a couple of cold ones," Nick said. "Long week."

"I can call in the order from the car." Richter put on his suit jacket. "Let's do it."

CHAPTER 68

On Monday morning, Andi was checking her e-mails when Monica came into her cubicle.

"Nick's not here yet," she said. "He's never this late without calling."

"So you're starting to fall for your stalker?" Andi teased her.

"I'm serious. He's usually in early. No one's seen him. His cell phone's going right to voice mail."

"Maybe he had a late start and got caught in traffic. Probably forgot to turn his phone on." Andi could see that Monica wanted to believe her. "I wouldn't worry. He'll show up."

Monica turned and stared out the window for a moment. Andi could tell there was something else.

"He didn't call me," Monica said.

"I know."

"That's not what I mean. He's been calling me on the weekends. He'll find some excuse to call, usually something stupid about work, then we talk for hours. He didn't call this weekend. I was a little worried, but then I figured he was trying something new to get me to like him, see if I missed him. Something's wrong."

"Did you guys have a fight last week?"

"No. When we said good night on Friday, I knew he'd be calling me. Andi, I'm going to call the police."

"Let's talk to Liz first." Andi led Monica into Liz's office. Connie, Mitch and Brendan were already there, trying to figure out who would cover Nick's cases until he got in. Andi was glad Connie was there. He'd know what to do.

"He wouldn't miss work like this," Monica said. "His job is everything to him."

"Maybe there was a little too much partying over the weekend," Connie said. Andi shot him a look, so he offered, "Maybe he hooked up with some buddies from law school. I'm sure he's fine."

"Monica, have you called around to the local hospitals to see if he got into an accident?" Mitch asked.

"Good idea," Liz said. "Andi can help you."

"Liz, I'll cover for Monica and Nick in the sessions." Brendan was already putting on his suit jacket.

By lunchtime, Liz had called Nick's parents in Roslindale. They hadn't heard from him either.

Connie pulled Liz and Andi aside. "I'm going to shoot over to Nick's condo. I'll take Mitch with me. I can have Alves meet us over there. If there's any problem," he whispered, "we'll have the police with us. I'll call as soon as I find out anything."

Even though Andi offered to get her some lunch, Monica said she wasn't hungry. The two of them had called all the local hospitals, asking about accident victims.

"What about the hospital the cops call the Stairway to Heaven?" Andi asked.

"Called it," Monica said. "Nothing."

The two women sat in silence. Monica seemed worn out. She hadn't bothered to put on her lipstick and her hair was uncombed.

Liz pulled up a chair and joined them, her face showing signs of strain. She studied Monica for a moment. "Connie called in from the condo. There's no sign of Nick. Let's notify the DA and file a report."

CHAPTER 69

Connie knew the two detectives from the Homicide Unit who showed up on Tuesday morning. The somber mood in the courthouse was heightened by their presence. Although no one wanted to think the worst, Nick's disappearance was being investigated like a homicide.

The detectives were a couple of old-timers named Taylor and Campbell who'd been assigned to Homicide for years and were biding time until their retirements. Connie had met them at several homicide scenes.

"What's up, guys? Anything new on Nick?" Connie asked as the two men walked past the secretaries toward Liz's office.

"Nothing," Taylor said. He looked worn down. "We need to talk with everyone in the building to see if they saw anything out of the ordinary last week."

"Connie," Campbell said, "when was the last time you saw Nick?"

"Friday night. We were both working late. Us and Mitch Beaulieu."

"Mitch Beaulieu?" Campbell asked.

"Another prosecutor. He's at his desk right around the corner if you want to talk with him."

"How late were you here?"

"I left around six thirty. Nick was still here. I'm not sure if Mitch was here."

"Did you leave alone?" Campbell asked.

"Yes."

"Where was Nick?"

"At his desk. Everyone else had gone home. The three of us were joking around about how we were big losers, working late on a Friday night. I told him I'd had enough, I was going home. He said he was going to stay a little longer, so he wouldn't have to come in on the weekend. We said good night. That was the last time I saw him."

"Did he say what he was doing over the weekend?"

"I didn't ask."

"Where was Mitch?"

"That's what I'm not sure about. He was working in the conference room, but kept coming back to his desk for stuff. I went to the bathroom before I took off. He wasn't at his desk, but I just assumed he was still in the conference room."

"I'll check with him," Campbell said.

"Did you see anyone hanging around outside when you left the building?" Taylor asked.

"It was deserted out there. This whole thing is pretty upsetting." Connie shook his head. "Could I have been the last person to see him?"

"You or Mitch," Taylor said.

"Do you guys think he's all right?" Connie asked.

"I don't know," Taylor said. "Nobody's seen him in more than three days. It doesn't look like he made it home Friday night. And it doesn't look like he's gone on a trip either. According to his parents, all of his luggage and travel bags were in his closet."

"And he didn't mention going away," Connie said.

"Let us know if you think of anything else," Campbell said. "I'm going to go talk with Mitch. You said he's around the corner here?"

Connie nodded.

"I'm going down to the clerk's office. I'll meet you back up here," Taylor said. He stopped and turned back to Connie. "How's everyone doing with this whole thing?"

"We're all a little shaken. Everyone's speculating as to whether this has anything to do with one of the cases Nick was prosecuting. It's a little unnerving to think that something may have happened to him because of the job. A few of the women are in the conference room, basically holding a vigil for him. The judges are giving us continuances on everything until we clear this up. The DA is sending a few victim advocates from downtown to make sure everyone's all right."

"You guys need to support one another right now. You shouldn't be thinking the worst," Taylor said. "At this point we don't even know that anything's happened to Nick. We always have missing persons who turn up after a few days. Sometimes the stress gets to people and they skip town for a while."

"I know how that feels. I've been so busy between court, prepping my cases, working at home all hours of the night. Throw in the Response pager and there are times I think I'm going to snap. That's when I stop and take some deep Yoga breaths to clear my head. But if that's what happened to Nick, why would he take off without any of his belongings?" Connie asked.

"That's the point. They want to get away from everything. That includes buying new clothes when they get where they're going. You said that the two of you were here late on a Friday night?"

"Yeah."

"There you have it. Who knows how late he worked after you left? Maybe it just got to him. Happens all the time. I know what you guys are worried about, but we have no reason to believe anything happened to Nick because of his work as a prosecutor. We called Liz Moore earlier, and she's pulling all the cases he's been handling so we can look at them. But we're just doing it as a precaution. We're also going to be increasing patrols in the area, so people should feel safe coming to and from the courthouse. We'll even give personal escorts."

"Thanks," Connie said as Detective Taylor moved down the hall. Connie knew Taylor would learn nothing from anyone in the clerk's office. That place was a ghost town by the time he left on Friday night.

CHAPTER 70

"Connie, where's Campbell?" Detective Taylor asked as he came running into the office. The detective probably hadn't exercised in a while, his face pale and damp with the exertion.

"I don't know," Connie said. "I think he's in Liz's office. What's going on? Did you get something on Nick?" It wasn't even noon yet. Taylor had been down in the clerk's office for no more than two hours. It certainly looked like he'd hit on something.

"I think I might have a lead on the Blood Bath Killer," Taylor said.

"What kind of a lead?" Connie asked as he followed Taylor into Liz's office.

"We'd better give Sergeant Mooney a call," Taylor said to Campbell.

Campbell pushed away a stack of files and stood, stretching as though he had been in one position too long.

"I was talking to one of the women in the clerk's office. She asked if we were going to solve Susan McCarthy's murder. I told her it was still under investigation. Then she tells me that McCarthy seemed like such a nice woman when she sat on a jury last winter. She recognized her picture in the papers and on television. Felt horrible about what had happened to her. Susan McCarthy comes to this courthouse for jury duty a few months before she gets killed. Now we have a missing prosecutor from the same courthouse. Maybe it's a coincidence, but it's worth looking into. This might be the break Mooney's been waiting for."

It appeared that Campbell didn't hear what Detective Taylor had just told him. He stood silently for a few seconds before looking from Liz to Connie. "Not a word about this to anyone. Not to other prosecutors, judges, anyone. We'll talk with the DA himself and the police commissioner. We're going to get Mooney and Alves over here ASAP."

Liz drew in a sharp breath of air. "Let us know if you need anything."

CHAPTER 71

Richter pushed the 350 pounds off his chest as if he were doing a push-up. It had been a hectic day, with Alves and Mooney and what seemed like half the police department swarming in on the courthouse by early afternoon. Judge Davis had closed the courthouse early but had all of his staff stay to be interviewed by the detectives. Alves and Mooney told Liz she could let her people go home as long as they were back first thing in the morning to be interviewed. Richter and the other guys went to relieve some stress with an afternoon workout.

One thing Angel Alves mentioned was that the police were having trouble getting the archived juror questionnaires. The Office of the Jury Commissioner had claimed that the forms were confidential records that couldn't be divulged, even for a homicide investigation. There had been a lot of legal wrangling, and the DA's chief legal counsel was going before a superior court judge in the morning to get a court order for the records. Richter enjoyed watching everyone scramble around.

Richter did nine more repetitions before he finally rested the steel bar back on the arms of the weight bench. While he was lifting the weights, he was in a zone, another world. He couldn't hear the others urging him on, or the pop music playing in the background, or the chatter of the people who came to the gym to socialize instead of lift weights.

Everything was working out well. In the locker room after their workout, Richter would take his time getting undressed and let the other two head for the showers first. Then he would be one step closer to deliverance.

CHAPTER 72

Still pumped from his workout, Richter followed Linda Bagwell as she left her office at Rosenthal & Fitch in the financial district. He kept his distance as she made her way down Federal Street and up Summer and then through the Boston Common and the Public Garden, heading toward her apartment on Marlborough Street. It was almost seven o'clock on a beautiful June evening, the first day of summer. A perfect night for a walk in the city. Richter pictured Linda shutting off her cell phone and relaxing on the couch with a book after a quiet dinner alone in her apartment.

As she approached the statue of George Washington on horseback, she suddenly stopped. Had she seen him? Richter turned toward a bed of deep purple pansies, kneeling as if admiring them. He watched her from the corner of his eye. She seemed to be overcome by the history that surrounded her as she gazed at Washington's statue at the west entrance of the Boston Public Garden, his stoic visage facing the statue of Alexander Hamilton less than a block away on Commonwealth Avenue. Comm Ave., a broad boulevard divided by a grassy mall and lined with stately brick town houses, was a taste of Paris in the heart of Boston, and any tourist who didn't realize that Commonwealth Avenue and the Public Garden were built on landfill in the nineteenth century might actually picture Washington and Hamilton meeting in that very spot, planning the American Revolution and the new government of the United States.

Richter touched one of the purple-and-yellow flowers that his grandmother said cheered her up. Each one was like a happy little face, she always said.

"Why's Gramma in bed crying?" the child asked. "Is she okay?"

The old man sat quietly in his rocker on the back porch loading his rifle. "She's fine, boy. Sometimes women just don't understand men's work."

"I understand, Grampa."

"Sure you do," the old man nodded. "How old are you now?"

"Seven," the child said.

"You want to help me do some men's work?"

"Can I, Grampa, can I?"

"You go find old Butchy and meet me out by the barn. We'll take him out so he can exercise his tired old legs."

The child was excited. He ran and found his grandparents' old mutt sleeping on the rug by the mudroom. "C'mon, Butchy," he said, shaking the dog. "We're gonna go play in the woods." The dog struggled to get his footing, before slowly standing up. "Let's go," the child called as he led the way out onto the back porch.

The child ran to catch up with the old man who had already made it halfway down toward the brook. Butchy was straggling behind, going at his own pace, stopping to sniff at old rabbit and woodchuck holes along the way. "What kind of manly stuff are we going to do, Grampa?" the child asked. "Are we gonna ride the tractor or feed the animals? Maybe we can milk the cows."

"Not everything is fun like that. Sometimes men have to do ugly work. Are you ready to do ugly work? Are you ready to show me you're a man?"

The child was frightened by the way his grandfather was talking, but he didn't want to show his fear. He wanted to make his grandfather proud. "I'm ready," he said.

"Good," the old man said as they crossed over the brook. "You like Butchy?"

"I love Butchy, Grampa."

"Well, old Butchy's not the same dog he used to be. He was a great

hunting dog, but now all he does is sleep and soil the rugs. We can't have that in the house. It's filthy."

The boy felt a coldness creep over him despite the warmth of the day. They were at the edge of the woods now and the old man took the rifle off his shoulder.

"I want you to show me how much of a man you are," the old man said, handing the rifle to the boy. "Butchy's not happy. He doesn't want to live like this. If you really love him, you'll take this gun and put him to rest."

The child pushed the rifle away. "I can't hurt him. I love him, Grampa."

"That's what I thought," the old man shook his head sadly. "You're no man. You're still that little boy who's afraid of the dark." The old man pointed the rifle at the dog. The dog looked in their direction, his eyes milky and unfocused.

"Don't do it, Grampa!" the boy yelled. He lunged for the gun, taking hold of the barrel and pulling it down as a round fired into the ground. The old dog didn't react to the crack.

"Don't you cry like a little girl," the old man said as he swung and hit the child firmly with the back of his hand. The child let go of the barrel as he fell to the ground. "You'd better start acting like a man or you're not going to last very long on this farm. If you don't care enough about old Butchy to put him down, I guess I'll have to do it."

The child lay on the ground sobbing as the old man raised the rifle and aimed it at Butchy's head.

The child covered his eyes and heard a loud pop. It seemed much louder than the first shot. And then silence.

Richter looked down. In the cradle of his hands was the small face of a pansy, snapped from its stalk. As if it were scorching the palms of his hands, he tossed it away and stood up.

Linda Bagwell hadn't seen him. Inhaling and looking around with great satisfaction, she continued her leisurely stroll up Comm Ave. She turned right onto Berkeley and then left on Marlborough.

Richter timed it so he caught up to her just as she reached her apartment building. He followed her up the granite stairs to the main entrance of the town house, which, like almost every other grand old home in Boston, had been converted into apartments or condominiums. She must have heard his footsteps, he must have startled her, because she spun around to see who was behind her.

"Oh my God, you scared me," she said, seeming to recognize him. She smiled. "You're the man from the district attorney's office. I sat on your jury last week. What brings you to the Back Bay? Do you live around here?" she asked with a smile. Richter could tell she was attracted to him as she tried to turn on her charm.

"I have a friend who lives on the third floor," he said. "I'm supposed to meet him for drinks. Do you live here?" Richter knew that she lived there, in the rear apartment on the first floor.

"I live here for now," she said as she unlocked the door, letting Richter into the main lobby. "Until I save enough to buy a condo on Beacon Hill."

He needed to take care of Linda Bagwell before Mooney and Alves got the archived juror questionnaires. Once they had those forms they'd learn that all the other victims had served their jury duty at South Bay. Then they'd be contacting every juror who had served in that court to let them know about the potential danger. Linda Bagwell might not have been as trusting of Richter if she'd received a call like that from the police.

As they entered the building Richter scanned the lobby to make sure they were alone. They walked toward the stairs, which were adjacent to her apartment door. As she reached to insert her key in the lock, Richter heard a loud mechanical noise and a bell at the end of the hall. It was an old service elevator. Apparently it was still functioning. Someone was coming. He had to act fast.

"It was nice to see you again, Miss . . . ?"

"Bagwell. Linda Bagwell. The pleasure was mine," she said as she opened her apartment door. "Maybe we'll see each other again sometime."

"Who knows?" he said. "With a little luck, maybe we'll be seeing a whole lot of each other."

Richter lunged toward her and grabbed her from behind. He slipped his left arm around hers and pulled it back into a chicken wing. At the same time he reached his right hand under her chin, pulling back and to the right so she couldn't make a sound. The Chin and Chicken was one of his favorite wrestling holds. Linda Bagwell was helpless. He lifted her into her apartment and kicked the door closed behind them. She'd done such a good job as a juror in his last trial that he couldn't let her get away. And he could set up her apartment as the crime scene that would finally point Mooney and Alves in the *right* direction.

CHAPTER 73

Alves stepped out of Linda Bagwell's apartment, nearly bumping into Mooney.

"It's definitely the Blood Bath Killer," Alves said

"Now I've got you calling him by that fucking name."

"Sorry, Sarge, how's this?" Alves said. "This case may be related to the open homicides we have where victims had their blood drained out of their bodies and into their bathtubs."

"Don't be a fresh prick. I'm not in the mood." Mooney was scanning the small studio apartment, focusing on the bed, a foldout couch from some tony furniture store. Alves had already determined that there was potential evidence from that source. "Don't push me, Angel. Not today."

"Sorry, Sarge." Alves realized that he'd crossed the line.

"What's her name?" Mooney asked.

"Linda Bagwell. Didn't show up for work this morning. Her best friend was worried because Bagwell always gets in early. She tried calling, but no one answered. After a couple of tries she called nine-one-one. Met the uniforms here with the spare key that Bagwell kept in her office for emergencies. The friend is outside with the paramedics in the ambulance. She freaked out after seeing the blood in the tub."

"No phone call from the killer?" Mooney asked.

"Not this time, Sarge. Maybe something spooked him and he had to get out quick."

"Maybe," Mooney muttered to himself, a sign he was deep in thought. "Have you talked with the friend yet?" Mooney asked.

"No, I told one of the patrolmen to bring her back in when she settles down."

"What do we have besides the blood in the tub?" Mooney asked.

"Her bedsheets look like a bloody shroud, like the towels on the bathroom floors at the other scenes. The killer must have moved her around on the bed. Maybe he sexually assaulted her there. It's hard to tell, but he did something with her. I've got the crime lab checking for semen, hair and fibers on the sheets."

"Did they find anything yet?"

"They've got some possible hairs and some sort of stain aside from the blood on the sheets. Looks like our guy may have been too tempted by this one."

"There goes your FBI profiler's theory that he's not a sexual predator."

"Sarge," one of the patrolmen interrupted them, "I may have found something out back. I was closing off the alley when I looked down the sewer grate back there. I saw a condom on top of the leaves. It seems pretty clean. I don't think it's been down there very long."

"If you think it's evidence, go back there and watch it before it washes away."

Alves remembered a story Mooney had told him about two detectives who were out with their wives when they got robbed at gunpoint and a round was discharged. When the district sergeant showed up, all three got into an argument over who should be in charge of the scene. Meanwhile, a city street sweeper came by and swept up the shell casing.

"Angel," Mooney said, turning back to Alves, "have the techs go out there and collect the rubber when they're done in here. I'm going to go talk with the friend."

Alves followed Mooney as he walked back out to the apartment threshold and inspected the door and its frame.

"I checked out the door and windows," Alves said. "There's no damage anywhere. She must have let him in."

An officer led a distraught young woman toward them. She looked to be in her mid-thirties. She was probably attractive, but now her dark mascara was running down her face.

"Ms. Shea. I'm Detective Alves and this is Sergeant Mooney."

"Hello, ma'am, sorry to meet you under these circumstances," Mooney said as he stuck his hand out. "You work with Ms. Bagwell?"

She nodded, unable to talk.

"Ms. Shea, I'm sorry, but I do have to ask you some questions," he said. "When was the last time you saw her?"

The young woman hesitated for a moment and then answered. "Last night. Around seven o'clock. We walked out of work together and said good night." Her shoulders shuddered. "We said we'd see each other in the morning."

"What time does she usually get to work?"

"We've been coming in at seven because we've got a deadline coming up on a project. We were behind because Linda had jury duty last week. She tried to tell the judge about our time constraints, but he made her sit on the jury anyway."

"Ms. Shea," Mooney said. Alves could see that this last bit of information had energized Mooney. "Do you know where she had jury duty?"

"I think it was that courthouse in Dudley Square."

"Thanks for your help, Ms. Shea," Mooney said. "Why don't you go with this officer?" Mooney indicated the same young patrolman who had ushered her in. "He'll take you back to work. We'll contact you if we have any more questions."

Mooney directed Alves to step back into the apartment. "Angel, I want you to finish processing the scene."

"Where are you going, Sarge?"

"I'd like to go to the jury commissioner's office and kill someone up there. We've got another dead woman because of those fuckin' assholes."

"There's plenty of time for that later, Sarge."

"And don't think I won't do it." Mooney paused, rubbing his temples. "I'm going over to South Bay to start looking through the jury forms. Meet me there as soon as you're done. If we confirm that each of our vics served on juries there, no one is leaving that courthouse today until we've taken a run at them. I want to know who would've had contact with them while they were there." Mooney dialed a number on his cell phone as he moved toward the door. "I've got to make some calls. I want every detective in the city working overtime to reach out to anyone who did their civic duty at South Bay over the past year. I want to make sure they're safe. Linda Bagwell is the last person this bastard's going to kill."

CHAPTER 74

"Boston Police Crime Lab, Eunice Curran."

"Eunice," Alves said, "I need some help." He was on his way to South Bay with his wigwags flashing. He left the siren off so he could talk on the phone. "We just finished processing Linda Bagwell's apartment. Your guys collected some evidence. They found hairs on the bed and a stain on the sheets. They also found a condom in a sewer that may or may not be related."

"What do you need?"

"I'm hoping we can get some DNA from the stain, the condom or maybe from a hair. In the meantime, if you find that the stain is semen or if you can tell anything about the killer from the hairs, let me know right away."

"I'll call you the minute I have anything. Is there a boyfriend or any guy she's been seeing who may have been at her place?"

"Her best friend at work told us she wasn't seeing anyone. Married to her work."

"Don't I know what that's like."

"That's why you're the best. I'm pulling up to the courthouse. You'll call me soon?"

"I'll give you an update in a couple of hours."

He hung up the phone and walked toward the building to meet Mooney. Alves knew they were close to solving the murders. He looked forward to getting his life back to normal. He had neglected Marcy and the kids and he wanted to make it up to them. But first he had a killer to catch.

CHAPTER 75

Angel Alves strode into the courthouse with a sense of purpose. He walked past the security officers without saying a word and headed straight for the clerk's office. Mooney stood, with the clerk magistrate behind him, going through boxes of forms. The clerk magistrate was responsible for maintaining the court dockets. He was a well-paid, elderly man who rarely showed up for work and drove an old Lincoln Continental Mark IV. Mooney once pointed out that it was the same car Frank Cannon drove in the old private investigator television series. "He has the shoebox mobile phone in there, too," Mooney insisted. The old man refused to retire. And why should he? He made as much money as a judge.

"How's it going, Sarge?" Alves asked as he approached the two men.

"Not bad," Mooney said. He gave a look indicating that the clerk had been no help. "We confirmed that each of the vics has been here. I've got all the questionnaires except for Bagwell's. I was hoping they might still have hers from last week, but the clerk's office sent them back on Monday."

"It should be easy to figure out who had contact with her, even without the questionnaire. She was just here. Someone will remember which trial she sat on. Let's start with the court officers. They spend the most time with the jurors. Then we'll know who the players were, including the judge and the lawyers."

Mooney looked at the clerk. "Can you help with that?"

The old guy looked as if they had interrupted his nap. "We have a regular clerk and court officer who work the jury session. I'll get the two of them." He waited to see if Mooney had anything else to say. Like maybe the sergeant would offer to get them himself. When nothing was forthcoming, the clerk magistrate worked his way out of his chair and slowly shuffled down the hall.

"Do the questionnaires list what trials they sat for? Can we start pulling those dockets? I'd like to cross-reference them and find a common denominator." Alves was anxious. They were close.

"That's being taken care of," Mooney said. "We've got people pulling the dockets and the attendance sheets. I've got a few of the district detectives supervising to make sure there's no funny business."

"So each of the vics is accounted for?"

"I'm not sure," Mooney said. "Something's been bothering me. Who was that woman from Area E who turned up missing last fall?"

"Emily Knight?"

"That's it. I've been trying to remember her name."

"You think she might be tied into this?"

"It's worth looking into. If she did her jury duty here, then she might actually be our first victim. I'm going to look her up right now. Once we have all the documentation we can start talking to some people around here. I haven't had a chance to go up to the third floor and check with the DAs."

"You want me to touch base with them?"

"Just ask the supervisor to give you their attendance records for these dates." Mooney handed Alves a sheet with each victim's name and corresponding dates of service. "Don't do anything else. I don't want to talk with anyone about specifics until we're ready. Let's see if we have a common denominator for all of these trials. Then we can interview that person together. I want to make sure we don't miss anything when we sit down with the bad guy. Make no mistake about it, Angel, today we're going to speak with him. He could be anyone in this building, including one of your friends in the DA's office. So no fucking around up there."

"I know, Sarge."

CHAPTER 76

Richter watched from the second-floor balcony as the detectives took over the courthouse.

This was it. Richter knew they would eventually figure out that each of the victims had been jurors at South Bay. What he couldn't believe was that it took them so long. But then, he *could* believe it. He'd been careful in selecting people who were nondescript in their appearance, people who wouldn't be remembered by the courthouse personnel once a little time had passed.

Richter had always waited a few weeks after their jury service before visiting each of them, except for Linda Bagwell. But there was a reason why he had to take care of her when he did. Nick's disappearance had brought the detectives right to the courthouse, and now they were looking into the juror questionnaires. Richter needed Linda Bagwell to create a diversion for Mooney and Alves.

Richter felt a surge of adrenaline. He had spent so many nights practicing for this. Preparation was the key. That way there would be no surprises. But he needed to give them a perfect performance, otherwise it would be over. He was certain they had no evidence tying him to the murders. He just had to stay focused and deal with them the way he had handled the detectives in Arizona so many years earlier.

CHAPTER 77

Connie spotted Alves walking toward his desk. Alves didn't seem to be his usual self. Something in the determination of his step. Something like disappointment in his face. "Connie, do you have a minute?"

"Sure, what's up?"

"We need to talk. But not here," he said, shooting a look at Brendan, who was trying to look busy at his desk. "Let's go into the conference room." Alves wasn't asking Connie, he was telling him.

Connie followed him. Sergeant Mooney was already there, waiting for them. "Hi, Sarge, what's going on?"

"Have a seat," Mooney said. "We need to ask you some questions."

"Sure, Sarge. Anything I can do to help." Connie was trying to be pleasant, cordial, although he knew that he was about to be interrogated. "Is this about Nick?"

"Connie, do you recognize this woman?" Mooney asked as he placed a photograph on the table in front of him.

Should he not answer their questions and ask for a lawyer? No. He would look guilty. Should he just come across as being helpful and completely forthcoming? No. How many people had walked themselves straight into a conviction by doing that?

The photo in front of him was of Linda Bagwell. One of his jurors. It looked like it was from her college yearbook. Her soft, brown hair was much shorter back then. Connie took his time and studied the photo while Mooney and Alves, he knew, watched his every move, his every change of expression. Mooney had a reputation as a skilled interrogator. "She served on my jury last week," Connie said. "Why?"

"She turned up dead this morning."

"Oh shit," Connie said.

Mooney leaned into the table and watched him. The room was silent for a full minute.

"Sarge, you don't think I had anything to do with her death, do you? Angel, tell him."

Alves didn't say anything. This was Mooney's interrogation and Angel Alves was just an observer.

Mooney continued, "Connie, we have to treat you like any other potential suspect in an investigation. You understand that, don't you?"

"I guess so."

"Where were you last night?" Mooney asked.

"I was home," Connie said. He felt his body start to slouch back in his chair. Mooney would think that his posture was a sign that he was lying. He forced himself to sit upright. Connie wanted his body language to show that he was telling them the truth right from the beginning.

"Alone?" Mooney asked.

"Unfortunately," Connie said. "I don't have any alibi witnesses if that's what you're after. I went to the gym with Mitch and Brendan after work. Then I was home for the night." Connie wanted to answer each of their questions even if the answers might be damning to him. He wanted them to see that he realized where the questions were headed and that he had nothing to hide.

"What about the night Susan McCarthy was killed?" Mooney asked. "Where were you that night?"

"You know where I was. I was with the two of you at the crime scene. Just like the Hayes and Ramos scenes. I guess I was home alone each of those nights, until I got called out. I live alone. Where else am I going to be on a work night?"

There was a knock on the door. "Excuse me," one of the secretaries said, "but I have a Eunice Curran on the phone. She'd like to speak with

Detective Alves. I told her you were all in a meeting, but she said it was urgent."

"Thanks," Alves said. "Could you send the call in here?"

"Sure thing," she said.

"Connie, could you step outside for a minute?" Mooney asked.

"No problem. I'll be at my desk."

"We'll only be a couple of minutes," Mooney said.

As Connie closed the door behind him he hoped that his interrogation was over.

CHAPTER 78

"Eunice, it's Angel. I've got you on speakerphone with Sergeant Mooney. What's up?"

"A couple of things. For starters, there was no biological matter in the stain on Linda Bagwell's sheets. No semen. No blood. No DNA. But it did contain a non-petroleum-based lubricant, the kind you find on latex condoms."

"What about the condom?" Mooney asked.

"Similar lubricant. I can't tell you they're a match with any scientific certainty, but the two lubricants are made up of a similar and distinctive chemical compound that contains a specific spermicide. I compared them to a database we use in rape cases. They're consistent with what is found on Sentinel condoms. I ran the condom through another database and the latex is also consistent with Sentinels. We went out and bought a box. On visual examination, they look the same as our condom. Same color and size."

"That's great, Eunice," Alves said.

"I found nothing on the inside of the condom, no cells or semen. On the exterior there were some epithelial cells. The type found on the vaginal walls and in the mouth, the ones we get when we take a buccal swab. What's significant about these cells, as opposed to the dead skin cells on the exterior of the body, is that these are living cells that have a nucleus and, therefore, DNA. I won't know if they're Bagwell's until we get the DNA results."

There was a momentary silence on the line before Eunice continued. "The other interesting thing is that there was a pubic hair inside the condom."

"What does that mean?" Alves asked.

"Our guy may have worn the condom but didn't, or couldn't, ejaculate."

"But if he wore the condom, wouldn't he have left cells?"

"Not necessarily. Another possibility is that he never actually wore the condom. He might have put the condom on some object and inserted it into her vagina or her mouth as part of his fantasy. I'm not a psychologist, but maybe this guy's impotent and that's why he's killing these women. Up to this point we haven't had any insight as to what he might be doing with their bodies after he kills them. This time he finally built up enough confidence to act out his fantasies in the victim's bed. But he wanted to feel as if he was really having sex with her."

"Do you think he took his clothes off?" Alves asked.

"I do. The hairs we found on the bed were inconsistent with her hair. I found some pubic hairs consistent with the hair on the condom, plus a couple of head hairs and an auxiliary hair. I can't tell if it's chest, arm or leg. It's hard to distinguish exactly where it came from. I've got roots on one of the head hairs and one of the pubic hairs so I may have some DNA for a match. There's no guarantee unless I've got some flesh attached. As for the pubic hair on the condom, it may have gotten there if he placed it on his penis. It may have been transferred there from his hand. I can't say for sure."

"Aside from the possibility of DNA," Mooney interrupted, "do the hairs tell us anything about this guy?"

"They do. The head hair is short, reddish in color, with Negroid characteristics."

"Negroid characteristics? So he's black?" Mooney asked.

"Probably. But not necessarily. I've seen white men with Negroid-characteristic hair, but it's rare."

"What about red hair with those characteristics?" Mooney asked, glancing over at Alves. "Is someone with that kind of hair more likely to be black or white?"

"I can't tell you anything for sure, but if I had to guess, and I'm do-ing a lot of guessing here, more than I'm comfortable with, I'd say he's a black male. But a very distinctive black male. Judging by the color of his hair—and there were no dyes used on the hair—he's probably light-skinned black. But the thing that makes him so distinctive is that hair. Very few black men have the red hair that our perpetrator does."

Mooney and Alves looked at each other. They were clearly both thinking the same thing as they got up from their chairs. Mooney was reaching for the phone to hang it up. "Thanks, Eunice," he said. "We have someone we need to speak with."

Alves turned to Mooney. "I know who you have in mind, but he doesn't fit your profile, Sarge. He doesn't fit anyone's profile. He's not a white male."

"Angel, he's one of the whitest black guys I've ever met. I don't care what the actual color of his skin is. That kid is a wealthy, white, privi-leged aristocrat in a black man's skin. He fits the profile perfectly."

CHAPTER 79

Connie stepped back into the conference room. "Connie, we have a few more questions before we interview some other people," Mooney said.

"I'm not sure if I want to keep talking. I don't like being considered a suspect," Connie said.

"You're not a suspect. But we have to treat everyone the same if we're going to get to the truth."

"It's hard when two guys you know and respect come to interrogate you for a murder."

"We can't spend any time crying about hurt feelings," Mooney said. "Connie, I need you to think back to your trial last week, the one where Linda Bagwell sat on your jury. Do you remember the trial?"

"Of course."

"Who watched the trial?"

"Just the usual people. Judge Samuels was presiding. Curtis Johnson was the court officer. I forget who the clerk was that day, but it should be listed on the court docket."

"I need you to think carefully about this. Do you remember who may have been in the audience watching the trial?"

"Yeah, I think the defendant's mother, sister and girlfriend were there trying to get sympathy points for the defendant." Connie took his time, thinking before he spoke.

"Was anyone from your office there during the trial?"

"We always watch one another's trials if we have the time. I'm sure Liz popped in and maybe Brendan and one of our interns. Oh, and Mitch sat in for that trial. He watches most of my trials."

"Most of your trials?" Mooney asked.

"If he could, he'd be there from the first word of my opening until the last word of my closing. I have more experience so he likes to watch me. He mimics what I do in his own trials. And it's working. He's won his last few."

"He may be doing more than just watching you to learn trial techniques," Mooney said. "He might actually be obsessed with your jurors."

"What are you talking about?" Connie asked, incredulous. "Are you crazy? You think Mitch killed those people? That makes no sense. He couldn't hurt anyone."

"Judging by the evidence against him, I'd say Mitch has been hurting people for some time now," Mooney said. "You wouldn't happen to know what type of sneakers he owns, would you?"

"I don't know," Connie said. "Why?"

"Think, Connie," Alves said. Connie recognized the desperation in Alves's voice. He *wanted* Connie to know the answer. "What does he wear to the gym?"

"He wears New Balance when we work out," Connie said, a tone of disgust that the detectives could even suspect his good friend in his voice.

"How do you know they're New Balance?" Mooney asked.

"I was with him when he bought them," Connie said. "I took him to the factory store in Brighton awhile back. I didn't find anything, but he got a pair of cross trainers."

"Thanks, Connie," Mooney said. "Do you know where he is?"

"I think he's back at his desk. You want me to get him so you can clear this up? I'm sure it's just a misunderstanding."

"That's all right. Angel can get him. Why don't you hang around, though, in case we need you?"

"I'll be at my desk."

CHAPTER 80

"Look, I don't know about anyone getting killed," Mitch Beaulieu said. He was unsettled by the detectives' questions. "Just because I broke up with my girlfriend doesn't mean I'm a killer. Not that it's any of your business, but I'm seeing someone else."

"That's convenient," Alves said. "What about your obsession with Connie's trials?"

"What obsession? So what if I watch Connie's trials? Everyone watches him—he's one of the best lawyers in the office. We watch him so we can become better trial lawyers."

"What about the condoms?" Alves asked.

"The condoms? Are you kidding me? What does that prove?"

"We're reasonable men, Mitch," Mooney said. "So, if there's a reasonable explanation for all of this, we're willing to consider it. We're just trying to get to the truth, and the evidence seems to point in your direction. We're giving you a chance to tell your side of the story."

"There's no story to tell." He was having a hard time keeping his hands still. "That's what I've been trying to tell you."

"We're getting nowhere with this," Mooney said. "Mitch, you don't mind if Connie joins us, do you?"

"I could use an ally in here."

"Angel, could you get him?"

The detectives had been grilling him for over an hour. At first it all seemed like a bad joke. But with each new volley of questions he felt himself more deeply implicated. A wave of panic began to surge through him.

Mitch wasn't so much concerned that the two detectives believed he was a murderer. What worried him was the evidence suggesting his guilt. Even though it was circumstantial, the evidence would make it impossible for an objective listener, a juror, to believe in his innocence.

As he waited for Alves to return with Connie, Mitch started to second-guess his decision to speak with the detectives. He knew that he shouldn't be talking with them. He was, after all, a lawyer. And the best advice a lawyer can give a client being questioned by the police is to shut up. *You have the right to remain silent, so shut your trap.* When the conversation began they'd even read Mitch his Miranda rights. And still he chose to talk. What an idiot. But why shouldn't he talk? If he chose not to talk he'd have looked guilty. But the more he talked, the more he realized how much evidence they'd developed against him. At least with Connie joining them, he'd have a friend in the room.

CHAPTER 81

Connie followed Alves into the conference room. The room where they had had so many good times with lively lunchtime discussions about restaurants, movies and philosophies of life seemed different. Now it was an interrogation room. Connie at least knew how to conduct himself during an interrogation. Mitch was falling apart. The features of Mitch's face seemed to be collapsing in, and Connie knew he was about to start crying. His skin was ashen and his eyes were pleading. But Connie couldn't help him. Mitch was on his own.

"Now, Mitch," Sergeant Mooney began before Mitch had a chance to speak, "the reason I invited Connie in here is to prove to you that Detective Alves and I aren't out to get you. We know that you and Connie are close friends. Connie will look out for your best interests. Do you agree?"

"Yes, but he's not really *my* lawyer. He still represents the Commonwealth."

"Agreed," Mooney said. "But are you confident that he'll protect your interests?"

"Yes."

"Good. Because what I'm going to do now is lay out all the evidence we have that points to you. I'm going to do this with Connie in the room as an objective listener. I think you even referred to him as one of the best lawyers in this court. I don't ordinarily do this, but I'm going to do it as a professional courtesy to you, not only because you're a prosecutor, but also because I trust Connie's judgment. He insists there's no way you could've been involved in any of these crimes."

"Thanks, Connie," Mitch said.

"After I lay out all of these facts for you, as a professional courtesy, I'm going to give you a chance to tell your side. At least help us to explain the evidence. If, at that time, you choose not to talk, all bets are off and we'll follow the evidence where it leads. If it leads us to your arrest, conviction and incarceration, then so be it. Are we clear on that?"

Connie nodded to Mitch, letting him know that it was all right to talk. "Yes," Mitch said in a barely audible whisper. He was clearly terrified by the gravity of the situation.

"Let's begin. Over the past six months or so, five women and one man who sat on juries in this court have disappeared, leaving bathtubs full of their own blood, so much blood that they're presumed to be dead even though their bodies have never been found. A sixth woman also sat on a jury and disappeared last September. Each of these people sat on cases that Connie prosecuted. And you spend a good amount of time watching Connie's trials, correct?"

"So do a bunch of other people. The same court officers always take care of the jurors. They have access to all the jury questionnaires that I've never seen. I don't know anything about these people. I don't know their names, where they lived, where they worked."

"But you do take the T to and from work every day?" Mooney asked. "Each of these murdered jurors also took public transportation to the courthouse, didn't they?"

"How would I know?" Mitch asked. "I don't know how people get to and from the courthouse."

"I'm telling you right now, Mitch, that every one of these people took the T into Dudley Square to perform their civic duty. And you want us to believe that you never bumped into any of them on the bus or the train?"

"I don't know. I may have. But I never pay attention to the jurors. When I'm in a courtroom watching one of Connie's trials, I'm focused on Connie, not studying the jurors."

"Did you just say that you watch Connie so that you can become a better trial lawyer, yet you don't study the jurors?" Mooney asked.

Mitch nodded his head.

"Let me tell you something that you may not realize I'm aware of," Mooney said. "Anyone who's ever spoken to Connie about trying cases knows that he believes jury selection is the most important part of the trial. So there'd be nothing more important than studying the makeup of the jury. Seeing how old they are, what they do for a living, what neighborhood they live in. These are the most important lessons you'd learn from Connie. You're heading down the wrong path if you're going to start lying to me, Mitch. You don't want to do that."

Connie didn't say a word. He was trying to give Mitch a chance to explain. But now he'd been caught in a lie. Connie knew Mitch had lied because he was afraid, but that wasn't how the detectives would see it. To the detectives it showed his consciousness of guilt.

Connie watched as Mitch's eyes glanced to the right as he tried to come up with an explanation. Connie had taken part in a course on the Reid method of criminal interviews and interrogation run by the National DAs Association. Most people's eyes drifted to the left when they were recalling something that actually happened. Their eyes moved to the right when creating "a fact" that never actually occurred. These were subconscious movements. Mitch's glance to the right didn't escape Mooney's keen eye either.

"Sarge, I didn't mean it like that," Mitch said. "I didn't pay much attention to how they looked. I'd notice their sex, their race, things like that, but it wasn't as if I sat there and studied their faces so I'd recognize them outside the courtroom. I never did that. You have to believe me."

The three men stared at him blankly. Connie looked at Mitch as though he didn't even recognize him, as if he weren't the Mitchum Beaulieu that he'd known and worked with. That the friend he'd had in Mitch Beaulieu had grievously disappointed him. Connie could see that the look he gave Mitch hurt him more than any of the questions thrown at him by the detectives.

"Let's say I believe you didn't get a good look at any of the victims.

And let's say I believe you never ran into them on the T. Should I then ignore that one of your co-workers has recently disappeared, possibly because he knew too much?"

"Wait a minute," Mitch said, finally indignant. "Are you suggesting that I killed Nick?"

"Who said Nick was dead?" Mooney asked coldly. "Do you know something we don't?"

"I don't know anything. You're the one acting like Nick's dead."

"Is he?"

"I don't know." Mitch sank deeper into his chair.

"Come on, Mitch," Mooney said. "Let it out. You'll feel much better not having all these secrets bottled up inside you."

"This is ridiculous." Mitch was angry again. "Nick was my friend. Sure, I worked late with him last week, but so did Connie. He and Connie were still here when I left, and Nick was alive and well. And you said yourself that the victims all sat on Connie's juries. Why are you coming after me?"

"Hey, what the fuck?" Connie said. "Why are you throwing me under the bus? I'm trying to help you out. If you want, I'll leave you here on your own." Connie stood up.

"I'm sorry, Connie. I wasn't suggesting you did anything wrong. I'm not trying to get you in any trouble. Please don't leave."

Mooney watched Mitch carefully as Connie settled back in his chair. Connie could see Mooney preparing to hit Mitch with another round of questions. He wasn't going to let up on him. Mooney probably figured Mitch was about to give it up.

"Mitch," Mooney said. "I realize this is difficult, but there's more evidence that points to you. I told you about the condom we found at the crime scene this morning? It was a Sentinel brand with a spermicidal lubricant. That is the brand you use, isn't it?"

"So what? It's a goddamn condom that they sell in every CVS, Walgreens and Seven-Eleven."

"And it's also the condom you use. Do you have any with you, Mitch?"

"No I don't have any with me. I'm at work. Why the hell am I going to bring condoms to work? They're at my apartment."

"Really? No luck with the ladies lately?" Alves joined the conversation. "Don't women just piss you off sometimes? A good-looking guy like you and no one wants to take you home for the night. Doesn't that bother you?"

"Who says I haven't been lucky?"

"Let me finish," Mooney said. "We found a shoe print in the dirt at one of the murder scenes. The print was left by a New Balance sneaker. Do you own a pair of sneakers, Mitch?"

"Of course."

"What brand?"

"New Balance," Mitch said. "Like a million other people wear."

"Well, Mitch," Mooney said, "this print was left by a New Balance cross trainer. Do you wear cross trainers?"

Mitch didn't answer.

"I'll take that as a yes. Did you pay cash for them?"

Mitch sat in silence.

"I'll take that as another yes. Are they size ten and a half?"

Mitch stared down at the floor. He suddenly seemed drained of any life.

"Mitch!" Sergeant Mooney shouted at him to get his attention. "Are your New Balance cross trainers a size ten and a half?"

"Yes."

"And are they irregulars that you bought at the New Balance Factory Store?" Mooney asked this final question slowly and deliberately. Connie had already given him the answer.

Connie watched as Mitch's eyes widened. Mitch looked as though he had just come to a realization. All of this circumstantial evidence against him couldn't be a coincidence. Everything else could be explained away. But how could his shoe print have been left at a crime scene?

"That's it, guys." Connie stood up. "No more questions." Although the detectives weren't finished, Connie could tell that Mitch was. It was time for Connie to end the interrogation.

"What did you say?" Mooney said.

"You heard me, Sarge. No more questions, at least not until I have a minute to speak with Mitch."

"Connie, you're not his lawyer. You're a prosecutor. You work for the state."

"I'm still a lawyer. As a lawyer I'm advising Mitch not to say another word until I have a chance to speak with him. Let us step out into the hall for a minute and we'll be right back."

It was obvious that Mooney didn't like what was happening, but he *had* told Mitch that Connie would be sitting in on the interview as an attorney. He'd only done that to gain Mitch's trust. Now it was backfiring on him.

"All right," Mooney said, "you can go out in the hallway, but that's it. And I'm going to be watching you the whole time, Mitch. Don't even think about running."

CHAPTER 82

Mitch tried to gather his thoughts as they stepped into the hallway. This could not be happening to him. He looked toward the stairs, then back over his shoulder into the DA's office. Mooney was watching him through the glass door.

"Mitch, you are fucked," Connie said.

"What?" Mitch asked.

"You heard me," Connie said. "You're fucked. It's time for you to shut up."

"Thanks for the advice," Mitch shot back, "but it would have been more helpful about ten minutes ago."

"I'm telling you now. Stop talking and tell them you want a lawyer, so they can't ask you any more questions. With everything you just said in there, you may as well have confessed."

"What do you mean, confess? I had nothing to do with any murders. Why would I confess to anything? You don't believe I killed anyone, do you?"

"It doesn't matter what I believe, it matters what evidence they have against you."

"It matters to me. Do you think I killed those people?"

"Mitch, I don't know what to believe right now. I know that you could never do anything like that. I told them as much. But the evidence they have against you is pretty compelling."

Mitch looked down at the marble floor, shaking his head. He could see that Connie was trying to remain loyal to him, even though he was having doubts about his innocence. "You actually think I did it. You're supposed to be my best friend."

"I am your best friend. That's why I'm telling you to shut the fuck up and say you want a lawyer. I don't care if I work for the government. They can fire me if they want. I'm not going to let you say another word. Otherwise you're just going to dig yourself deeper."

Mitch thought he saw his father's face in the pattern of the marble. He closed his eyes to see his face more clearly, seeking guidance. Thinking of his father, the idea came to him. At first it was just a flicker in the back of his head, but as he focused, the plan crystallized in his mind. The stress he had been feeling for months was suddenly gone. He was at peace. "There's only one way out of this," Mitch said, lifting his head, a feeling of resolve coming over him.

"I know. There *is* only one way out of this and that's for you to be quiet while I call you an experienced defense attorney."

"That's not what I'm talking about, Connie. No lawyer's going to get me out of this. The evidence they have against me isn't just circumstantial, it isn't all a coincidence. Don't you see? Someone set me up. They planted this evidence against me. *I* know that's the truth. If you don't believe it, why should I expect a jury to believe it?"

"You can't think like that, Mitch. We'll get you the best team of lawyers. If you didn't do this, they'll get you off."

"*If* I didn't do it?" Mitch asked, disappointed. "You're right, Connie, I am fucked. Like Mooney said, I'm going to be convicted and spend the rest of my life in prison. I can't survive in a place like that. You know that. There's really only one way out of this. You've been a good friend to me and you understand why I have to do it this way. And because you understand, I know you're not going to do anything to stop me."

Connie watched him without saying a word.

Mitch looked into his friend's eyes once more. Then the two turned toward the district attorney's office.

Connie saw that Mooney was watching them through the glass. Connie stood in the frame of the door, blocking anyone from coming out. Mitch, a step behind him, pivoted on his heels and turned toward the balcony. Now the sergeant was moving toward Connie and the door, shoving aside chairs and a startled secretary. But it was too late. Mitch had a good head start as he began to sprint for the railing. Within seconds he was on the rail and airborne, his arms by his side and eyes closed. He never uttered a sound as he fell three stories and his skull hit the polished marble floor below.

CHAPTER 83

"**W**hy the hell did you let him do that?" Mooney shouted at Connie. He moved quickly, following Connie and Alves as they ran for the stairs.

"I didn't *let* him do anything. We were heading back inside." Connie took the stairs, two at a time, pulling ahead of Mooney and Alves. Connie had let Mitch jump the rail, but he had to. He at least owed Mitch that much, letting him go out on his own terms, instead of being led out in handcuffs.

On the second-floor landing, Brendan Sullivan called toward Connie, "What the fuck happened?"

"Mitch jumped."

"Mitch?" Brendan joined them as they ran down the last flight of stairs. Down in the lobby Mitch's prone body was surrounded by the court security officers. One look and Connie knew his skull was crushed, his body motionless.

There was a piercing scream from the balcony. Above them, Monica and Andi stood on the third floor. On the second floor, spectators, witnesses, officers, even the judges had piled out of the courtrooms to gawk at Mitch's body.

"Why did he do it?" Brendan asked Connie.

Connie turned from the unfolding chaos back to Brendan. "They were questioning him. About the murders. I stepped out of the office with him. One minute he's talking with me," Connie explained, "next thing I know, he's running for the balcony. He was upset, but I . . . I never expected. . . ."

Mooney was right behind them. "What did you guys talk about?"

"I told him he needed to get a lawyer. He wanted to clear things up. He was scared. I tried to tell him that everything was going to be all right. That he needed to shut up. I thought we were in agreement. I had no idea he was . . . going to. . . ."

Mooney looked toward Mitch's body. "This was no one's fault but Mitch's," Mooney said, turning to Connie and Brendan. "You may find it hard to believe, but your friend was a murderer."

"What are you guys talking about?" Brendan said. "Mitch couldn't kill anyone."

"He saw his world crashing down around him," Mooney continued. "I never should've let him walk out of that room."

"What next, Sarge?" Alves said.

"We'll need warrants to search Beaulieu's place, his car, his desk at work. If he had a locker at the gym, we'll need that too."

"Mitch's body isn't even cold and you're talking about warrants?" Brendan said.

"At this point, we don't know if anyone else is involved. We don't want evidence suppressed. The case isn't over by a long shot. We're going to search every part of his life. I'm going to find those bodies."

Mooney turned and walked away through the gathering crowd.

CHAPTER 84

The church had been almost empty, and Connie felt bad about that. Usually when a prosecutor or police officer died there would be standing room only at the service. But nobody showed up except for Mitch's closest friends. There was no family left. Even the district attorney was a no-show, to avoid any controversy and risk losing votes in the next election. The pastor at Mitch's church had performed a moving ceremony at the Faith Baptist Church in Cambridge. The ceremony was dedicated to celebrating Mitch's life rather than mourning his death. There'd been no mention that Mitch was believed to be a killer.

Sonya's and Mitch's friends from Harvard Law School had sat together at the church and now huddled in a small group at the cemetery. Sonya was holding a man's hand. Apparently she'd moved on with her life while Mitch had kept dreaming of getting back with her. The pastor drew in toward the casket with the group from Harvard. Connie and the other ADAs remained back at a distance. Sonya and company hadn't made them feel overly welcome, refusing to acknowledge their presence. There was no eulogy at the cemetery, just a reading of some Bible passages by the pastor.

"For God so loved the world, that he gave his only begotten Son, that whosoever believeth in him should not perish, but have everlasting life."

"That's John 3:16," Connie whispered to Andi as she held his hand.

"Mitch believed in Christ. He went to church every Sunday, you know. I really think he's in a better place now. He's been granted eternal life."

"Connie," Andi whispered back. "I know you keep trying to block it out of your head because he was your friend, but Mitch was—"

"I *can't* believe that," he said.

"Connie, they found his hair and DNA at the last murder scene. They had all that other evidence. He used his work computer to Google those women to learn more about them before he killed them. Alves even told you about the locked room in his house. The creepy shrine for his father, with religious artifacts and family heirlooms. Crazy stuff. Serial-killer type stuff. I'm sorry, Connie."

"If he did kill anyone, it's because he was sick. Something had to have been wrong with him. You didn't know him like I did. I should have been there to help him before it went this far. I should've stopped him from jumping over that rail."

"Listen to me, Connie," she said, turning to face him. "You're not responsible for Mitch's death. And you're not responsible for anything he did. You simply didn't know him as well as you thought you did. The police have done their investigation. They're satisfied that Mitch was the killer. He knew he'd been caught. That's why he killed himself instead of calling a lawyer. He knew a lawyer couldn't help, because he really was guilty. You have to stop taking the blame for this."

"She's right," Liz interrupted. She'd come up quietly behind the two of them. "Connie, you can't keep beating yourself up. Mitch was sick and under a lot of stress. Unfortunately, none of us realized how bad things were. But we can't lose sight of what he did to those poor people. And maybe what he did to Nick too."

"You know what's bothering me the most about this whole thing?" Andi said. "I keep thinking about that Christian Burial case we talked about when I was prepping that motion a while back. I can't help but think how horrible it is that none of Mitch's victims received a proper burial and their families haven't been able to lay them to rest. I pray Nick is okay, but I can't help thinking of his body lying in the woods somewhere. It was selfish of Mitch to kill himself without letting someone know where the bodies are."

"And for that he should never be forgiven," Monica said, the venom in her voice surprising all of them. Monica had given her notice to the DA and was talking about teaching high school history.

Connie and Liz didn't say anything. They listened silently as the pastor read some final passages. It had been cloudy and raw all morning. Now the sky opened, and a cold, bleak rain began to fall.

"Hey, guys," Brendan said as he moved in close to them. "Why don't we get out of here before we get soaked? We're not welcome anyway. What do you say we go to Kilronan's and talk about some of the good times we had?"

"That sounds good," Andi said. "Connie, there's nothing left for us to do here. Let's get going."

"Sure," Connie said. He took off his jacket and draped it over Andi's shoulders. He put his arm around her and pulled her close as they walked back to their cars. "If it makes you feel any better," he whispered in her ear, "I'm sure that Nick and the others are in a better place now, regardless of whether or not they received a proper burial. I truly believe that with all my heart."

CHAPTER 85

Connie looked around the courtroom. It was small but impressive. The walls were dark paneled, solid cherry, leading up to the judge's bench. The same beautiful cherry made up the rail in front of the jury box. Connie leaned forward and picked up the pitcher of water on the table. He poured some into his glass and took a small sip, placing the cup back on the table. Finally he stood up from his chair, walked behind it and slowly pushed it in toward the table. His ritual. He had that well-rehearsed, concerned look on his face so the jurors would think he didn't know where to begin his opening.

When he knew that all eyes were on him, and there was absolute silence in the courtroom, Connie looked up at the jury and scanned the entire panel before speaking.

"Good morning, ladies and gentlemen, my name is Conrad Darget and I represent the Commonwealth in this case." He paused for a moment. "On October seventh of last year this defendant"—he pointed to the defense table—"Jesse Wilcox, was in possession of a nine-millimeter semiautomatic Glock handgun, twelve rocks of crack cocaine and fifty packets of heroin."

Connie had to be careful not to mention the items the police recovered in Wilcox's apartment, the large rock of crack that hadn't been packaged yet, the three fingers of heroin that hadn't been cut, the scale with the cocaine residue on it or the $4,530 that was stuffed in an envelope under the mattress. He couldn't talk about any of it because it had all been suppressed from evidence. In a sense, the whole trial would be a sham. Everyone in that courtroom knew about this evidence except for the people that mattered—the eight jurors.

"On that evening Detective Angel Alves and two patrolmen responded to a radio call for a domestic dispute at Ten Franklin Street, third floor. When they got there, they heard a woman screaming and a baby crying. They forced their way into the apartment. There they found the defendant casually sitting on a couch next to an open window on a chilly night. His girlfriend was sitting at the kitchen table with her six-month-old baby, both of them crying. The officers searched the area below the open window and found a gun and drugs. They were clean and dry except for the dirt on the barrel of the gun, which was next to a divot in the sod, as if the gun had just been thrown from a window."

Connie hated being dishonest, not mentioning the evidence the police had recovered in the room. But it was the law. Rules were rules. When a judge decided the police had violated someone's constitutional rights and that the items seized could not be used as evidence, he had to live with it.

Connie continued with his opening statement, making eye contact with each of his jurors. He looked back to Emily Knight, his foreperson. There was a time when he believed she was his best juror. But then she'd let him down. This was her chance to redeem herself and put Jesse Wilcox in jail where he belonged. He gave her a slight smile.

He moved on to the other jurors. It was a diverse group. He was proud of his jury-selection skills.

He locked eyes with Robyn Stokes. She was a strong woman. He respected her more than any of them, because she came from nothing and had made so much of her life. She was wearing one of the oversized, brightly colored shirts she wore as a nurse. She had earned her position as a charge nurse and deserved to be recognized by the others for her accomplishments. As the sole African American on the jury, Connie knew that Robyn Stokes would fight to keep her neighborhood safe.

Jill Twomey, Michelle Hayes and Linda Bagwell were upright and alert, ready for him to continue.

On the left side of the jury box sat Edwin Ramos. Blue-collar, a true craftsman. A man like Ramos would bring common sense to the table.

And Nick Costa.

Nick would provide the perspective of a first-generation American, with the background of his Mediterranean immigrant parents.

Connie was very pleased with how Nick Costa and Edwin Ramos balanced his jury. They were the only men, but they'd certainly be able to hold their own in deliberations with the women. Though Susan McCarthy might give them a run for their money. She was a fighter.

The scene was almost perfect. The only thing missing was a judge on the bench and someone second-seating him at the prosecution table, an attractive woman, someone like Andi Norton. That would certainly help complete the scene. He would love to make those additions to his courtroom, but he couldn't risk it. Not right now. After all, the police thought that they had their killer.

Poor Mitch. Connie had no choice but to frame him—with the hairs he took from his stuff at the gym, the condom, wearing his sneakers at the McCarthy house—but he'd never imagined things would work out so neatly with Mitch killing himself. The shrine to his father in that locked room was the final puzzle piece. Connie felt bad for him. They were friends. But he couldn't allow feelings to interfere with the natural order of things. Mitch's sole purpose was to provide an escape for Richter, just like a rabbit's sole purpose in life was to provide food for the wolf.

Connie looked back at his jurors, seated in the jury box in his basement courtroom, a mockup of the trial session in South Bay, which he'd built after killing Emily Knight. He continued his opening, knowing that he needed to connect with each of them in order to win a conviction. The real trial would begin in the morning. This was going to be a tough case. Jesse Wilcox always seemed to find a way to avoid going to jail. This time, with the right preparation and with some help from his attentive audience, Connie would get his conviction.

ACKNOWLEDGMENTS

Thanks to Lin Haire-Sargeant, Peggy Walsh and Candice Rowe, the members of my writers' group, for their critical observations, encouragement and support; to Mark Meadows, always a hospitable host serving us delicious desserts at each of our meetings; to Paul Treseler, a prosecutor and a friend, who turned out to be a great editor as well; to MaryKay Mahoney who graciously read early drafts with a keen eye.

Special thanks to Kevin Waggett, a Boston Police sergeant detective, lawyer and friend who had great passion for the novel, spending many hours on the phone, day and night, imparting his police knowledge and critical insight.

Thanks, too, to my two favorite forensic scientists, Kevin Kosiorek and Amy Kraatz of the Boston Police Crime Lab, for lending me their expert advice; to Bob Lawler of the Lawler and Crosby Funeral Home in West Roxbury for ensuring that my details were accurate; to my good friends Paul Curran, Paul Leonard and Paul Toomey for answering my technical questions; to Jeremiah Healy for his support and expert editorial advice; to my father and my brothers and sisters for keeping me out of trouble; to Henry for his unconditional love; and, of course, to all of my friends in the Suffolk County District Attorney's Office, the Boston Police Department and in the Trial Court.

I am also fortunate to have an insightful and thoughtful editor at

Ballantine in Mark Tavani and a brillliant agent in Simon Green at Pom, Inc.

Most important, this novel would never have been written if not for the love, support and encouragement of my wife, Candice Rowe. She has taught me to be a better writer and a better person.

ABOUT THE AUTHOR

RAFFI YESSAYAN spent eleven years as an assistant district attorney in Boston. Within two years of becoming a prosecutor he was named to the Gang Unit, ultimately becoming its chief. He recently left the DA's office to go into private practice. He and his wife live in Massachusetts. This is his first novel.

ABOUT THE TYPE

This book was set in Requiem, a typeface designed by the Hoefler Type Foundry. It is a modern typeface inspired by inscriptional capitals in Ludovico Vicentino degli Arrighi's 1523 writing manual, *Il modo de temperare le penne*. An original lowercase, a set of figures and an italic in the "chancery" style that Arrighi helped popularize were created to make this adaptation of a classical design into a complete font family.